DESTINED STORM

NEPHILIM'S DESTINY: BOOK 4

TESSA COLE

Gryphon's Gate Publishing

Destined Storm

Copyright © 2019 Tessa Cole

Cover Design by Melody Simmons

Gryphon's Gate Publishing

550 King St. N.

PO Box 42088 Conestoga

Waterloo, ON

N2L 6K5

ebook ISBN 978-1-988115-72-6

Print ISNB 978-1-988115-71-9

CHAPTER 1

My senses reeled from the power channeled by the glyph witches we'd fought on top of City Hall moments ago and from my crash into the alley, while my body burned with pain and power and Cassius's rage. His grip on my throat tightened, and his fire, searing bands of flame securing my wrists, burned my skin and controlled where I pointed my palms, as if he feared I'd blast him with divine light.

With a snarl, he pressed me harder against the garbage bin, drawing agony through ribs that had to be broken. The reek of the alley's bin in the early summer's heat, even perpetually shaded in the alley across from City Hall, made me gag. Wings I didn't know I'd had until a few seconds ago twitched and slapped against the metal side with a dull thud, as my pulse roared and my thoughts whirled.

I had wings.

I. Had. Wings.

I couldn't make my mind work past that thought.

I had wings.

I wasn't supposed to have wings. I was a powerless nephilim, more human than angel. How the hell did I have wings? Wings ruined everything. Made me a liar, and a monster.

I didn't want to believe I was more like Michael's nephilim than I was human. I didn't want my nature to change, to become violent or bloodthirsty. All I wanted, all I ever wanted, was to help others.

Behind Cassius, Kol howled and wrenched in Gideon's grip, swiping his blade at me, desperate to kill the monster. Me. His face was a mask of pure panic and rage, and his emotions turned the air frigid. All sense of the flirtatious, wicked incubus was gone, and my throat tightened with grief and rage. A reaction like that meant his experience with Michael and his nephilim had been worse than he'd made it out to be. Horrifyingly worse.

Cassius pulled a red zip tie with a power containment spell on it from his pocket and, with his fire whip, yanked up one of my hands, burned and bleeding from my own power. He slipped the tie over my wrist, and the world darkened and snapped cold. My buzz's stinging inferno stuttered along with the lurching temperature from Cassius's fury and Kol's fear, but that only made me more aware of the pain in my body, adding a dislocated shoulder to my broken ribs and the agony in my back where my wings had ripped free.

"Her wings aren't magical constructs. The zip tie would have dispelled them. They're real." Cassius's gaze locked on me, his angel glow blazing in his eyes. "Get Kol back to the roof to guard the witches then get the SUV."

"Cassius—" Gideon started.

"She's a nephilim."

From the corner of my eye, my vision lurching in and out of focus, I saw Gideon stiffen. But I was afraid to look at him and see the same hurt and betrayal in his eyes that I'd seen in Kol's the moment my wings appeared.

"She's my mate." The force of Gideon's words made my soul sing, but when I raised my gaze, my vision darkened and his expression was strange. Had he really said that with conviction or was that just what I wanted to hear? God, it was so hard to focus.

"And she's a war criminal," Cassius said.

"Cassius—"

"We'll deal with this back at Operations. In private," he said, cutting Gideon off again. Then his tone softened a bit. "Get Kol to the roof and get the SUV. We have to get her back to Operations before someone sees her."

Gideon opened his mouth to say something but another billowing wave of spinning darkness swept over me and when my vision cleared, he was hauling Kol, still out-of-his-mind screaming, out of the alley.

Then Cassius wrenched back to me, his fury so strong it snapped to cold. "Where are the other nephilim?"

"There are no others," I gasped. I still couldn't figure out what had happened. The guys had been fighting the witches. Kol had been knocked off the roof. I'd tried to catch him and—

"There are always others. Your kind can't be alone. You don't know how to be alone. You're pack animals."

"There are no others." I was alone all the time. I had

been for so long I hadn't realized how empty I was until I'd found my guys. God, my guys—

Cassius jerked me forward and slammed me back against the full garbage bin with a thud. Hot white agony shot through my chest and the world darkened. I fought to catch my breath but couldn't, each inhalation blazing torment through me.

A part of me prayed I'd pass out, in part to stop the pain, but more because I wasn't ready to face my guys. Kol had been instantly horrified. I was still confused about Gideon's reaction, and I had no idea what Jacob's would be. Marcus's, without a doubt, would be furious. He, above all, had completely believed I was human and that I wanted nothing to do with the supernatural world. He'd sacrificed years being apart from me because he'd thought that was what I wanted.

Except now the truth was out. Would his wolf still see me as his mate? Was that a bond that could be broken, unlike the unbreakable angelic mating brand I shared with Gideon and Jacob?

My throat tightened and tears stung my eyes. It had all happened so fast, and it was all too soon. Maybe if I'd had time to show them who I was, they'd have been able to forgive the lie. But they barely knew me, even Marcus. I was a monstrous abomination, my kind responsible for the torture and death of so many people, and Gideon, Jacob, and Kol all had first-hand experience with nephilim.

Cassius slammed me against the garbage bin again. "I said, what's your plan?"

I dragged my whirling thoughts back to him. "No plan."

"Tell me your plan. You infiltrated Operations. You branded my brother." His grip on my throat tightened, and I fought to breathe. "I can't kill you, but I can make the rest of your life miserable. Without your magic, you won't be able to kill yourself to end it or my brother." His fire whips tightened around my wrists, and I panted against the pain. "Didn't your siblings tell you to kill yourself the second you were caught?"

"I don't have siblings. I'm natural." *God, please just believe me.*

He barked a bitter laugh. "There's no such thing as a natural nephilim."

"Please," I begged, the alley spinning faster and growing darker.

Cassius said something, but I couldn't focus past the pain to understand him.

Time lurched and Cassius shoved me into the SUV— I had no idea how I'd made it to the mouth of the alley. I tried to drag my gaze up to Gideon in the driver's seat, but couldn't raise my head. My heart was breaking. I had to know how he felt. I couldn't be alone again, an outcast without a family. Please. I needed them, needed to belong, needed to be loved for who I was.

Except I hadn't been loved for who I was. Not all of me. I'd never be fully accepted and it had been foolish to think I could keep my secret and my guys. Now I had neither.

The darkness surged again and my stomach churned. I had to have a concussion. It was the only explanation for why I couldn't think straight, couldn't get my vision to clear.

Another lurch in time and we were in the Quarter. I'd missed the entire ride from City Hall.

"Go around to security," Cassius said. "Let's not parade her in front of every angel in Union."

Gideon parked on the other side of the building in front of a metal door instead of pulling into the garage, and Cassius hauled me out of the SUV. He pressed his thumb to a fingerprint reader and marched me into the secure part of Operations, where they kept the holding cells and interrogation rooms. I leaned my forehead against the cool cinderblock wall and squeezed my eyes shut, but the world wouldn't stop spinning.

"Go back to City Hall. Deal with those witches." That sounded like Cassius.

"Chris and Nathaniel are—"

"Not the team's leader." Cassius's voice was strangely gentle, with no sign of the fury I'd seen in the alley. "You have an optics problem already. You can't afford to let head office think they should replace you. I've got this."

Someone said my name. I was pretty sure it was Gideon. Or maybe I'd just imagined it. Then there was a long pause... or I blacked out again. I wasn't sure which.

"God damn it," Gideon hissed. "Fine."

I forced my eyes open and managed to raise my gaze to look at him, but he'd already strode halfway out the door.

Cassius unlocked the interrogation room beside us, shoved me into the plain gray space, and down onto a metal chair. He cuffed my hands to the bar in the middle of the stainless steel table, and a freezing, aching hollowness filled my chest as the magic containment cuffs locked away my power. Without a word or a second glance, he stormed out of the room.

I sagged forward, leaning my forehead on the cool table, trying to draw a breath that didn't hurt and fighting my tears. I was a survivor. I could survive this.

Except I couldn't. Even if a miracle happened and I managed to escape, Gideon and Jacob would be able to find me through the brand. And even if they let me go, I was broken without them. I didn't want to be. I wanted to be strong, independent, but the magic that bound our souls together was stronger than me. I couldn't fight it for the rest of my life. Hell, I could barely fight just thinking about fighting it.

Come on. There had to be a way out of this, a way to break the bonds, to escape, to—

But I didn't *want* to do any of that. I wanted to stay. I wanted things to go back to this morning when I'd woken in Gideon's arms, and Marcus had kissed me, and all my guys loved me.

Didn't they still love me? They had to sill love me. Didn't they?

But I was now a monster, a war criminal. Unless I could convince Cassius otherwise, I was going to be locked up for the rest of my life even if they did love me.

This couldn't be my fate. I couldn't live like this.

Please, love me.

I knew I was being irrational, that my emotions were going crazy, but I couldn't get them under control. It was as if a dam had broken and I couldn't stop the flood. I bit back a sob. Even if my guys did want me, the best I could hope for was magical stasis. Cassius would put me to sleep, and I'd never wake up.

Which wasn't God damned fair. I wasn't one of the nephilim from the war and I didn't have an ulterior plan. But I already knew life wasn't fair. My mom gave up everything for me and she'd died too young. My father had given me up completely. I'd never known him and I'd like to have thought he'd have wanted to be in my life if it hadn't risked revealing my half-angelic nature.

The door banged open, and instinct jerked me up, my wings slapping against the back of the chair. Blazing white agony sliced through my chest and my throat tightened again. Cassius. Not one of my guys.

Jeez, come on. Get a grip. Focus.

"Gideon—"

"—is none of your concern now," he snapped, and I knew there was no way in hell he'd get any of my guys for me no matter how much I begged... if they even wanted to see me.

He sat in the chair across from me, fire licking over his hands as if he were so angry he couldn't fully control his power. "It'll be easier on you if you just tell the truth."

I sucked in a shallow breath. "I'm a natural nephilim." I forced out the words, words I'd never thought I'd ever say out loud, let alone twice and to an angel. "I was born before the war. I was seven when Michael fell."

Please believe me.

"The truth." Cassius's fire snapped from his fingers and brushed my knuckles. I jerked back, yanking my wrists in the cuffs securing me to the table and slicing more agony through me. "You bound my brother's soul to yours," he snarled. "You've poisoned something beautiful and sacred. For what? What's your plan?"

"There's no plan." He *had* to believe me. My *guys* had to believe me. *Someone* had to. But my mother had warned me. No one would. I was impossible, and no one wanted to risk letting one of Michael's monsters go free by believing a lie.

"There's always a plan." Cassius's fire flared, making me jerk back again. "Tell me."

"There's no plan." There never was a plan. All I wanted was to live a normal human life. All I wanted was to not be alone.

"I'll get it out of you," he said, his voice dark.

Except there was nothing to get, and he wasn't ever going to believe the truth. No one would.

My eyes burned, my tears threatening to release. I had no idea why I fought them. It didn't matter if Cassius thought I was weak. I couldn't convince him of the truth, and my emotions were just too overwhelming.

God, why did I have to have wings? Why couldn't they have shown up later when Cassius was gone and my guys truly knew me?

But that wasn't the way it was and I had to pull my shit together.

"Tell me the plan." His fire swept over my hands and up my wrists.

A strangled scream escaped my clenched jaw. The room darkened again, but I didn't pass out. I had to think. *Come on, think.*

"Lawyer," I gasped.

"You're a terrorist. I can hold you indefinitely without cause."

"Lawyer." There wasn't anything else I could say, although I didn't believe for a second he'd get me a lawyer or that a lawyer would even believe or, hell, represent me. All I could hope was that I'd buy some time while waiting for a lawyer to arrive... if a lawyer arrived, for my head to clear. "I have rights."

"JP law doesn't recognize nephilim as people. You don't have rights," he said. "Tell me where your siblings are. How many of you are left? What's your end game?"

"Lawyer." I couldn't lie about having nephilim siblings to get him to leave me alone. He'd just come back more enraged. A part of me wanted to say I'd only tell one of my guys, but that would only add to Cassius's belief that I had a plan.

He jerked to his feet and slammed his palms on the stainless steel table. His flames swept around him. "Tell me your plan or you'll wish you never perverted the mating brand and hurt my brother."

And that was what hurt the most. Even if I hadn't meant it, I'd betrayed Gideon and Marcus and Jacob in a way that couldn't be forgiven. I'd let them believe I was something I wasn't, and it didn't matter if I'd shown them my true self or not. That one fundamental lie put everything else in doubt, most of all whether they'd really fallen in love with me or if I'd manipulated them.

"Tell me." Cassius leaned closer, his fire searing over my arms.

I jerked against the cuffs, unable to stop myself, and

blazing agony sliced through my chest, forcing me to pant shallow, ragged breaths.

"Tell me or I'll bring in Yadveer and have him tear into your memories."

My pulse skipped. He thought that was a threat, but having the lethe demon see the truth and then show it to Cassius might convince him I wasn't lying.

"I consent," I gasped. "I consent to the lethe demon reading my memories."

"You're not a person. I don't need your consent." He shoved back from the table. "Don't think you can give consent and then hide the truth from Yadveer. You can't hide anything from him. He's cracked more powerful supers than you."

He stormed from the room, and I sagged my head onto the table, sobbing. A flicker of electricity, the gentle hum I recognized as Gideon's power, whispered through our brand, finally noticeable past my buzz because the containment cuffs had silenced it. Guess the containment cuffs didn't affect the magic of the mating brand.

But that only made me ache more. I yearned to talk to him, to see him, but feared to at the same time. We'd finally agreed to start figuring out our relationship. Hell, I was just starting to figure out my relationship with all my guys.

And now—

My throat tightened and more tears plopped onto the metal table.

Gideon's electricity, still filled with warmth, affection, honor, and determination, the part of him that resonated core-deep with my essence, grew stronger. It slid up my arm into Jacob's brand, and I felt his powerful stillness and intense certainty.

My guys were coming closer. *Please open the door. Please tell me everything is going to be okay.*

But a small voice, the voice I'd lived with all my life, said that they wouldn't. And even if they did, what did I say to them? What *could* I say to them?

It always came back to that. I couldn't possibly be what I was. And even if I was, I'd still lied.

The minutes ticked by. Cassius didn't storm back in. He was probably trying to make me sweat, building up my fear about what was to come in hopes I'd confess. But having my memories read was my only salvation. Gideon and Jacob got a little closer, but not close enough to open the door. They probably weren't even in the secure section of Operations. And, now that I'd had time to think about it, the strange tone of Cassius's voice earlier had been calm and consoling. Without a doubt he'd lied to Gideon. Which, for a second, shocked the hell out of me, because that was a very unangelic thing to do. But Cassius was more emotional than the typical icy angel, and I didn't doubt he'd lie to protect his brother. Except that meant none of my guys knew where I was. They were probably going along, business as usual, dealing with the glyph witches and the mess at City Hall.

My thoughts muddled, and my body grew heavy. I dreamed of Gideon arguing with Cassius, the light in his eyes blazing, his expression furious. In fact, all of my guys stood up for me and demanded my release. Gideon was yelling, his voice hard and icy, Marcus barely had his wolf contained and was snarling, Jacob radiated more vampiric intensity than I'd ever felt before, and Kol—

Wasn't there. Even my psyche knew no matter what I wanted or craved, I'd lost our friendship by just being what I was.

Besides, it was just a dream. I was a monster.

Except I wasn't a monster. I was a naturally born nephilim.

But that didn't mean I wasn't a monster.

And that was the fear the zip overdose had brought to life, the fear I'd been hiding from myself my entire life. What if Michael's nephilim weren't monsters because that was how he'd made them, but because that was just what nephilim were? Human DNA twisting angel DNA because the DNA of a being of celestial light was supposed to be incompatible with anything else. Except if that was true, then I shouldn't exist—

Or I wasn't natural.

The door banged open, and I jerked awake, the sudden movement again shooting agony across my chest and stealing my breath.

Cassius stormed in again, fire still licking over his hands and now curling up his forearms to his elbows. Yadveer, Operations' resident lethe demon, shuffled in behind him, looking as elderly and weathered as I remembered. Pricks of red light glowed in his dark eyes, the only indication—at this distance—that he was anything other than human.

He settled on the chair across from me and held out his hand, radiating the telltale heat of a demon. "You want to know everything?" he asked Cassius.

I shuddered at the question, even though I already knew that if Cassius went ahead with his plan for Yadveer to read my memories, my entire life, every hope and dream and fuck-up, would be exposed. I wasn't sure if it was a good thing or not that I hadn't slept with Gideon. If I had, then Yadveer would be able to show Cassius how much I cared for Gideon and how connected we were... and how much his rejection was going to hurt.

"Make it fast." Cassius crossed his arms and glowered at me. "My brother's life is in danger. All of Operations could be in danger."

"Fast will be painful." Yadveer's gaze dipped to my burned and bleeding hands cuffed to the bar at the center of the table. "She's already injured. She could lose consciousness."

"Will it kill her?"

"Not likely," Yadveer said.

"Then my only concern is learning the truth and keeping my brother and everyone in this facility safe. You do what you have to do."

Yadveer's gaze rose back to mine, not a hint of sympathy in his eyes. "As you wish."

CHAPTER 2

A HARD BALL OF ICE FORMED IN MY GUT AS YADVEER TOOK my hand, and I tried to fight my fear. This was the only way to prove my innocence. Hopefully it would be enough so I wouldn't be locked up like a criminal for the rest of my life. Except the alternative was to be studied like a lab rat to learn how I was even possible.

Yadveer closed his eyes, and fire, not the gentle heat from when he'd read my memories before, scorched into my hand and up my arm with a pain as powerful as my buzz. I tried to bite back a scream but couldn't stop it. The inferno seared into every cell of my being, diving deep into me, threatening to control me like the archnephilim had—

I slammed against an alley wall, agony shooting through my chest. The archnephilim wrenched me close, his power and darkness whirling around me, turning my buzz into an inferno. Then he poured his smoke into my mouth, and I fought to breathe, to move, to do anything. But the archnephilim kept pouring his essence into me, trying to control me. *No, please. I won't let him. He can't take me—*

Except he *had* controlled me. He'd made me burn Kol—

I wrenched around as divine light burst from my hands and slammed into Kol's chest. He staggered, and everything lurched into terrifying slow motion, every detail crisp, perfect, as if Yadveer's magic enhanced everything I'd seen but hadn't noticed.

More divine light blazed from my palms, and terror filled Kol's eyes as I grabbed his head, sending all that power into his face, burning his skin, the charred bitter smell of blood and burnt flesh filling my nose.

Kol screamed. The sound tore at my soul, making the part of me that knew this was a memory, that Kol was all right, writhe against Yadveer's power. This wasn't who I was. The archnephilim had made me do it. I hadn't wanted to hurt Kol.

Please. Look at the good I've done, the people I've helped. I strained to direct Yadveer to the years I'd been a cop, but my memory jumped to a dark dusty living room.

My thigh was on fire. A shifter, his eyes filled with wild feral intensity, dug his claws deeper into my leg and yanked me close, while a massive gray wolf snapped its jaw around Marcus's arm. Marcus screamed and the wolf wrenched him to the floor.

My memory lurched again. Blood dripped from Marcus's elbow onto a floor with a thick layer of disturbed dust.

Another lurch. A vampire with pale skin, black eyes, and animalistic hunger in her gaze snarled at me. Blood, so much blood, smeared down her chin and soaked into her filthy torn shirt from the zip addict she'd just killed. Her fingers were extended into short, sharp claws, and the reek of rotting human flesh made bile burn the back of my throat. I had a magazine of enspelled ammunition in my hand, ready to load into my Glock, but lightning, like a Taser blast on its highest setting, shot through me. My thoughts jerked to Gideon. He was in trouble, hurt, dying, and I couldn't lose him. God, please. I couldn't lose him.

The thought crushed me and I couldn't breathe, but my memories jerked again, not releasing me.

I sat in a bland beige hospital room, my mother's frail hand held gingerly in mine. Her skin was so thin, so pale, like fragile gauzy fabric, and the monitor beeped, loud, slow, horrible chirps. She'd collapsed again and against her wishes I'd called 911. I knew it was too late to save her, but I couldn't sit by and watch her suffer any longer. She hadn't wanted me to spend my escape money on her, hadn't wanted to burden me with medical bills or questions, and we'd fought about it the last couple of days. My last words to her had been frustrated and angry.

Please wake up so I can tell you how much I love you. I slid into bed beside her and wrapped my arms around her. *Please don't die. You're all I have.*

My memory lurched again. We still lay in bed, but this time Mom had her arms around me, and I had my pink princess comforter pulled up to my chin. I was warm and safe and Mom smelled fresh and sweet. It was a few days before we'd had the first JP agent scare—or at least the first one I could remember. I was five? No, four, and I'd known nothing about the Joined Parliament or nephilim.

"Tell me again about Daddy."

Joy and awe lit up Mom's eyes with a look I never got tired of seeing. True love. Love I'd hoped to have one day.

"He's the most beautiful angel I've ever seen. His hair is brown but looks like copper if the sun hits it just the right way, just like yours." She pressed her lips to my forehead. "And his eyes are warm and brown with flecks of gold. Angel glow radiates from his eyes even when he sleeps and his wings—" Her voice turned wistful and sad, like it always did when she talked about Daddy. "His wings are pure white, and he'll fly back to us soon."

Except 'soon' turned into 'someday', which turned into 'couldn't' because it was too dangerous. Daddy would never be able to hide his true nature and look human, while Mom would never be anything but human, and that would make too many people ask too many questions about me.

My memories lurched again, whirling faster and faster, the fire of Yadveer's magic searing into my cells. Hiding in an abandoned house, shaking with fear. Playing with three other kids on the banks of a shallow creek beneath an overpass, bright with wonder. Teased by Marcus while on patrol, hot with desire.

I fought to breathe, to think, to do anything other than feel the blaze of my memories, each one growing stronger, the emotions more powerful, as Yadveer yanked me around in my mind. Frost covering the backs of my hands, scared. Lying on soft grass in the backyard, safe. First day at the police academy, determined. Burying my mother by myself, empty. Seeing my guys for the first time, dread. Gideon. Jacob. Kol. Marcus. Anger. Joy. Desire. Fear. Whirling and lurching and burning and—

Nothing. No pain, no memory, and no magic. Just peaceful black oblivion. For a second, no longer than a fluttering heartbeat, I floated in a water that wasn't water. I was safe... but still alone. I ached for my guys. This wasn't where I was supposed to be. Except I no longer knew where to go or how to get there.

A thread of agony blazed through the darkness, and I gasped shallow breaths, desperate to ease the pain.

"—didn't get it all, but—"

"Then wake her up and finish it," Cassius snapped.

Another slice of pain cut through my chest.

"The block is magical," Yadveer said. "I think it's crumbling, but it's still too strong for me to break through. It also doesn't feel like her magic."

"So someone else put it on her?"

"Yes."

"Who?"

"I won't know until the block comes down," Yadveer said.

I cracked my eyes open to see an out-of-focus table edge and floor. I'd passed out on the table, putting pressure on my broken ribs and dislocated shoulder. Blood darkened the side of my T-shirt and hip and dripped off the side of the chair into a pool on the floor. I couldn't figure out how I was bleeding. Yadveer's magic was purely mental and it didn't make sense that Cassius would hurt me while Yadveer worked.

With a snap of mental fire, residue of Yadveer's

magical intrusion, my memory leaped back to the alley. Kol had attacked me. I must have been in too much shock to notice he'd actually cut me before Gideon had yanked him back. I tried to concentrate on my brands to see if I was drawing strength from Gideon and Jacob, determine if they were in danger of my dying, but couldn't focus past the pain.

"We're not waiting for the spell to fail. Call Bane. Tell him we need a spell broken, and I don't care what it costs." Cassius's feet strode into sight, and he grabbed my arm with the dislocated shoulder.

I screamed as agony exploded in my shoulder and chest. My wings jerked, hitting the back of the chair, and the room went dark.

"—and how could you not know she was bleeding?" That sounded like Amiah and she sounded pissed.

I cracked my eyes open again. My head was back on the table, and pain flooded every inch of my body. I must have passed out again.

"I know now, so heal her," Cassius said.

Amiah's black practical shoes came into sight. I tried to raise my head to look at her and Cassius, and hell, anyone else in the room, but couldn't find the strength. She grabbed my shoulder and the lightning of her magic erupted inside me, blazing through my body until darkness enveloped me again.

"—her essence."

I strained against the darkness, trying to figure out who had spoken, where I was, and what was going on. There'd been pain, so much pain, and—

I bit back a sob. My guys knew the truth.

"We'll deal with it when Bane gets here." That sounded like Cassius.

I'd passed out again? At least this time, although I could still feel the world spinning even with my eyes closed, the pain of my injuries was gone.

"He's a mercenary," Amiah said. "Do you honestly think we can trust him with this?"

"The replacement spell-break charm is still on backorder. He's the only one in Union City who might have quick access to one and be powerful enough to break the spell on her," Cassius said.

I forced my eyes open as he grabbed my upper arm and hauled me to my feet. The room darkened and lurched and my wings bashed against him, but I didn't pass out again.

He jerked me around the table, my mind stumbling over the fact I was no longer handcuffed to the bar. Amiah glared at me—

No, not a glare. Something else. I couldn't read her expression. It was hard and concerned... and something...But with the containment cuffs still around my wrists—at some point the zip tie had been removed—I had no idea what she was feeling.

She stepped away from the door to let us pass, and Cassius hauled me into the hall and deeper into the secured section of Operations. The fluorescent lights above were too bright and even though Amiah had healed me—or at least mostly healed me—I still couldn't get my head to stop spinning.

We reached a T-intersection and turned left into a long hall with half a dozen metal doors on either side.

Cassius marched me to a door halfway down and unlocked it with his thumbprint. Inside was a narrow gray cell with a stainless steel toilet and sink and a hard, wide bench running along one side.

I shuffled inside—thankful he didn't push me—and the door closed with a heavy *thunk*. With a groan, I eased onto the edge of the bench, since my wings wouldn't let me sit back. And while I really wanted to lie down, I didn't want to deal with the frustration of figuring out *if* there was a good position to lie with them sticking out of my back.

Cassius hadn't removed the containment cuffs, probably because he didn't want me to turn my power on myself and commit suicide. Not that I'd ever consider hurting Gideon and Jacob that way. He probably thought the cuffs would piss me off, but I was grateful they were still on because they silenced my buzz. And once the cell stopped spinning from the blast of Amiah's healing magic, I was going to feel better than I had in days... physically, at least.

My back still stung, though, so I rolled my no-longer-dislocated shoulder, confirming it was back to normal, and felt my ribs and side for tenderness. Nothing. Guess Amiah's healing hadn't dealt with the effects of whatever magic had ripped my wings out from inside me.

I shifted, and my wings extended and banged into the walls on either side. Jeez, they were going to take some getting used to, and not only did my back still sting, but the muscles ached as well. I contemplated trying to pull the damned things back into my body, but I had no idea how to do that or if the containment cuffs would even let me.

Wonderful.

Okay, think. There's a way out of this. There had to be. *Please let Cassius believe the memories Yadveer pulled from my mind and let Sebastian confirm that whatever spell was on me wasn't my doing.*

My thoughts tripped over that. Someone had put a spell on me. Was that why my eyes hadn't glowed until after I'd blasted myself with divine light? Or why I barely had any magic? I'd thought I was more or less powerless because my human half was stronger than my angelic half, that it was just the way nature had combined my parents' DNA in me. But maybe nature had nothing to do with it.

Sebastian had said that every time I'd used my divine light, I'd burned through the concealment spell on my contacts. That was basic concealment magic one-o-one. What if my father had placed a powerful spell that concealed my true nature and my magic even from me?

I had no idea if that was even possible or the kind of power it would take for a spell to last thirty years without failing. Which made me wonder who my father was and just how much power he possessed.

The lock on the door clicked, and I jerked awake. Somehow I'd managed to lean my head and shoulder against the cell wall without twisting or crushing my wings too much and passed out. I rubbed my face, emotionally and physically exhausted from everything that had happened in the last couple of days, and knowing I needed to stay calm. Freaking out wouldn't help Cassius believe I was harmless and meant what I said when I claimed to be a naturally born nephilim.

Except it wasn't Cassius who stepped into the cell but Sebastian. His nearly translucent skin glowed with cold white-blue light, and his eyes, such a pale blue they were almost clear, leaped from my wings to my face. His lips curled back in a wicked smile, still filled with sexual invitation even though I was clearly a nephilim, and for the first time I didn't sense there was something else going on behind his smile.

"So that's what you've been hiding." He let the door close behind him but didn't draw closer. Which bothered the hell out of me.

"I don't bite."

"What if I ask nicely?" He still didn't move from the door.

"I'm—" My throat tightened and I snapped my mouth shut. I'd been about to say I was taken. But I didn't know if I was any more. I sagged back, painfully pinched my wing between the wall and the bench, and jerked forward.

God damn fucking wings. How the hell had I ever dreamed of having them so I could fly like Gideon? They ruined everything, and now I couldn't sit or move the way I wanted to. "Just do whatever Cassius is paying you to do."

"He wants to know why you have no memories of your siblings or your plans to infiltrate Operations."

"Because I have no siblings or plans." I don't know why I kept saying it. No one was going to believe me. "I'm an only child, naturally born."

Sebastian crossed his arms, straining his white button-down against his muscular shoulders and showing the shadow of his black tattoos twisting over his biceps. "Angels claim that's impossible."

"So I've been told."

"Did you have a spell put on you to hide your nature?"

"You mean the spell that Yadveer says is blocking my memories?" He wasn't going to believe the truth, either. "Just go digging around or spell breaking or whatever it is you're supposed to do. Cassius doesn't believe me. Why would anyone else?"

"I do." Sebastian eased onto the edge of the bench beside me. "I knew you were hiding something, but I never sensed insincerity from you."

He pressed a hand to his ribs, activating one of his magic glyphs. Light blazed from a swirl of black tattoo, making his white shirt see-through, revealing thick black tattoos covering his entire chest and abs and disappearing past the waistband of his slacks. "Take a breath and close your eyes."

I drew in a breath—an honest-to-goodness deep breath—and closed my eyes. Sebastian pressed his palms to my temples and lightning shot into my brain while power clenched inside my chest. I gasped and instinctively opened my eyes, meeting Sebastian's gaze.

A universe of icy light snapped in his irises with blazing power. It poured into every cell within me just like Yadveer's fire and the archnephilim's smoke, but instead of burning or consuming, it lit me up. My skin glowed, my divine light bleeding not just from my palms but every pore, and for a moment I felt like a true being of celestial light. I wasn't just half angel and mundane human. I was living, breathing light. It crackled along my nerves and radiated around my heart. My angel brands blazed a brilliant gold, swirling from my forearm to my shoulder, the light shining through the fabric of my T-shirt.

Sebastian's eyes widened and the icy power flared, the weight of the universe in his gaze crushing me, making my own light blaze brighter with a pressure that kept growing. It threatened to rip me apart, disintegrate my physical form until all that remained was light.

Tears raced down my cheeks, but I couldn't close my eyes, couldn't look away from all that power. I'd never felt anything like it before and doubted I would ever again.

A scream tore from my throat and my light erupted into a blinding explosion. My body went limp, but Sebastian caught me, pulling me against his chest before I could fall back and twist my wings. His breath came too fast and his body shook.

"You're not at all what you say you are," he gasped.

More tears rolled down my cheeks and soaked into his shirt. "So I am one of Michael's puppets and didn't even know it?" Were my mating brands with Gideon and Jacob even real? I loved them. I knew I loved them. But that didn't mean it wasn't part of some greater plan that I knew nothing about.

Oh, God, even my memories could be fake, magical constructions. All the time I'd spent with my mom, the heartache of losing her, my whole life up until I'd been assigned as Marcus's partner. I had no idea how any of that made sense, how anyone could have known being Marcus's partner four and a half years ago would get me close to the JP team, but I no longer knew what was true.

"Esther, you're not a puppet." He cupped my cheeks with his palms and nudged me back to look him in the eyes. The icy universe and his enormous power were gone. His eyes were back to their unusual, almost-clear blue. "You're not human."

CHAPTER 3

My thoughts tripped over his words. "Of course I'm human." How could I not be human? "My essence says I'm human." My whole life, every super I'd come across who could read essences had thought I was human. Except my whole life might have been a fabrication.

"You're not. Someone hid your true essence with a powerful spell—" Sebastian frowned and his grip on my cheeks tightened as he drew nose to nose with me. "Gold flecks."

"Gold what?"

"Flecks. In your angel glow."

"What does that mean?" I tried to keep my voice steady while my thoughts spun. I didn't think I was ever going to feel steady again. I had to have gotten the flecks from my father, the man I'd dreamed about yesterday. Maybe Sebastian knew who my father was.

"It means you're at least half archangel," he said, a tremor racing through him. With a strangled groan, he pressed his forehead to mine, as if it were too heavy to hold up. "It's going to take at least another attempt, probably more, to break the spell on you."

"My father was an archangel?"

"Your mother, too, possibly."

"My mother, too?" I couldn't wrap my mind around that, especially since he was saying my mom couldn't possibly be my mom.

He had to be wrong. I couldn't be a full angel. My mom *was* my mom. A human. Angels didn't die from cancer and the doctors had been clear, cancer had killed her, but— "I'm an angel, not a nephilim?"

"Yes," Sebastian gasped. "There's nothing human about you."

The cell door banged open, making me jerk back from Sebastian, who stayed sagged forward, hands on his thighs to keep himself from collapsing face-first into my lap.

Gideon stormed in, the glow in his eyes radiating brilliant white light, and my heart stuttered with yearning and fear. Even with his beautiful blond hair buzzed short like his brother's, he was breathtaking with his chiseled jaw, broad muscular shoulders, and narrow hips.

Except I'd never seen him this cold before, every inch of his posture screaming death and vengeance. This was an avenging angel, the kind people had talked about from the war. Powerful, brutal, and if they possessed any emotion at all, it was hard and icy.

A shiver swept over me, and a vise squeezed around my heart. I yanked my gaze to the floor. He was furious.

I'd lied to him, and as far as he knew, I was an abomination. Our bond wasn't enough for him to love me. I knew it wouldn't be, not faced with the truth so soon, but that reality crushed me, making my soul hurt even more than my body did.

"Move away from her, Bane," Gideon said, his voice low, hard.

Because I was a monster.

Sebastian shuddered, groaned, and didn't move.

"Bane!"

The sharpness of his tone yanked my attention to Gideon as Sebastian gasped and jerked back, falling off the edge of the bench onto his butt. "It's not what it looks like."

"Then what is it?" Gideon growled. "The brand lit up with power."

"All her power."

Gideon leveled his gaze on me, and I shrank back, squeezing my wings against the wall. "Nephilim don't possess that kind of power."

"Yeah, about that—"

Jacob and Marcus shoved into the doorway, pushing Gideon further into the cell. They were opposites in size, Jacob bulky and big with his barrel chest and bulging biceps, and Marcus with his wiry compact form. Jacob's complexion was too pale, but I couldn't see any injuries and his clothes were clean. He must have changed, after the fight on City Hall's roof with the three glyph witches, while I was in the interrogation room. Marcus also looked like he'd changed, and he must have shifted and healed his injuries because he looked fine. At least they'd gotten through the fight okay.

My heart swelled with joy, then plummeted a second later as my brain caught up with my situation. I yearned for Marcus to wrap his arms around me, pull me tight to his lean-muscled body, and tell me everything was all right. But it wasn't all right. If Gideon was furious with me, Marcus certainly was as well. He, out of all of them, had the biggest reason to be livid.

"The brand started burning." Jacob turned all his vampiric intensity to Sebastian, who shuddered and groaned again.

"Not my power."

"He says the power was Essie's," Gideon said.

Jacob shifted his gaze to me, and for the first time the strength of his vampiric intensity terrified me. "Nephilim don't have that kind of power."

"No shit," Sebastian snapped.

"For fuck's sake." Marcus shouldered past Jacob, knelt in front of me, and grabbed my hands. His wolf darkened his eyes, its feral intensity threatening to take over, but not with rage. No, with ferocious, protective love.

My thoughts tripped over that and my throat tightened.

"Are you all right?"

Was I all right? He wanted to know—

Tears burned my eyes. One simple question and I knew Marcus didn't care what I was. He didn't care that I'd lied to him and we'd wasted years apart because of my fears. He still loved me.

"I'm getting you out of here." He pulled a handcuff key from his pocket and unlocked the cuffs.

My buzz exploded with a fiery agony, stealing my joy that Marcus was still my mate. Every inch of my skin burned, and my muscles twitched and clenched. It was worse than it had ever been before, and it had been overwhelming while standing on City Hall's roof.

"Marcus, please. Put the cuffs back on." I wasn't going to be able to stand, let alone think straight. And with Gideon still looking like he wanted to run someone through with his divine light sword—most likely me—I wasn't going to beg to hold his hand.

Jacob dropped to his knees beside Marcus. "We're not letting you stay here. We know *who* you are, what kind of person you are. We don't care *what* you are."

"Then you won't care that she's a full angel with at least one archangel parent," Sebastian said.

Gideon glared at him, the strength of his anger turning the air sweltering. "You should have led with that."

"You try breaking a spell designed to permanently hide even half of an archangel's power."

"Marcus, please," I gasped. The muscles in my back contracted, and my wings smashed against the wall and buffeted the guys.

Marcus's grip on my hands tightened, sending his frosted fear curling over my wrists and up my arms. "Pull your wings in."

"How?"

His eyes widened with surprise. Yeah, bet he'd never

had an angel ask him how to pull her wings in. "You just — Don't you know?"

"I didn't even know I had wings until this morning."

"Concentrate on drawing them into your body," Jacob said.

Sure. Concentrate. A muscle in my thigh clenched, and I yanked my hand from Marcus's grip and dug my knuckle into my leg, trying to get the spasm to release. But the movement only sent more stinging fire up my arms that did nothing to burn away Marcus's frost.

"Take a breath, Essie," Marcus said, "and pull them in."

I tried to take a breath, but my shoulders seized, cutting off my air with a sharp snap.

Come on. Concentrate. Pull them in. I fought to imagine my wings drawing into my body. The muscles between my shoulder blades seized again, and my wings slapped Jacob and Marcus. "Just put the God damn cuffs back on."

Gideon grabbed Sebastian by the arm and hauled him to his feet. "What's wrong with her?"

"Hell if I know."

"It'll be easier to get you out of here if you pull your wings in," Jacob said. "Gideon. Help her."

"I can't concentrate. I'm on fire." I was going to burn up— No, I was going to combust and take all my guys with me. The thought made my pulse trip and my gut clench with fear.

"Oh, fuck." A shudder raced through Sebastian. "The concealment spell must finally be weak enough that her power is trying to break through. Get her wings in and get those cuffs back on."

"I'm not handcuffing my mate." Light flared from Gideon's eyes.

"Please," I begged.

"Until we can figure out how to contain her, it'll be safer for everyone," Sebastian said.

Gideon glanced at Marcus and Jacob and the cell's temperature plummeted. The frost on my hands and arms thickened.

"Fine." Gideon shoved Sebastian toward the door. "Everyone out."

Marcus jerked to his feet and snarled at Gideon. "I'm not leaving her."

"Then duck when she turns around and keep your wolf under control." Gideon lifted his gaze to mine and beneath the rage I saw absolute terror.

I wrenched my gaze from his, stood, and turned, trusting the guys to get out of the way. "I'm sorry. I—" The muscles in my side clenched, making me whimper.

Gideon brushed trembling hands along the top of my wings. My buzz dimmed at the contact, but didn't vanish like it had when he'd touched me before. I fought back a sob of frustration.

"We'll deal with the power after we get your wings in," he said, his voice low and soothing, no sign of the fear I'd seen in his eyes or felt in his hands. "Concentrate on the spot between your shoulder blades."

His fingers grew steadier and skimmed closer to the base of my wings. The muted fire of my buzz turned sultry with desire, but the pressure inside me still threatened to explode.

He shifted closer. Gentle warmth radiated from his body that did nothing to melt the frost on my arms, and his breath feathered across the back of my neck.

"Imagine a spark of magic right here." He slid his thumbs along the base of my wings, the movement slow and sensual.

My breath hitched, desire rushing low within me. I hadn't known the base of an angel's wings was an erogenous zone, but just one touch and I was melting with need. I ached for him to draw closer and press his body against mine, preferably without our clothes on. So far we'd only kissed, but I needed him as much as I needed my other guys, and I had to solidify our bond before a part of my soul completely shattered and couldn't be fixed.

His lips brushed the hollow behind my ear. I gasped at the sudden kiss and tipped my head back against his shoulder. A low moan escaped his lips and vibrated to the core of my being. The pressure of his thumbs against my wings grew, the movement rougher, faster, as his breath picked up. But just like the last time we'd kissed, the force of my magic inside me grew with my desire. It swelled and mixed with the electric crackle of Gideon's power radiating from his brand, taking it and entwining it with mine.

His magic surged up my arm into Jacob's brand, who gasped as the surge pulled power from him into me. It rushed around my heart, churning stronger and stronger, filling me, burning through every inch of my body, seeping into every cell, and threatening to erupt in a violent explosion. Fear soured my desire and the knot in my gut tightened. I was going to hurt Gideon again. I was going to hurt all of them. I couldn't control myself.

"I can't do it. Put the cuffs back on." I jerked forward to put some distance between us, but he shifted forward with me, pinning my legs with his against the bench.

"Focus right here," he whispered.

"I can't. I'm going to hurt you."

"Right here." He ran a sensual firm stroke across the base of my wings again, making my breath catch and my attention jerk from my roaring power to my back. As if thinking about it refocused it, my power surged to where he touched me. "Fill the area with power and squeeze your shoulder blades together."

My stomach churned. *Pull in your wings. Come on. Please. I can do it. Just pull them in.* That was all I had to do. Just pull them in. *Please. Don't let me hurt them.*

"Squeeze your shoulder blades, Essie."

My power burned hotter, crackling along the top of my wings and sparking from the tips, and my muscles clenched and snapped. I couldn't make them work, couldn't draw my shoulder blades together.

Just pull them in.

The frost on my skin thickened into ice, but I couldn't feel the cold any more. There was only fire, burning me up, threatening to explode and burn my guys up, too.

Come on. Come on. I could do this. I *had* to do this.

I clenched my jaw and with a strangled scream wrenched my shoulder blades together. Gideon snapped electric power from his thumbs into my back, and my body flexed. Light blazed behind me, and my wings contracted and slammed inside my chest.

Oh, thank God.

But my power, without me trying to focus it, rushed to my palms and filled them with blazing, burning divine light.

Shit shit shit.

"The cuffs," Jacob said.

Marcus grabbed my hand and snapped a cuff around my wrist. All my power leaped to my free palm and blackened the cell wall.

God, no. I fought to hold it back, the pressure threatening to rip me apart and turn everything to ash. I was going to turn all of them to ash.

Marcus snapped on the other cuff and my power vanished, whooshing out of me, taking all my strength and leaving me shivering and hollow. My knees gave out and Gideon caught me before I fell, lifting me with ease, and cradled me against his chest.

I pressed my face against his neck, my pulse racing and tears burning my eyes. I couldn't do this. I'd almost lost control again, almost killed my guys.

"Put me down. I have to stay here," I said. The last time I'd kissed Gideon, my magic had blazed out of control. Just having him stroke me made it worse. It wasn't safe for me to leave this cell. "I'm too dangerous. I'm going to hurt someone."

"You're not," Marcus growled. "We're leaving and—"

Cassius stormed into the doorway. "What the hell is going on?"

Gideon's arms around me tightened, and he turned to

face Cassius, whose fire crackled over his hands, his anger just as strong as it had been before. Behind him, looking around his shoulder, was Amiah, her eyes narrow and gaze hard.

Marcus raised his chin in defiance and his fingers extended into claws. "We're taking our mate out of here."

"You're not taking her anywhere," Cassius said.

Jacob shifted to stand beside Marcus. "It's three against one."

Cassius's gaze jumped to Gideon. "Is it?"

"You lied to me," Gideon said.

"I said I'd take care of it and I did."

The light in Gideon's eyes flared. "You arrested her."

"Of course I did," Cassius snapped. "She's a war criminal. A monster."

"No, she's not," Gideon snarled, and Marcus growled a warning.

The muscles in Cassius's jaw flexed. "That's the brand talking."

"It's a true brand. Fate would *never* bind me with a monster." Gideon clutched me tighter. "Besides, she's not a nephilim."

Cassius turned his glare to Sebastian.

"Look at her eyes," Sebastian said with a shudder, his body still tight with pain.

With a huff, Cassius strode into the cell toward me. Gideon held his ground as his brother approached, but his body tensed and his electric power crackling up my arm swelled.

I met Cassius's gaze, praying he'd see what Sebastian had seen, and there wouldn't be a fight. If I wanted to look stronger, more in control, I should have asked to be put on my feet, but I needed Gideon's embrace right now more than I needed to convince Cassius of my power.

"Gold flecks." He didn't sound happy about that.

"So she *is* an angel, even if her essence doesn't say so," Amiah said, also not sounding happy.

"Glad you're so excited she isn't a nephilim," Marcus said, his tone thick with sarcasm. He turned to Gideon and Jacob, who gave him a tight nod, before returning his glare to Cassius. "We're leaving."

Cassius, his expression still hard, reached into his pocket and pulled out the handcuff key. "I'll remove the cuffs."

"No!" the guys said in unison.

Cassius's eyes widened with surprise.

"Not until I can figure out how to contain her power," Sebastian said. "She—"

A blast of all-too-familiar magic slammed into me, stealing my breath and blazing under my skin, as if the containment cuffs hadn't cut off my buzz. I was on fire again, my whole being caught in a whirling inferno of power, just like when I'd been on City Hall's rooftop and the guys had been fighting the three glyph witches. Except this was ten times more powerful.

Sebastian released a strangled cry and dropped to his knees. "What the fuck is that?"

"The glyph witches," I gasped.

Sebastian shuddered and hugged himself. "A glyph witch isn't that powerful."

"There are three of them," I said.

He groaned. "That's more power than even three glyph witches can summon."

"It's not the glyph witches. They're locked up under power containment wards," Cassius said. He looked fine, as if he could handle all that power pounding into him—

No. As if he couldn't feel it. I dragged my attention to Marcus and Jacob. They didn't look as if they felt it either, and Gideon's posture hadn't changed, so...

"Sebastian and I are the only ones who can feel it?"

"If she can feel glyph magic with the cuffs on, she must be an archangel," Amiah said.

"They're either not glyph witches," Sebastian said, "or they're getting outside help."

The pressure from the power swelled, and I bit back a whimper.

"We have to get to their cells." Cassius jerked to the door, his fire crackling over his hands and up his forearms.

"No. Get back here!" Sebastian pressed his hands to his chest and light burst from a swirling glyph hidden in his tattoos, making his shirt see-through again. The glyph curled from his right hip across his chest to his left shoulder and, when he leaned forward and pressed his hands to the floor, I could see the tattoo finished in the center of his back. "As close to me as possible. Now."

Gideon knelt beside Sebastian, still holding me, and Marcus and Jacob pressed close. Amiah gave Cassius a questioning look.

The witches' magic swelled again. I panted, trying to catch my breath around the agony, and Sebastian doubled forward in pain.

"Move. Now!" Gideon said.

Cassius grabbed Amiah's hand and jerked close to Jacob. Marcus caught Amiah as she stumbled into the group. She locked gazes with him, and the shadow of something dark and sad passed across her expression, before the witches' power exploded and I was blinded by agony.

CHAPTER 4

THE FORCE OF THE WITCHES' SPELL RIPPED THROUGH MY essence, stealing sight, breath, and thought. One of the guys screamed. Someone else yelled something, but power rushed in my head, stealing the words.

"—the hell was that?" Marcus asked. "Bane? Bane!"

I blinked black specs from my vision. Gideon still held me, his forehead pressed to mine, his body curled forward, protecting me. Sebastian had collapsed on the floor, his cheek against the concrete, his eyes half closed, his breath shallow. Amiah dropped beside him and grabbed his shoulder. Light flashed from her hand as she used her healing magic, and he jerked up with a strangled gasp, his pale eyes jumping to her in shock.

"What was that?" Cassius asked, his expression dazed.

"One fucking powerful spell." Bane stood, but his legs shook and Marcus grabbed him before he collapsed.

"I have to check on the witches." Cassius raced into the hall, his fire curling over both his arms, dripping from his hands, and sparking on the floor.

Gideon rose. "Jacob, you're the weakest right now. Take Essie."

"I can stand," I said. The roar of the witches' power was gone and so was my buzz again.

"Gideon," Cassius yelled in the hall. "I need you."

Gideon set me on my feet and rushed to help Cassius. Marcus and Jacob followed him. Amiah helped Sebastian stand, and I shuffled to the doorway, dizzier than I'd expected.

Power flickered at the edge of my senses, and Cassius tumbled past the door. Then a thick vine seized his leg and yanked him out of sight.

"Amiah, call for back up." I peeked out the door. With the cuffs on, I was powerless, even if it seemed I could still feel when the witches were activating the glyphs on their bodies. Only Marcus and Cassius had a key, and I wasn't sure I wanted to release my power. I was just as likely to blast one of my guys as one of the witches.

All three glyph witches were out of their cells, and had made it to the main hall leading to the double set of security doors separating the secure section of Operations from the rest of the building. Vines from one of the dark-haired swarthy-skin witches squeezed Jacob, pinning his hands to his sides and drawing a scream. Gideon sliced through the vines with his divine light sword, while Marcus lunged at the witch with bright red hair, his fingers extended into claws.

The vine, still wrapped around Cassius's leg, slammed him against the ceiling. He sliced the vine with a whip of fire and crashed to the floor. The third witch, with similar dark hair and skin to the vine witch and a dark tattoo covering her entire right arm, raced into the hall toward the doors.

"Stop her," Gideon yelled. "Don't let her get out."

Marcus shoved past the red-haired witch, but she pressed a hand to her forearm, activating a glyph hidden in the colorful tattoo on her arm, and yelled a guttural word. More power shuddered against my senses, stronger this time, and a flicker of buzz sliced through the magic of the containment cuffs as Marcus slammed into an invisible wall.

"I don't think so." She pressed a different tattoo and lunged in, a blade of ice forming in her hand.

Marcus jerked to the side. The blade skimmed his ribs, slicing shirt and skin. A vine shot from the floor, seized his leg, and tossed him into Gideon. They slammed into the wall and sagged to the floor. Cassius leaped past them and snapped a whip of fire at the vine witch, who blocked it with another vine.

Jacob dove for the vine witch as well, slicing through a vine that wrapped around his wrist with his short, sharp claws. But another, bigger vine seized him around the chest and squeezed, drawing another scream.

Bane staggered to the doorway beside me. "They're so powerful. How the hell did you apprehend them the first time?"

"I have no idea. Kol was with them and Jacob wasn't as hurt, but—" Even if Kol was fighting now and Jacob was stronger, the witches would still be kicking our asses.

Cassius roared and snapped a whip of fire around the vine witch's neck. She screamed and he yanked her to her knees. Marcus sliced through the vine holding Jacob, who gasped for air and staggered to the wall to keep standing, while Gideon swung at the red-haired witch, who shot shards of ice at him. He deflected the blasts with his sword and swiped at her. She wrenched back, his blade nicking her side, but the vine witch heaved a vine in Gideon's way and tripped him.

"Stop the witch from getting out," Gideon yelled. "Marcus. Cassius."

But neither could get past the vine witch. Even with the four of them, they weren't strong enough to subdue the witches.

A vine speared through Cassius's shoulder. His fire flickered, going out for a second, then flared back to life. The red-haired witch blasted a pillar of ice at Gideon, too big for him to dodge. I screamed as it slammed him into the wall. I had to do something to help them. I couldn't just stand by and watch.

"The witches should be out of magic by now," Sebastian gasped.

I glanced back at him and Amiah. "Where's the back up?"

"No one is answering their phone," Amiah said.

The red-haired witch leaped around the corner, and the vine witch sent a flurry of vines to cover their retreat. One vine seized Jacob's leg and slammed him against the wall, another speared Cassius through the gut. Marcus twisted out of the way and slashed the vines coming after him, while Gideon shoved aside the ice pillar.

The guys staggered around the corner after the witches. Someone screamed and my pulse froze. The witches were going to kill them. Even if I couldn't control my power, I had to use it. It was the only thing that might tip the balance of the fight in our favor. "Sebastian, can you uncuff me?"

"That's not wise," he said. "You can't control your magic."

"So you *can* uncuff me."

Another scream. Jacob flew back into the hall I was in and crashed against the wall, leaving a blood smear. His head lolled forward and he didn't move.

"Sebastian, please." I couldn't just stand there and watch. I had to do something.

"It's too dangerous."

Even with the handcuffs, my buzz was growing under my skin, making it hard to tell if Gideon or Jacob had started pulling strength from me through our brands. "My power is going to break free whether you unlock the cuffs or not."

"Fuck," Marcus yelled, his voice strangled and filled with pain.

Divine light swelled in my palms and Amiah's eyes widened.

"Sebastian!" I couldn't let them die. I had to save them.

He activated a glyph on his wrist and grabbed the cuffs. They popped open and my buzz screamed through me. I gasped, the agony dropping me to my knees.

"It's too much, Essie. Put the cuffs back on," Amiah said.

"No." I had to help them.

Jacob had regained consciousness and was trying to stand. Marcus swore again, and my divine light swelled, turning both my hands into blazing white nimbi. I fought to hold it back, to make sure I didn't hurt my guys in the blast. The agonizing pressure swelled within me, and I rushed to the T-intersection and turned my attention to the fight in the hall. But my thoughts tripped at what I saw.

Chris and Nathaniel stood by the first of the security doors, frozen in mid step, unaware of the chaos approaching them.

"So that's what they were casting," Sebastian said at my shoulder. "A time spell."

Between me at one end, and Chris and Nathaniel at the other, were my guys and the three witches. Blood wept from dozens of cuts on Gideon's body and he held his arm tight to his ribs as if they hurt. His breath was shallow and fast, and his divine light sword flickered in and out of existence. Marcus had somehow managed to get close enough to the vine witch to slice four deep gashes in her cheek, but her vines now crushed him against the ceiling, while Cassius had a fire whip around the other witch's neck.

She howled in pain and pressed a tattoo near the inside of her elbow, making my buzz blaze in response to the rush of her magic. Hundreds of spiders surged from the floor and swarmed over Cassius. He screamed, dropped to his knees, and his fire vanished.

Gideon turned to help him, but the red-haired witch shot another pillar of ice at him. He jerked to the side but there wasn't enough room to get out of the way.

I wrenched my palms up, straining to focus my divine light. My power blasted from my hands into the pillar. It exploded in a shower of ice shards and water and all three witches jerked toward me.

"Kill them," the red-haired witch said, shooting a spear of ice at me.

Marcus leaped up, taking the spear in his shoulder before it could hit me. I jerked my hands away at the last minute before I hit him, sending my blast into the ceiling above the vine witch. She made a canopy of vines that protected her, and seized the larger chunks of concrete from the ceiling and tossed them at Marcus. He twisted to the side but wasn't fast enough to get out of the way of all of them.

Gideon grabbed Cassius's arm and yanked him back. Cassius staggered but couldn't get to his feet.

"Defensive position," Gideon gasped.

"No, to me." Sebastian dropped to his knees beside Jacob, pressed both hands to his thighs, and power erupted from the floor in a circle around him. "We're getting the hell out of here."

Gideon's eyes widened with surprise before his attention locked on me.

"Get in the circle, Essie," he said. "Close to Bane."

I didn't know what Sebastian was doing, but if Gideon said get close, I was getting close.

Marcus grabbed Cassius's other arm and helped Gideon heave him into the circle as magic sliced into my body.

I screamed, my power erupting from me, but Sebastian's magic devoured it as it also devoured me. The spell tore into my cells, ripping me apart until I was nothing but blinding pain, a bolt of white agony blazing through black emptiness.

Then the pain tightened, grew, reformed me with my buzz burning me from the inside out. My knees slammed onto the floor, my wings tore from my back, and my power threatened to explode again from my hands. I pulled my palms to my chest, unable to see anything with the bright specks of light snapping across my vision and terrified I'd hurt one of my guys.

"Everyone okay?" Gideon asked.

"Get the cuffs back on Esther," Sebastian gasped.

Someone pressed a hand to my spine between my shoulder blades. "Pull your wings in," Gideon said.

With a moan, I fought to concentrate on sending power to my back. I imagined yanking my wings back into my body, and Gideon's magic snapped, stronger than the last time, with a painful bite. My wings slammed into me as if I'd been punched in the chest, and the cold metal of the containment cuffs clicked around my wrists.

I raised my gaze, my vision clearing, and met Jacob's dark eyes. His fangs were fully extended and he radiated his full vampiric intensity. Blood soaked his T-shirt and jeans from dozens of gashes, and his complexion was even paler than before and tinged gray. Strength seeped from me through his brand on my biceps into him. It also seeped from Gideon's brand into him as well. Both of my guys were seriously hurt.

I shifted to look at Gideon behind me, who groaned and pulled his wings into his body. He too was covered in gashes, his breath shallow as if it hurt to breathe. Beside him, Amiah and Cassius also had to pull in their wings.

Cassius's skin, beneath nasty red, swollen spider bites, was grayer than Jacob's. He collapsed face first to the marble floor, making my thoughts stutter. Marble. We weren't in Operations anymore.

Instead, we were in a large, opulent living room with a vaulted ceiling covered in a white and silver fresco. Sunlight, tinted slightly purple, blazed through gauzy curtains hanging across tall windows along the back wall, reminding me that it was still the middle of the morning. A large silver and crystal chandelier hung from the center of the ceiling, catching the sunlight and sending refracted light onto a conversation area consisting of two blue-gray couches and a pale-wood coffee table.

"Where are we?" Amiah asked.

"My place," Sebastian said, not moving from the floor, his eyes unfocused. His skin was even more translucent, his glow brighter, colder, and his ears were more pointed than I remembered.

"In Rouge?" Jacob asked.

A massive black wolf drew up beside him and snarled at Sebastian.

"Hey, I didn't have a whole lot of time to think when I cast the spell," he said.

The wolf huffed and turned a piercing green gaze to me.

My breath caught. "Marcus?"

Yeah.

I wrenched back. "Holy shit, you have telepathy!"

Sebastian groaned. "She's the most powerful super in the room and doesn't even know shifters have telepathy in their shifted form. Have you been living under a rock?"

His tone broke something in me and I wrenched to face him.

"I've been trying to," I snapped. I'd tried so fucking hard. "As far as I knew, I was a powerless nephilim. So yeah, I stayed as far away from the supernatural world as humanly possible. And now I'm a— a—"

My anger lurched to confusion and grief. I couldn't catch my breath. I wasn't a despised, unnatural nephilim. I was an angel. And I had no idea who I really was or who my parents were. The woman who'd raised me, loved me, and left me too early wasn't my mother.

My throat tightened, and I heaved my gaze back to Marcus's.

He limped to me and bumped his head into my chest. *It's okay. You're okay.*

I don't know if I am. I sank my fingers into his thick ruff and pressed my cheek against his. I needed to feel him, to feel all of my guys, to reassure myself they were all still alive.

"Why did you shift?" I asked, trying to think of anything but my situation.

"It's the teleportation spell," Gideon said, his attention locked on Sebastian. "It reassembled us in our supernatural forms. Something a glyph witch shouldn't be able to cast."

"Yeah, well, you can tell by the ears and glow I'm not a faekin glyph witch." Sebastian groaned and pressed his forehead to the floor. "And if you tell anyone I'm full fae, I'll kill you."

"Depends on how much you plan to charge us for

that rescue." Gideon coughed, the sound wet and rattling in his chest.

"I'll let you know how much when I can see straight."

I should have been surprised and awed that I was sitting next to a full fae, but I must have been numb from the cuffs and my new reality and, quite honestly, I was exhausted. All I wanted was to hold all my guys and cry with joy and grief. My whole life, I'd been terrified that my true nature would be discovered, only to learn I'd had no idea what my true nature really was, and that my guys loved me regardless. On top of that, we were all seriously hurt, the witches had cast some kind of freezing time spell, and the cop in me wouldn't just let that thought go.

"Those witches had wanted to be caught," I blurted out.

"Agreed," Jacob said. "We have to figure out their plan before people get hurt."

Amiah looked up from Cassius, who groaned, his eyes squeezed tight in agony, a thick sheen of sweat slicking his face and neck.

"You mean *more* people get hurt," she said.

"Okay." Gideon rubbed his face, coughed again, and drew in a ragged breath. "Healing first. Bane, have you got a guest room Essie and Jacob could use?"

"I live above a vampire nightclub. I've watched them feed." Sebastian grabbed the edge of his couch and climbed to his feet.

"I'm sure, but—" Gideon glanced at me. His summer-sky eyes filled with yearning and uncertainty captured my soul, and the pieces that were still fractured from fighting our bond ached for him, for his touch, his body, his love.

Then he blinked and his desire disappeared behind a mask of professionalism. He wasn't trying to avoid me, not like he had before, but healing our bond wasn't a priority. Healing Jacob was... and before I'd fallen into his gaze, he'd been asking me if I wanted Bane to know I was bite-locked.

My body and soul hurt too much to keep anything secret. Besides, Sebastian had already seen me naked. "I'm bite-locked, so even if I didn't want to give you a show, you're getting one."

"I would love a show," Sebastian said with his usual wicked grin, but it didn't reach his eyes. "Except I suspect your mates would then kill me. So... I'm going to my office to try to figure out how to deal with your magic without you destroying the building. Take any room except the one at the end of the hall, and call me when you want to talk about the witches." He staggered to a hall on the other side of the room near a grand piano, and opened the first door on the left.

"I'll call Kol." Gideon stood, drew in a ragged breath, and coughed blood into his hand. "With luck, he was still melting down over Essie and hadn't returned to Operations when the witches cast their spell. I'll tell him to avoid Operations and bring us clean clothes."

Amiah pointed to the couch. "No, you're sitting here until I heal you. Then you're calling Kol, then having a shower, *then* you're planning your next move." She snapped her attention to me and held out her hand. "And you. Hands."

I shifted closer to her and raised my hands. They were bloody and oozing from blasting my divine light at the witches. She grabbed my wrist, thankfully not touching my burned hands, and sent an agonizing blast of magic into me. I gasped and while I couldn't tell for sure beneath the blood if my hands were healed, they no longer hurt—and hell, I hadn't even realized how much they'd hurt.

"Come on," Jacob said to me as he climbed to his feet, his face contorted in pain.

Gideon caught my attention, the light in his eyes flaring for a second, making my pulse skip a beat. "Make it quick. We don't know what the witches are planning but they clearly wanted to disable Operations."

Are we even strong enough to stop them? Marcus asked.

Gideon coughed more blood. "I have no idea."

And that was what terrified me. The witches were more powerful than anything we'd faced before and my guys were duty bound to confront them.

CHAPTER 5

JACOB SHUFFLED INTO THE HALL AND HEADED TOWARD THE
end. I hurried to his side, helping him catch his balance
against the wall as he staggered. His skin was freezing,
proving just how serious his injuries were, and my pulse
tripped with fear.

"Thanks." He drew in a breath almost as ragged and
wet as Gideon's had been and left a thick blood smear on
Sebastian's white wall.

I opened the closest door, even though it was clear he
was trying to pick a room away from Sebastian in his
office. *Please let this be a bathroom so we can clean up.*

Inside lay a bedroom with en suite bathroom, just as
opulent as the living room. It was decorated in the same
white, silver, and blues as the living room, and I was
starting to feel like Sebastian lived in one big, icy crystal.

I helped Jacob inside, ignoring the king-sized bed
with its pristine white duvet and pillows, and turned
straight into the white marble bathroom with its large
vanity, fluffy white towels, and shower that would have

been big enough for a normal person but a tight fit for the two of us.

Trembling, he sagged onto the closed toilet lid. I pulled off my runners and knelt before him to help him unlace his boots.

"I was hoping things wouldn't be so dire the next time we had sex." His dark gaze met mine, filled with sorrow and love, making me ache with a confusing mix of emotions.

My throat tightened and tears burned my eyes. I didn't want to have a breakdown. Really, I didn't. But in the blink of an eye, I'd thought I'd lost everything, and in another blink saw that love could conquer everything... and then had almost lost them again fighting the witches. I'd run out of strength and just couldn't hold it together.

"Hey." He cupped my cheeks with his large hands.

"If Sebastian hadn't been able to cast that spell—"

"We're okay."

"I'd hate to see your definition of not okay."

"Not okay is not being with you."

He dipped in and brushed his lips against mine. It was a tender whisper of a kiss that made a tear break free, not because I was sad but because there was just too much emotion and all of it was mine.

"Marcus was going to raid the armory then break you out," Jacob said, "and I was going to help him while Gideon distracted Cassius when the brand lit up."

"Even though I'm a nephilim."

"You could have been a hellfire prince and we would have come for you." He brushed the tear from my cheek.

"I meant what I said. We know who you are. Fate would never bind us with someone evil."

"You didn't doubt the bond? Didn't think I'd falsely branded you like the archnephilim had branded me?"

"Never. None of us." Jacob chuckled then gasped in pain. "You should have seen Gideon lose it on Cassius."

"You need to feed." I grabbed the hem of his T-shirt and rose, peeling off the wet, sticky fabric. Deep gashes covered his massive chest, oozing blood over his bulky muscles and into the waistband of his pants.

"And you need to know how I feel about you." He tugged me into his lap, tangled a cold hand into my ponytail, and captured my lips with his.

Even without my empathy, I could feel his desire and love for me in his kiss. It was tender and certain. He had no doubt about having his soul forever bound to mine.

Need swelled within me, and his kiss deepened as if he knew exactly what I craved. His tongue slid into my mouth, languid strokes that fueled my desire, making my breath pick up.

"I wish I didn't have to feed," he whispered against my lips, "that I could use my magic to bring you pleasure because I want to, not because I need to."

I kissed my way along his jaw, sliding my neck closer to his lips. "I love you, too."

It was crazy that I'd fallen in love with him so quickly, but the thought of losing him, of losing any of my guys, filled me with absolute panic. And I knew as soon as I said the words that they were true. I was in love with him and Marcus and Gideon.

And, God help me, I thought I was in love with Kol. It

broke my heart to have seen and felt his horror when he'd realized— or rather, *thought* I was a nephilim. I could only hope my full angel status would be enough to save our friendship.

Jacob slid his hand up my back and tightened his grip in my hair. His fangs slid into my neck with a sharp bite of pain and then bone-melting desire rushed through me. I moaned and leaned into him. Just like Marcus's ferocious passion, I didn't think I'd ever get tired of Jacob's tender touch combined with the rush of his magic.

He took a long pull on my neck, and his magic surged. Another pull, and his erection swelled hard under my thigh, revealing he was just as turned on as I was. His fangs still in my neck, he lifted me, carried me into the shower, and set me on my feet.

I eased back, drawing his fangs from my skin, as he turned on the shower and protected me from the cold spray with his body. Not that I would have felt the cold with the heat of my desire flooding me. Blood caked his chest and crusted the line of fine hair disappearing into his pants, but the gashes were already starting to seal shut.

His dark, intense gaze locked on mine and a warm smile curled his lips. My breath caught. God, he was stunning. Powerful and strong, every inch of him sculpted, hard muscle.

"You're so beautiful," he said, his voice that low rumble that made my cells thrum, aligning my essence with his.

He pressed close, capturing me between the shower

wall and his massive body, and kissed me again. His lips tasted coppery with my blood, and his magic rushed in my core. He hooked his nails into the neck of my T-shirt, one on either side, and ripped the fabric along my shoulders, so he could draw my shirt down my body without it getting caught on the containment cuffs.

With a groan, he sank his fangs into my neck again and skimmed a hand over my too-sensitive skin into my bra. He tweaked my nipple in a tight bud, sending bites of pleasure racing through me, then moved to the other breast. His magic throbbed, growing stronger. My pulse roared and I ached for satisfaction.

I undid his pants and slid my hands inside, wrapping my fingers around his thick, hard erection and drawing a groan. The sound vibrated against my skin and more of his magic flooded me, melting me with pleasure, forcing me to use the wall to keep standing.

Hot water sprayed around us, a glimpse of the sultry heat I knew I'd feel if the cuffs were off, and my desire twisted tighter, teasing me with the promise of a release that I couldn't have until Jacob brought me to climax.

He sliced the straps of my bra and unhooked it, letting it fall to our feet. His fangs left my neck, and he slid down my body, sucking on my nipples as he undid my jeans. Then he slid them and my underwear down my legs, and knelt before me.

My breath hitched, my soul captured by the intensity in his gaze. It held a hunger for me that was more than just a vampire's need to feed. It was deeper than that. Light flickered from the brand on his arm, catching in the water running over his body.

I ached for him, body and soul, not just because of his magic whirling in me. I needed him in me, filling me. I needed him feeding, taking his fill, and healing. I couldn't feel my strength seeping into him through our bond anymore, but his complexion was still gray. He hadn't taken enough.

"You have to take more." My breath came faster with the anticipation of his magic building until I burst, and his erection driving into me.

"I don't want to take too much." He brushed his fingers over the angry red line in my side where Kol had cut me and Amiah had done the bare basics to heal it shut.

"I trust you. You won't." I hooked my fingers under his chin, urging him to rise.

But instead he nudged my legs open and sank his fangs into my thigh. I gasped, his magic jolting through me. With a groan, he slid a finger into my wet core and my muscles clenched around him, already on the edge of climax.

He took a long, hard pull, and slowly slid in a second finger. I dug my nails into his scalp, my head spinning as he drew out and slowly pushed back in. Sensation roared in every cell, building and twisting tight. He teased my clit with his thumb, making me jerk, my climax trembling on the edge. Then he stilled and let me tremble without crashing over. My breath stalled in my chest and I squirmed my hips, flexing, trying to drive his fingers deeper into me, rub my clit, anything to satisfy the pressure building inside.

He kept me teetering on the edge, drawing long sips

of blood, until I was panting and moaning. Then a whisper of healing magic sealed the bite on my thigh shut, and he rose and pulled off his pants. His erection slid between my open thighs and brushed my folds.

God, yes.

With a low guttural moan, he grabbed my hips, lifted me, and slid inside, slowly burying himself to the hilt. He filled me, so big he stretched me with a whisper of delicious pain. Then he slowly drew out, building my pleasure beyond what I thought possible. I hooked my legs around his waist and my arms over his head and hung on, giving him control over my body. There wasn't anything I could do but ride this glorious wave.

The promise of my climax tightened until every cell within me strained for release. His pace grew faster, his breath as ragged as mine, until he was driving into me with delicious force. With a roar, his body tensed, his climax seizing him, and he sank his teeth into my neck.

My climax ripped through me and his magic exploded with blazing ecstasy through every cell. I screamed his name and our brands lit with golden light. For a second, no more than a rapid beat of my heart, I feared the screaming frozen pain from that last time we'd had sex would devour me, but another wave of pleasure swept through me instead, leaving me trembling and dizzy.

Jacob sagged to his knees. His healing magic warmed my neck as he pulled out his fangs and wrapped his arms around me in a tight embrace. His love filled me, an honest to goodness emotion that somehow seeped past the power of the containment cuffs. Maybe it was because of the brand. The cuffs didn't seem to affect that. But a part of me knew it was because our connection was that powerful. My empathy would be able to seek him out no matter what magic tried to contain it.

We sat there in the shower's spray, trying to catch our breaths. I knew we needed to finish up and get back to the rest of the team, but I didn't want this moment to end. I wanted to stay in his arms forever.

Someone knocked on the wall, and I dragged my attention to the still open bathroom door.

"You guys alive in there?" Marcus asked. He stood in the doorway looking as ruggedly handsome as ever, without a hint of jealousy or anger in his expression.

He was dressed, which meant Kol had arrived with a change of clothes, since the magic that let him shift had destroyed his clothing when Sebastian had teleported us. A part of me ached to reach out and invite him into the shower to join us. But we didn't have time. Not to mention I didn't know what either guy would think about that, and the shower was too damned small.

"Yeah," Jacob said. He pressed a kiss to my forehead. "Can you stand?"

I had no idea.

Marcus set a stuffed plastic bag on the floor and grabbed a towel as I stood on shaky legs. The bathroom darkened and spun a bit, reminding me that Jacob had taken a lot of blood, and I shouldn't make any fast movements.

"Kol's here," Marcus said, "and Amiah's gotten Gideon back on his feet."

"Which means he wants to get back to work," Jacob said, using the shower wall to steady himself.

Marcus wrapped the towel around me and pulled me into a firm embrace. "You're too pale. You told him to take too much."

"He didn't take more than I could handle, and right now the only thing I'm good for is keeping you guys alive."

"That's not true."

I eased out of his embrace and raised my handcuffed hands. "I'm not taking these off until we can figure out a way to control my power, which means I can't go into the field with you."

"You'll always be more than just keeping us alive, even if you couldn't ever go into the field again." He turned his attention to Jacob, who was scrubbing off the blood from his now-healed injuries. "And you, you should know by now that she has no sense of self-preservation."

I grabbed Marcus's jaw and urged him to look at me. "I'm fine. Now help me at least put my pants on, since I'm not going to be able to pull on a shirt."

"I'm hoping you can hold your power in for a few seconds." He pulled a handcuff key from his pocket. "I'd rather you not be hanging out at Bane's in a towel."

"It's not like he hasn't seen me naked," I said.

Marcus groaned. "I'm not sure I want to know."

I pulled a pair of cargo pants out of the bag that were way too big for me, and set them on the vanity for Jacob. "Didn't Jacob tell you he helped us flee Rouge when our brand formed?"

"I left out the bit about you being naked." Jacob shut

off the water and grabbed a towel. "Although if Marcus had been thinking about it, he'd have figured it out. He knew I'd brought you home wearing nothing but a sheet."

"I was a little distracted at the time by my mate being in dire need of an incubus's body heat."

"Speaking of our resident incubus..." I fished a lacy white thong and matching bra out of the bag. Not in the least practical for field work, but at least he'd thought to bring me underwear. I didn't know if that meant he wasn't freaking out over me being a nephilim or if Gideon had ordered him to buy them.

"He just arrived and he's feeling no pain right now." Marcus chuckled. "Even being a few blocks away wasn't enough to protect him from the release of your bite-lock."

"I hadn't realized it was that powerful." I stepped into the thong and a pair of cargo pants that were my size.

"Not sure he realized that, either," Marcus said.

Jacob toweled off and grabbed his pants. "We're going to need to figure something out for him if we want him to be able to do his job."

"Does he know I'm not a nephilim?" I didn't want him looking at me like he had in the alley ever again. All that pain and horror. I didn't want to think about what he'd gone through to have a reaction like that.

"Gideon told him." The muscles in Marcus's jaw flexed. "Not sure if he believed him."

Great. I didn't want to hide in the bedroom and wait for the team to leave. I wanted to be part of figuring out what we were going to do about the witches, even if I couldn't help in the field.

"He's here. Means he's had a chance to cool down since you saved him from a sixteen-story fall," Jacob said.

"I just don't want to trigger him again." Except right now, if I didn't want to hide in the bedroom, there wasn't anything I could do about it.

But maybe I should hide. I was exhausted, and if I was being honest with myself, still reeling over everything that had happened.

I bit back a sigh and held out my hands. In the very least, I could put a shirt on. And I was God damn going to hold my power back long enough for that. "Let's do this."

Marcus unlocked one of the cuffs. My buzz exploded into agonizing pain and my knees gave out. Marcus's eyes flashed wide, and Jacob grabbed me and steadied me on my feet.

"Just put me down," I gasped. "It'll be easier to get dressed without you holding me." Divine light blazed from the palm of my free hand and I clenched it in a fist, fighting to hold it in. The pressure inside me swelled, and my whole body blazed with fiery stinging bites.

Marcus put my arms through the bra straps—not bothering to hook it behind my back—then grabbed the T-shirt.

I strained against the agony, desperate to hold my power in. I could do this. I could hold it in. I wouldn't burn him like I'd burned Gideon. I wouldn't do that to anyone again.

The pressure grew stronger and darkness clouded my vision, then Marcus snapped the cuffs back on and my buzz vanished. I sagged into Marcus's arms, panting, my throat tight with tears.

"Come on, what's the hold-up?" Gideon asked, striding into the bedroom. "Kol and Bane are wait—" His gaze locked on mine and his angel glow flared as he dropped to the floor close behind Marcus. "What's wrong? What happened?"

"We needed to uncuff one hand to get her shirt on," Jacob said, his tone grim.

"I'm okay." I tried to push out of Marcus's embrace, but he held tight. "Marcus, I'm okay."

He growled and his grip relaxed, but I could still feel the tension in his body.

"Tell me Bane has figured out how to help Essie," Marcus said, his pupils slitted and his canines partially extended, his wolf threatening to take over.

I cupped his cheeks and forced him to meet my gaze. "I'm okay. He'll figure it out." My clothes were still just on my arms, so I settled the bra over my breasts. Jacob hooked it behind me before I could even ask for help— since I couldn't reach behind my back with the cuffs on— and I pulled my T-shirt over my head. I was still exhausted from feeding Jacob and terrified of hurting my guys, but this was the best I was going to get for the moment. "Tell me Kol isn't going to freak out if I step out of this bedroom."

"You're part of the team. You're not hiding in the bedroom." Gideon held out his hand to help me up, and I met his gaze. The warmth and worry in his eyes stole my breath. It was so different from how he'd been looking at me before that it almost didn't seem real. He didn't hate me. I wasn't the worst possible thing that could have happened to him. And while I knew he still loved and mourned Zella, I also knew he wanted our bond as much as I did.

We belonged together.

That was a destiny we couldn't deny, and we had to solidify our bond. The need crackled along the fractured edges of my soul, an aching desire I wasn't going to be able to resist.

The muscles in his jaw tightened. His worry slipped into a need as powerful as mine, and made my buzz whisper under my skin, reminding me that my desire for Gideon was dangerous.

With a quick breath, he shoved his desire back under a mask of professionalism, reminding me that no matter what I ached for—even if my power didn't release and burn him up—we were in the middle of a crisis.

Right. Jeez. We were adults. We could resist the pull of the bond long enough to figure out what we were going to do about the witches.

I took his hand, my fingers sliding over his palm, making his breath hitch and my pulse trip, and rose unsteadily to my feet. The room darkened and spun, and Marcus grabbed my hips to steady me.

I leaned into him, in part because I needed his support, but also because his wolf needed comfort. If the situation wasn't what it was, I'd tell Jacob to get out, and take Gideon then Marcus to bed. But pressing close to Marcus and holding Gideon's hand was the best I was going to be able to offer them.

We left the bedroom and headed down the too-short hall, my pulse picking up with each unsteady step. I needed Kol to not fear and hate me. My need was so deep it scared me. He wasn't one of my mates, I didn't have a connection to him like I did with the others, but I still desperately needed him.

He and Bane were both on the blue-gray couch facing me, but my attention instantly locked on Kol, looking sexily disheveled and exhausted and strained. It made my heart ache. I wanted to ease his pain, tell him everything would be all right, but I didn't know if it would be.

His gaze locked on mine and hellfire blazed in his eyes. His expression was strange, hard, but without my empathy I had no clue what he was feeling. Whatever it was, it wasn't good.

CHAPTER 6

He held my gaze and a hint of heated desire unfurled within me. It made my pulse trip with hope. Maybe he'd believed Gideon and knew I wasn't a nephilim, or maybe, after the initial shock of seeing what I was, he'd remembered *who* I was.

The desire swelled, the hellfire in his eyes burning brighter. My thoughts leaped to the dream I kept having of him caressing and kissing me, begging to satisfy me like my other guys could. To hell with it being his incubus nature influencing me. I wanted him sexually and emotionally as much as I wanted my other guys. Yes, we didn't have a magical bond, we weren't destined to be together, but I wanted him in my family. From the moment we'd met, he'd always been there for me, supported me, held me, made me laugh. We could make this work. We could—

He jerked his attention to the floor, his body tense and his heated desire vanishing, leaving me cold and aching. So much for being high and happy on my sexual release. My throat tightened, and I stumbled. Marcus growled and lifted me in his arms, carrying me the rest of the way to the seating area.

"This is a bad idea," I whispered against his neck. Especially if I was going to start crying every time Kol gave me a hard look. I hadn't even cried this much when Gideon had been trying to keep his distance and I'd had our bond slowly shattering inside me.

I needed time to still my whirling thoughts and regain my bearings, and the best way to do that would be sleep. Lots and lots of sleep. Something I hadn't really gotten in a long time.

"Deal with your shit later, Shaw," Marcus growled. "We need to figure out what the hell we're doing about these witches." He sat on the couch, but kept hold of me as if he couldn't bring himself to let me go, belying his harsh words.

Gideon sat beside us and placed a hand on my knee. It was a small gesture, but it spoke volumes to anyone who knew our situation. He was onboard with everything I was and everyone I was mated to. His electric power whispered over our brand, making my nerves thrum with need. I fought to concentrate past that, as well as the feel of Marcus's hard body against mine, determined to be a useful member of the team.

Sebastian shifted beside Kol, his icy eyes filled with worry, and jerked his thumb over his shoulder. "There's juice in the fridge."

Jacob strode past him to the far side of the living room area and disappeared through a wide archway into a room just as white as the living room.

"Have you found a way to deal with Essie's power?" Gideon asked.

Sebastian rolled his eyes. "It's been what? Less than twenty minutes? I haven't even pulled all the books I want to look at from my shelves."

"And that's not the issue," I said, as much as I really wanted my power under control and the cuffs off. "The witches let us arrest them and cast whatever they'd cast on Operations. They've got to be planning something. You said it was a time spell?"

"A temporal freeze," Sebastian said. "It temporarily stops time on every organic thing within the spells radius. Which I bet is all of Operations. And while I managed to protect us from the initial blast, if we'd stayed at Operations much longer, we would have been caught in the spell as well."

"We know what a temporal freeze is," Marcus said.

"If Esther didn't know you have telepathy in your wolf form, I'm pretty sure she doesn't know what a temporal freeze does."

"Glyph witches aren't powerful enough to cast a temporal freeze spell," Kol said, his words slightly slurred, the only hint so far that he'd been flooded with too much sexual energy. His gaze lifted for a second then jerked back to the floor. His breath picked up, and he leaned forward and tightly clasped his hands.

Sebastian rubbed his face. He looked as exhausted as I felt, and I couldn't help wondering how much magic he'd drained protecting us from the temporal freeze and then teleporting us to safety. "Obviously they're not glyph witches or they got help."

"Obviously," Jacob said, striding across the living room toward us with a huge glass of orange juice. At least he finally looked better. He'd been running on low for days now, barely recovering because I was barely recovering. I was sure he still needed more blood and sooner rather than later, but maybe I could convince Marcus to allow Jacob to feed on him and use his magic this time. Surely we could spare enough time to bring Jacob up to full, and I could spend some quality time with my angel and my wolf.

Jacob pressed the glass into my hands, sat on the arm of the couch beside Marcus, and rested a big hand on my shoulder. I wasn't sure if he'd done it on purpose to reinforce to Kol where they stood with me, and if he did, it didn't matter because Kol hadn't looked at me since I'd entered the room.

I shoved that thought away before my emotions overwhelmed me again and took a sip of juice. "On City Hall's roof, it felt like the witches' power kept growing, as if they were tapping into a source outside of themselves."

"That's what it felt like to me in Operations," Sebastian said. "They should have been out of magic after casting the temporal freeze, but they just kept casting stuff."

Marcus's grip on me tightened. "So even if we figure out what they're planning, they have an unlimited supply of magic?"

"Possibly. And you're going to want to hurry," Sebastian said. "The temporal freeze will only last for about twelve hours, no matter how much power is put into it."

Marcus groaned. "That's just fucking great. They're

planning something that's going to happen in less than twelve hours and we have absolutely no clue what."

"We must know something," Gideon said, "or they wouldn't have needed to freeze Operations."

"Well, I have no fucking clue what that would be." Marcus's wolf darkened his eyes. "And we still have no way to stop them. I'm not letting you guys endanger Essie's life by running blindly into trouble. The dangers of mating brands go both ways, you know."

"We need an area containment master ward," Gideon said.

"We don't have an area containment master ward," Marcus growled. "Only head office has an area containment master ward and I wouldn't want to bet on us being able to get it in time."

They glared at each other, then turned their attention to Sebastian.

He raised his hands in defense. "I don't have one, either."

"But can you find one on short notice?" Gideon asked.

"With enough money, I can find anything." He flashed a smile, but it was a ghost of what it usually was.

"What about dispelling the temporal freeze?" Jacob asked.

"It'd be easier to find an area containment master ward." Sebastian's gaze dipped to mine. "But that means Esther's problem will have to wait."

"That's fine. The cuffs are holding my magic back," I said. Keeping the city and my guys safe took priority over my comfort every time.

Kol raised his head and for a second I thought he'd

look at me again, hoped, prayed, *please, look at me again*. But his hands clenched tighter and his gaze remained locked on the bowl of large clear marbles in the center of Sebastian's coffee table.

I fought back tears. Jeez. I really was exhausted if him not looking at me made me want to sob. But it was because I knew just looking at me caused him pain. As much as I couldn't get the memory of my sexy dream of him out of my head, I also couldn't get rid of the look on his face when he saw my wings.

Time. Just give him time. I could get back the easy friendship we'd had. I just had to be patient. Except a part of me feared I wouldn't get it back, that my wings had permanently changed everything between us. No more cuddling on the couch watching movies, no more jokes or teasing or playful wicked smiles.

"Okay." Gideon rubbed his palm against my knee, reminding me that we were working things out. And things would work out with Kol, too... even if we didn't share a soul bond. "In City Hall, the red-haired witch came from that back hall by the elevators. Let's go back there and see if we can figure out why they were there. With luck, it'll be connected to whatever they're planning in the next twelve hours."

"I'll start hunting down an area containment master ward." Sebastian stood with a groan and headed back to his office.

"How do we get out of here without Victoria or her offspring seeing us?" Jacob asked before Sebastian made if halfway across his massive living room. "I don't want to run into her, and I don't want her to know Essie is under her roof."

And if I hadn't been so exhausted, I would have thought about that already. I'd severed her link with Jacob when our brand formed two days ago, and while I didn't know how she felt about that, I'd place my bets on pissed.

"I have a private entrance." He jerked his thumb to a heavy door inset with a large frosted white and blue stained glass window. "Take the stairs to the left."

"I didn't know you had a private entrance," Gideon said.

"You're not paying me enough to know I have a private entrance."

"We pay you a lot," Marcus said.

"Yeah." Sebastian opened his office door. "So think about how much you'd have to pay to get prime customer service and go beyond the office I rent two floors down." He stepped inside his private office and closed the door.

The door on the other side of the hall opened and Amiah stepped out, quietly closing it behind her. "A word before you go, Gideon."

Gideon's strokes on my knee shifted higher, sliding up my thigh. My pulse picked up and a whisper of my buzz tickled my skin.

His gaze lifted to mine for a second, stealing my breath, then he realized what he was doing and jerked away to talk with Amiah.

A part of me ached at his absence, even though he was only a few feet away.

Jeez. Be an adult. But it wasn't that I couldn't be responsible. It was that my bonds with all my guys were too new, and the one with Gideon was still in danger of shattering. Except if my powers blazed out of control every time he touched me in a sensual way, we might never fix what we'd broken.

"Sebastian's going to hold this mess over us for a long time, isn't he?" Marcus said to Jacob. "I don't want to see what head office says when they see the final bill."

Jacob sighed. "One problem at a time."

"You're going out?" Amiah asked Gideon as he drew close, her voice low, only audible because Jacob's claim enhanced my hearing... or was it because I was really part archangel? I had no clue what powers an archangel possessed beyond those of a regular angel, only that they were powerful.

"How's Cassius?"

"Not good," she said, her gaze darting to the door she'd just closed. "I've managed to stabilize him, but the poison from those spiders is magical. I'm having trouble purging it from his system and it's still slowly killing him."

Kol stood, unsteady on his feet, and Jacob hopped off the couch arm and grabbed his elbow, steadying him before he banged his shins on the coffee table. "You're going to need to bleed off some of that excess magic."

"When I'm away from *her*," he mumbled, and headed to the door with the stained glass.

Marcus pressed his lips to my forehead. "Finish the juice." His warm breath caressed my skin, drawing a shiver of desire. "And get Amiah to heal you."

"She's probably running low, as well. I'm fine." I lifted my lips to his and kissed him.

He groaned and slid his tongue into my mouth, adding fuel to my desire. His ferocious passion thrummed in his body, his muscles tense, his hold on me firm. I ached for all that power and desire to take me, fill me, send me spiraling with bliss.

"Come on, Marcus," Gideon said, his expression strained. "You can give her a few minutes to recover from Jacob."

"Yeah, I know," he mumbled against my lips. "But part of my wolf still feels like he has to protect her from Cassius."

Gideon's angel glow darkened, clouds passing over his summer-sky eyes. Cassius might have brought the full force of his rage against me when he thought I'd wrongfully and permanently bound his brother's soul to mine, but he was still Gideon's brother. I'd watched my mom die, so I could imagine how much Gideon hurt right now —and I didn't need my empathy to figure that out.

With another groan, Marcus slid me from his lap onto the couch cushion and followed the rest of the guys out of Sebastian's apartment.

I sagged back, tugged the elastic out of what was probably a disastrous ponytail so I could comfortably lean my head back, and took a long sip of juice. I wanted to comfort Marcus and Gideon, but given our deadline to who-knew-what disaster, there wasn't time for either. But Gideon and I had lasted apart for this long, so another day or so couldn't hurt, and Marcus already knew how I felt about him. He could wait, too—a shiver of desire swept over me—as much as I craved his ferocious passion.

My thoughts drifted to the last time we'd had sex. His wolf had been anxious, afraid I would choose Gideon over him, and I'd made a point of showing him how I felt. The attraction sizzling between us had been there from the moment we'd first met. It had survived my biggest screw-up, and I knew with certainty that we were mates. Just like I knew Gideon and Jacob were my mates, as well.

The electricity in Gideon's brand tickled over my forearm and sank into the intense stillness of Jacob's. A whisper of emotions that weren't mine ghosted through me, love, fear, determination, certainty. I couldn't tell which of my guys they came from, probably a bit from everyone, and I let myself sink into it, allowing sleep to drag at my senses. There wasn't anything else I could do right now, as much as that drove me crazy. Even if I could control my power, I was still exhausted. That made me a liability, and with our lives as entwined as they were, it was too dangerous to put me in the field. The best thing to do was get some sleep.

Something creaked, it sounded like a door opening, and soft footsteps drew close. They didn't sound heavy enough to be Sebastian's, so it was probably Amiah headed to the kitchen or something.

"You're pale," Amiah said, her tone brusque.

My eyes flew open and I jerked, nearly dropping my half-drunk glass of orange juice.

She stood near the couch, her arms crossed, her expression hard. "I've heard it can be difficult to say stop when they feed, for both of you, but that's why you need to set ground rules before you get started."

"He needed as much as I could give."

"I'm sure you'll say that every time," she said.

I met her glare. "For all of them. You'd do the same."

"Don't assume to know me. I'd never lie to my mate. Ever."

"You have a mate?" I hadn't seen her showing affection to anyone other than Marcus, but then I'd been trying to avoid all the angels at Operations in the short time I'd spent there.

"Of course not." Her angel glow flared, turning her summer-sky eyes, so similar to Gideon's, icy. "But if I did, they wouldn't have been blindsided by something as important as not being human."

"Oh, and you would have just come out and told them you were a nephilim?" Easy for her to say. She hadn't spent her entire life fearing that everyone wanted her dead.

"But you're not a nephilim. Even your essence has changed. It's muddled and still doesn't say you're an angel, but you're clearly not human."

"Except I didn't know I was a full angel." I set my glass on the coffee table, forcing myself not to slam it down. "I wasn't going to break Marcus's and Jacob's hearts by telling them I was a monster."

"You're still going to break Marcus's heart. You've branded Gideon and Jacob. If you were truly Marcus's mate, you'd have branded him, as well."

For the love of— Get over him already! I jerked to my feet. The room darkened and spun, but I gritted my teeth and kept standing. "What I have with Marcus is as strong as what I have with Gideon and Jacob. And who I love is none of your God damned business."

I grabbed the glass and wrenched around to head to the bedroom where Jacob and I had cleaned up to lie down, when blazing white lightning exploded from Gideon's brand. All my muscles seized, like I'd been hit with a Taser. My thoughts leaped to Gideon, my pulse racing. He was hurt. Oh, God, he was dying.

CHAPTER 7

MY THOUGHTS WHIRLED, TRAPPED IN A BODY FROZEN IN agony. I had to save Gideon. I couldn't lose him. *Please, God.* I could feel his life draining from him, the brand consuming my strength to keep him alive. *Save him. Save him.*

The lightning suddenly stopped and all my muscles went limp. The glass shattered on the floor, the juice an orange spray on the white marble, and I slammed down onto my knees, falling forward and narrowly catching myself on my hands before smacking my face.

"Sebastian!" I screamed.

I had to get to Gideon. Now. He wasn't going to last long. There wasn't anyway I could get to City Hall... if he was even at City Hall. I had no idea how long I'd been dozing. A few seconds? A few minutes?

"Sebastian!"

I scrambled to my feet. *Please. I can't lose him.*

Another blast of lightning ripped through me,

blazing from Jacob's brand. I crashed back to the floor, every muscle seizing. *Not him, too.*

Amiah dropped to her knees beside me, all anger at what I was doing to Marcus gone, her eyes filled with terror, her expression hard, as if she were trying to lock away all that fear.

Every cell in my body screamed. *Do something. Save them.*

The second blast released me, and I tried to stand, but Amiah placed a hand on my shoulder. Her magic flared to life and I jerked away.

"Save it for them. Please." She was already low. I couldn't let her waste her magic on me. "Sebastian." I could barely get his name out. My ragged breath sawed in my lungs as if I'd run a marathon, and I couldn't get my muscles to support me even to rise to my hands and knees. "Sebastian."

He rushed into the hall, his exasperated expression snapping to shocked. "What?"

"You have to save them," I gasped. *Please, God, save them.* "I can't lose them. They're dying. Teleport them. Please."

Amiah reached for me again, and I managed to shove her hand away. "No. They need you."

Strength poured from both of the brands on my arm into Gideon and Jacob. Their injuries were bad. They weren't going to last. And God, I had no idea if Marcus or Kol were as badly hurt.

"Please, Sebastian." He was the only one who could get to them fast enough. My throat tightened and tears spilled down my cheeks.

"I don't have the power to teleport." He dropped to his knees beside Amiah. "I'm too magically exhausted to draw that much raw magic from the Realm of Celestial Light."

No. No no no. He had to help. He was the only one who could. I couldn't lose them, I wouldn't survive their deaths, and I didn't want to.

"I'll call—"

"Sebastian," I begged. "Now. They need help now." *Save them. Save them.*

A sob broke free. Divine light blazed from my palms even with the containment cuffs. Maybe I could teleport, maybe that was a power I'd inherited from my archangel parent. Except I had no idea if archangels could teleport or, even if I could, how. I had so much God damned power, it blazed through me, filling me with agony, screaming at me to use it, save them, and there wasn't anything I could do. All I could manage was to focus it on them, send it through the brand, and pray it was enough for them to hold on until they could get back here.

But it wasn't going to be enough. They weren't going to last. *Save them. Save them.*

"Esther, I can't draw in enough power."

My thoughts stuttered. I was bursting with useless power. "Take mine."

"I—"

"Sebastian, please. Take mine, take it all. Save them."

"Can you do that?" Amiah asked.

"I'm not tapping directly into the power from the Celestial Realm of Light, there's less chance of burning up, and her magic is divine light," he said. "That's the O negative of magic. Any being can use it."

"Sebastian, please."

Gideon's electric magic flickered in his brand and chilled. My pulse froze, my whole essence froze while my soul wailed. I shoved magic through the brand and his power flared, searing through me, ripping a scream from my clenched jaw. He was out of time.

"Let me get the charm for the transfer."

"No time." I grabbed Sebastian's hand and imagined the rest of my magic flooding into him, not burning—*please don't let me burn him*—but pouring into his essence and igniting it into a roaring magic.

His head jerked back with a howl of pain and divine light blazed from his eyes. "Slow it down," he gasped. "It's too much, Esther."

I tried to stem the flood, to pull some of it back, but my desperation had control. Sebastian needed it to save my guys and he was getting it all.

My power screamed through my body and poured into him, searing my magical channels. Sebastian wrenched his head down and squeezed his eyes shut, but divine light blazed from under his lashes, hell, it blazed from every inch of his exposed skin. "Call one of them. I need a living connection to know where to teleport."

Amiah pulled out her phone.

"Call Kol." My hands blistered and bled. So too did Sebastian's, but I kept hold of him, kept pumping magic into him. "He's the fastest healer. If they're all mortally wounded, he's the most likely able to answer."

They can't die. I can't lose them.

Amiah dialed.

"Amiah—" Kol moaned.

"Got it." Sebastian wrenched his bleeding hand from mine. A small circle of light burst around him, swarmed over him, and tore him to miniscule pieces.

"Bane is coming," Amiah said into the phone.

"How?"

"Essie." Amiah stared at me with a mix of horror and fear.

A ball of light exploded on the other side of the couch by the front door. Gideon appeared on his knees. His wings shot out with a burst of light and he collapsed, face first onto the floor, his wings splayed. Jacob lay on his back and blood rushed onto the marble around him the moment he'd fully materialized. Marcus materialized as his massive black wolf lying on his side, panting fast and shallow breaths, while Kol curled into a ball moaning as his phone clattered to the floor.

Sebastian took a staggering step forward then his eyes rolled back and he dropped, cracking his forehead on the arm of his couch.

"Oh, my God," Amiah said as she scrambled to the group.

"Save Gideon and Marcus." *Please save them.* I stood, making the room darken and whirl, and seized the back of the couch to keep standing. "I can save Jacob and Kol."

My stomach clenched, fear and physical weakness churning into nausea, and I staggered to Jacob's side. A massive hole had been punctured through his chest, terrifyingly similar to the injury he'd taken fighting the archnephilim.

I shoved half of what little strength I had left into his brand—praying he wouldn't need more in case Gideon also needed help. His eyelids fluttered opened and his gaze locked on me with the crushing power of his vampiric intensity.

I can't lose you. I can't lose any of you. Please let me have enough in me to save them.

I shoved my wrist against his mouth. For a second he hesitated, probably thinking about how much blood he'd already taken from me, then sank his teeth into my flesh.

His magic swept into me, muting my panic and making every terrified cell thrum with instant desire. I shoved my free hand under the back of Kol's T-shirt and pressed my burned palm to his skin, then set my forehead on the marble floor and closed my eyes, giving in to the sensation. I was exhausted liquid bliss. Jacob's power rushed to my core, and I ached for satisfaction, but I was also too weak to do anything about it.

My strength continued to bleed through the bonds, but it slowed from a torrent to a stream. A little more and they were going to make it. A sob broke free. I tried to raise my head to check on Marcus and Kol, but couldn't. *Please let them be okay. Please.*

Jacob groaned against my skin, and his magic twisted tighter within me. My breath came too fast, adding to my dizziness, but his magic wouldn't let me pass out. I needed a release so much it hurt.

A whisper of warmth caressed my wrist and Jacob

sealed his bite shut, but he hadn't taken enough. Strength still seeped from our brand. I tried to tell him to take more blood, but my lips were numb.

"Will Gideon live?" Jacob asked.

"He's stable," Amiah said. "And Marcus, don't you dare shift."

I'm not as hurt as they are, Marcus said, his mental voice tight with pain. I knew he was talking to Amiah, but he'd included me in the conversation to reassure me.

Another sob ripped from my throat. *Thank God. Oh, thank God.*

You need to release her, Jacob.

"I know. Just—" He sat up, groaned again, and picked me up, his skin radiating cold through his clothes. "Just working up the strength to move us."

He trembled as he staggered to his feet and shuffled to the bedroom we'd used before. My eyes kept fluttering open... or did they keep fluttering shut? I wasn't sure. Everything spun with pain and exhaustion and need.

He sagged on the bed and propped himself against the headboard, cradling me in the V between his legs. His massive body wrapped around me, strong, secure, and deliciously powerful. Even seriously injured, his erection pressed hard against my back.

His hand slid down my abdomen and into the front of my pants and underwear. I shuddered, the promise of a climax taunting me, and the bedroom spun faster.

"You need to take more."

"No," he said, his voice rumbling through his massive chest, making my essence vibrate.

"You're still pulling strength through the brand. Please, Jacob." I might be weak, but I could handle this. "Amiah can't really heal you, but she can heal me. I'm not going to lose you."

He growled and sank his teeth into my throat. I gasped at the bite of pain and violent explosion of magic in my core. It rocked my hips, pushing his fingers into my curls and closer to where I needed him.

Every cell in my body throbbed, painful and full with his magic. I couldn't catch my breath, and I squeezed my eyes shut before the whirling room made me throw up. I could handle this. I had to handle this. He just needed a little more, just to stop the brand from pulling my strength into him.

He took a long pull on my vein, twisting his magic tighter. I moaned, bucking up again, urging him to release the climax clenching within me.

Another pull, and he slid two fingers inside me, slowly pumping in and out as he swept his thumb over my clit. The pressure of my climax grew. I panted, desperate, but knew I'd shatter and never recover if he didn't release me gently.

His breath came fast, too. Hard exhalations sweeping over my neck, ratcheting up my desire. His free hand slid under my T-shirt, and he roughly kneaded my breasts as his hips rocked beneath me.

My climax trembled, faded, trembled again, and with a final rock of our hips, rushed through me, blazing through my cells and sending sparks flashing across my vision.

Darkness followed, and I yearned to sink into it, but his brand still sucked my strength.

"It wasn't enough," I said, fighting to stay conscious. "Take more."

"No. Amiah can't heal you if you're dead."

"Jacob—"

He wrapped his arms around me and held me tight to his massive chest. "We can wait for her to help Gideon."

I concentrated on Gideon's brand. Weak electric magic danced under my skin, not nearly as powerful as it should have been. He wasn't pulling strength, but he was on the very edge of needing it.

"She has helped him."

"Then we can wait for her magic to recover." Jacob drew in a ragged, wet breath and groaned.

"Or I could help," Kol said from the doorway. He looked like shit, his body bloody and bruised. A massive gash, only partly healed, sliced from his forehead to his jaw, barely missing his left eye, and the front of his T-shirt was shredded, revealing more partially healed gashes all over his chest. Hellfire blazed from his eyes, and he gripped the doorframe with both hands as if he needed the help to keep standing.

My breath caught with hope that we were going to be okay, then he dropped his gaze.

"I can give Essie a boost," he said, his voice heartbreakingly soft.

"Don't. I don't want you doing something you don't want to do." Especially since giving me a magical boost meant he'd have to kiss me.

"You're also still weak," Jacob said. "Last time you saved her, it knocked you out for hours."

"Release your bite-lock again, and I'll get it back and a bit more." His knuckles turned white, his grip on the doorframe tightened.

"Kol, don't." It was clear just being near me hurt him.

His gaze rose and captured mine, the hellfire in his eyes stronger than before, bleeding light across his cheekbones. "I know you're not one of them. I just—" He swallowed hard and took an unsteady step into the room. "You saved us. Let me help you save your mates."

"No more than you can handle," I said.

A hint of his wicked smile pulled at his lips, but it didn't reach his eyes. "You should talk."

He staggered to the bed, one arm held tight to his body as if his ribs hurt, and sagged to the mattress beside Jacob's leg. The hellfire fully consumed his eyes and with the gash on his face, he looked dangerous, not the playful, devastatingly handsome incubus I'd come to know.

I wanted to tell him I wasn't going to hurt him, that I thought what had happened to him had been horrible, but the words wouldn't form in my muddled mind.

He leaned forward and cupped my cheeks between warm, trembling palms. A whisper of his heated power slid under my skin, and my pulse picked up in anticipation. His gaze dipped to my lips, and he squeezed his eyes shut, his face tight with pain.

This wasn't right. I couldn't ask him to do this.

"Kol, don't—"

His lips captured mine and his magic swept into me. I gasped, and he deepened the kiss, sliding his tongue against mine, pouring his power down my throat. It rushed, blazing liquid desire straight to my core, and spun my nerves into breathtaking sensitivity.

Instinctively, I grabbed his wrists to hold on, the flood of his magic overwhelming, but he tensed and his trembling increased. My throat tightened. I couldn't let him do this to himself. Jacob and I would find another way. Kol didn't have to fight his fear to help us.

I tried to pull away, but his hold on me tightened. "Don't fight me."

I wasn't, not like I had when I'd been shot and he'd stabilized me enough for Gideon to get me to Amiah. "You don't have to do this."

"Just take the magic," he said against my lips. "Please." His voice was thick with emotions. I just couldn't figure out which. Pain? Desire? Fear? I wasn't sure I'd be able to figure it out even with my empathy.

"Okay." I clutched the comforter to keep from reaching for him again and gave him full control.

His magic rushed into me, sweeping me into desperate aching need. It was similar to Jacob's magic, powerful, twisting, bone-melting, but so much more. It poured into my cells and made every inch of me hypersensitive. His lips were firm and hot and hungry. His grip on my cheeks tightened, sending more swelling power into my core. Beneath me, Jacob's breath picked up as if touching me connected him to Kol's magic.

Every breath I took sent the promise of a climax trembling through me, rubbed my body against Jacob's, brought me closer to Kol with his glorious heat. I was caught between hot and cold and wanted them pressed against me, capturing me with their bodies.

Kol's magic surged, rushing fast down my throat and entwining with my magic. He started to shake, and with a groan, he pulled his lips away. My magic clung to his for a second, curling wisps of red smoke between our lips, before he jerked back, putting too much distance between us and severing the connection.

I squirmed with need, no longer bone-weary. I was still tired, but I felt more like I had when they'd first arrived. Marcus padded into the doorway, still in wolf form, and his green gaze slid over the three of us.

"I didn't even pass out this time," Kol said. He stood, and his eyes rolled back and his knees gave out.

With a growl, Marcus lunged for Kol, shifting as he moved, catching him before he cracked his head on the floor. He leaned him against the wall, close to the bed but out of the way, then turned to me. Without his clothes, I could see every gash and bruise on his beautiful body, now partially healed because he'd shifted. I could also see his desire for me.

"You're still too pale," he said.

"Jacob is still too weak. We're running out of time to stop the witches and I—" Panic from almost losing my guys snapped through the desire from Kol's magic. "I can't lose you. Any of you."

"It'll be okay," Jacob said. "I'm okay."

"I can feel you're not." I pressed my hand against the delicate gold threads of our brand on his biceps.

The muscles in Marcus's jaw flexed. "Feed on me."

Jacob tensed beneath me. "Not without my magic like

last time. And you're hurt, too. I wouldn't be able to take a lot from you."

"Then both of us," Marcus said.

"I still might not be able to get up and leave when—" Jacob said.

"That's not what I'm proposing." Marcus's piercing green gaze, filled with desire and need, locked with mine.

Holy shit, he'd been serious about the threesome.

CHAPTER 8

My mouth went dry while the rest of me throbbed in anticipation of two of my guys in bed with me.

"I'm in if Essie is," Jacob said, his voice a low, sensual rumble.

I held out my hand to Marcus, unable to speak, inviting him to join us. His wolf darkened his eyes and his breath picked up. With a low growl, he crawled onto the bed and captured my lips in a fierce kiss.

His fear and love and need filled my chest, the magic of our connection, even without an angelic mating brand, defying the power of the containment cuffs. Amiah was wrong when she'd said Marcus wasn't my true mate because I hadn't branded him. I loved and needed him as much as Jacob and Gideon.

I dug my nails into his scalp, his passion making the remains of Kol's magic swell low and sultry. He leaned closer and reached past my head, offering Jacob his wrist. Jacob shifted, digging his still-hard erection into the small of my back, sending a thrill of pleasure racing through me, and sank his fangs into Marcus.

Marcus froze, his lips pressed against mine, his breath ragged. "Good Lord. I thought I knew what you felt when we released his bite-lock, but this—"

He moaned into my mouth and trembled with what I knew was an aching, twisting need. His hips dropped, and he ground his erection against me. I shifted so he hit my clit, shooting sudden pleasure to my core and nearly coming again.

"Not yet," Jacob said, placing a heavy hand on my head and tilting it to give him better access to my neck.

I shuddered, and Marcus deepened his kiss as Jacob sank his fangs into my neck.

Consuming desire swept through me, stealing all breath and thought. There was only the feel of hard muscle capturing me between them and the ferocity of their desire for me. Jacob took a long pull on my neck. His magic overwhelmed me, and I tipped my head back, knowing my guys had me, that they'd satisfy me. Marcus scraped his nails down my body with enough pressure to make me squirm but not enough to tear my T-shirt. He skimmed the sides of my breasts, my skin hypersensitive from Kol's and Jacob's power.

Jacob took another pull on my vein, twisting his magic tighter. My breath came fast, my body aching for release.

Marcus hooked his fingers into the waistband of my pants and pulled them and my underwear off. He sat back and swept his gaze over me, his eyes filled with awe and desire. His erection jutted from his body, thick and hard, and I shuddered, knowing how he'd feel sliding into me, driving me over the edge.

Another pull on my neck, and my eyes rolled back. Jacob's magic teased me with the promise of another mind-blowing climax, and Marcus trailed his claws up the insides of my thighs. I squirmed, pushing my legs wider, inviting him in, and he settled between me. His erection brushed my folds, and my breath hitched. *Yes, oh please, yes.*

Jacob's grip on my head tightened, and he pushed his other hand under my shirt and palmed my breast. He ground his erection into my back and rumbled with pleasure, a low vibration that radiated through me. I arched into Marcus, and his tip slid into me. Jacob's magic jerked, a sudden almost blast of climax, making all of us gasp.

Marcus slid in deeper. I squirmed, rubbing against Jacob's erection. His rumble turned to a groan. He needed a release as much as Marcus and I did, but with my hands handcuffed together, there wasn't much I could do.

Then Marcus thrust into me in a hard, fast stroke, and Jacob rocked his hips, pushing mine up and driving Marcus in deeper while grinding his length against me, and all thought vanished. There was only sensation.

I shuddered, my climax teasing me, my body aching for release. Slowly, agonizingly slowly, Marcus withdrew until just his tip was inside me, then he thrust again. Jacob matched him with another rock of his hips, and the pressure of Jacob's magic swelled. I squirmed, deliciously trapped between them. Another withdraw and thrust, faster this time, and another.

Marcus's wolf rose to the forefront, darkening his eyes and slitting his pupils. His canines extended and his thrusts grew more ferocious. He grabbed my hips for more control, and Jacob's hand left my breasts and dipped into my curls to rub his thumb against my clit. The pressure of his magic and Marcus's wild passion pounded tighter and tighter until my climax ripped through me, shooting stars across my vision and making me scream with pleasure.

Both guys tensed with their own release, and Kol jerked upright as if he'd been struck by lightning.

"Holy fuck," he gasped, then his dazed gaze focused on us. "Holy. Fuck."

I murmured my agreement and slid into a warm darkness. My guys were safe, and I was boneless and thoroughly satisfied. God, I loved them—and not just for the pleasure they'd given me. They were the family I'd never known I'd ached for. I yearned to lie, safe and loved, in their embrace forever. And now that I wasn't a nephilim, I could.

My dreams drifted from the warm darkness to the warm water that wasn't water. I gently bobbed, up and down, up and down, the motion calm, relaxing. A handsome angel with brown hair and gold flecks in his angel glow smiled back at me. My father. Now I knew he was an archangel. I just didn't know which one... and I didn't want to think too hard about that, given that I'd been hidden my entire life and my father hadn't come back for me once the war was over. Which meant he'd died, either defending humanity or trying to exterminate it.

A bang thudded far off in the distance, then another.

My father glanced over his shoulder, but I couldn't see where he was looking. Only foggy darkness lay behind him, distorted by the not-water.

He pressed his palm against something between us and the warmth in the not-water swelled. It wrapped around me with a gentle embrace and the foggy darkness billowed until it was all I could see. A masculine voice murmured something to me. I wasn't sure who, but it had to be one of my guys. *My guys.* God, I loved thinking about them like that. I lay caught between two hard, muscular bodies, boneless from an amazing climax and craving more.

I slid my hand out to caress whichever of my guys lay in front of me but didn't touch muscle, only mattress. My mind stuttered. I wasn't embraced between my guys. I was alone—

"Agent Shaw," the voice murmured again from close behind me.

That made my pulse skip. Had Gideon stopped using my name? Was he back to addressing me formally? Perhaps old habits died hard? Or he'd changed his mind about being one of my many mates? The fractured part of my soul ached at that thought.

"Gideon, please." I rolled over, my sight blurry with sleep and my eyes sore from still wearing the contacts I no longer needed. I blinked my vision clear enough to see eyes with a pale angel glow.

Except they weren't blue and his hair wasn't buzzed short or blond. Not Gideon.

My pulse lurched. He wasn't Gideon, and this angel

didn't know I wasn't a nephilim. I needed to run. Find my guys. Now.

"Agent Shaw." The man pressed a warm hand to my forehead and gentle heat seeped into me, easing my panic. "I'm Priam. Amiah asked me to help heal you."

My pulse returned closer to normal. Amiah knew I wasn't a nephilim... unless she was trying to get rid of me to save Marcus.

Except I was still in the same white and blue bedroom in Sebastian's apartment. The blankets had been pulled over me, while the white comforter, bloody from Jacob and Marcus's injuries, lay in a heap on the floor where Kol had been sitting.

"Is she awake?" Amiah asked, striding into the room.

"Just," Priam said. He was handsome—like most angels were—but in a casual, boy-next-door kind of way, not strikingly handsome like Gideon.

"Good." She looked pale and haggard, and my stomach plunged for a second before I realized she was probably just exhausted, physically and magically. Neither Gideon nor Jacob were drawing strength from the brand, Kol had gotten a pretty big infusion of sex magic, and Marcus had been healthy enough to help with that amazing orgasm.

"Are *you* okay?" I asked her.

She looked surprised that I'd even ask. "I just need to recover my magic, maybe sleep for a week."

Priam gently squeezed her elbow and gave her a warm smile. "Just like the good old days when we worked emerg at Mercy Memorial."

"Which I left for this very reason." She squared her

shoulders, her angel glow billowing. "The guys are waiting for you in the living room. I'll give you a minute to get dressed."

She and Priam left. I retrieved my underwear and pants from the floor and put them on. My shirt was bloody from lying on Jacob's ravaged chest, but I didn't have a spare and didn't want to risk taking off the cuffs to change. I also really wanted to pull my hair back in a ponytail, but I had no idea where my hair elastic had gone, so I did a few quick combs with my fingers then left the bedroom.

At least I felt a hundred times better than I had before. In fact, save for a burning headache that came from having used too much magic too quickly, I felt better than I had in days. The cuffs contained my buzz so my skin was no longer on fire, and Priam must have healed me completely because I couldn't feel a hint of having been drained of blood, twice, in the last handful of hours.

Everyone except Priam and Cassius sat in Sebastian's living room, and all eyes turned to me the moment I stepped out of the hall. My guys rushed to my side, and relief flooded me. They all looked healthy and well. Gideon's expression was strained and his face was still bruised, but at least the bruises looked a few days old instead of a few hours. Jacob looked fine, and when he wrapped his arms around me in a firm hug, his body was even warm. Marcus took over when Jacob released me, capturing my cheeks between his palms and kissing me with one of his ferocious, quick kisses that always left me breathless. There wasn't a hint of bruising on his face, and while his new, clean clothes made it impossible to tell if he was still covered in wounds, he didn't move as if he were still hurt.

Marcus released me, but threaded his fingers between mine as Gideon brushed a kiss over my forehead. God, I needed him to kiss me in full. But if his kiss had been as deep as Marcus's or his embrace as encompassing as Jacob's, my need to solidify our bond would take over and I'd drag him back into the bedroom. He hesitated, his body close, his power humming through his brand. I could feel his need to stay close, and hear his struggle with his ever so slightly too-fast breath.

Please kiss me.

Please don't.

I wanted both. I wanted him. I didn't want to be responsible for people getting hurt.

With a groan, he stepped back and crossed his arms, as if he were trying to keep his hands to himself.

Kol had risen from his seat on the couch but didn't approach. The nasty cut on his face was gone, and he no longer pressed his arm against his ribs. Hellfire flickered in his eyes, banked and contained, but his expression was tight. Things still weren't right between us, but it was complicated and not easily fixed.

Heat swept up my neck and across my cheeks. He'd seen me with Marcus and Jacob. Which had been amazing, and satisfying, and something I wouldn't mind repeating. And while I doubted Kol would judge my sex choices, I still couldn't help feeling awkward and embarrassed about desires I hadn't known I had.

Sebastian, still sitting, watched me from the seat

beside Kol with that calculating look that made me feel
like he was seeing into my soul. He didn't have a welt on
his forehead from where he'd smacked his head and his
hand was no longer burned, so Amiah or Priam must
have healed him, too. But my divine light still bled from
his eyes in tiny droplets that, every couple of blinks,
rolled down his cheeks then sank back under his skin.

"How long was I out?" I asked as Marcus led me to the
couches, sat, and pulled me onto his lap, even though
there was space for both of us.

Jacob pushed the coffee table aside and sat on the
floor at Marcus's feet, Amiah took the seat beside me and
Marcus, while Gideon perched on the couch's arms—
close but not touching.

Please, just touch me.

Jeez, my willpower just wasn't going to last the day, let
alone the next couple of hours.

"Less than an hour," Marcus said. "So we've still time
to deal with the witches."

"Tell me you've called for backup." I didn't want them
to face the witches again, but I knew my guys wouldn't
give up. It was their job to arrest the witches, and it wasn't
in their nature to quit.

"The closest team in Los Angeles is dealing with their
own problems, and head office doesn't know when they
can get agents to us," Gideon said. "We're on our own."

Jacob rested a hand on my calf, his still intensity
helping me to focus past the yearning of my bond with
Gideon. "And we still don't know what they're planning
or where they are."

"Even if we get backup, we still need a way to cut off

their power before we face them again." Kol's gaze jumped to mine for a second then slid away. "That ambush in City Hall nearly killed us."

"Like I said five minutes ago," Sebastian said, his tone exasperated, "I'm still waiting to hear back from a few sources about your area containment master ward."

"That wasn't a criticism," Kol said. "Just a statement of fact. I'd rather not have those witches hand me my ass again. I doubt you'll be around next time to teleport us out of there."

"I don't know. I might be. Essie made one hell of a payment to save you, and she hasn't come close to spending it all." He shuddered and wiped a trickle of divine light from his cheek. "Archangel divine light is some potent shit."

"And you're never getting her power again." Gideon glared at him.

He raised his hands. "Never going to ask for it."

Something passed between the two men, a warning from Gideon to Sebastian, but I couldn't figure out for what. Gideon didn't strike me as the jealous type. He'd only been concerned about me having multiple mates because of Marcus's possessive wolf.

"So," Marcus said, breaking the tension. "What's the plan?"

Gideon opened his mouth to respond, but his phone buzzed. He checked the display and didn't answer.

"Apparently it involves continuing to avoid the mayor," Kol said.

Gideon set the phone to silent and shoved it back into his pocket. "I'll deal with him when we have a plan."

"And to do that, we need to figure out what the witches are planning," Jacob said. "I doubt they're still at City Hall."

"Sure, what are the odds they'll ambush us twice in the same place?" Marcus barked a bitter laugh.

"City Hall was a lucky guess," Jacob said.

"I'm not willing to risk that it wasn't." Gideon's angel glow flared. "These witches are powerful. I wouldn't put a scrying or tracking spell past them."

"It takes a shit load of power to cast anything like that," Marcus said.

Gideon met his gaze. "I know."

I didn't like the sound of that. "So if they're watching us right now, they know where we are and what we're planning. Whatever we do next, we could be walking into a trap."

"Not right now," Sebastian said. "I have a concealment glyph on my apartment."

"But as soon as we leave..." Kol ran a hand through his hair, mussing it and no doubt not realizing how sexy it made him look. "We need our concealment charms."

"But they're in Operations and even if we could get them, we don't have a witch who can set them." Jacob glanced at Sebastian. "Unless you can set a concealment charm, among all the other things you can do."

"I can't set charms, but I know who can." Sebastian pulled out his phone. "So long as you promise not to arrest her."

"I promise not to arrest her for giving us concealment charms," Gideon said, since only the JP and certain branches of the army were allowed to have those—

although that didn't mean there weren't witches willing to make and set them for enough money.

Sebastian gave Gideon a dry look. "You can be a little less specific than that."

"Fine," Gideon sighed. "I promise not to arrest her for anything seen or done during this one exchange with her."

"Better." Sebastian typed in a text. "You'll have to go to her. She won't come to you."

Gideon pulled out his phone and checked the text.

"You know where that is?" Sebastian asked.

Gideon gave a tight nod. "I do."

"Good. You'll also need the right payment to cover all five of you."

"Four," Marcus growled. "Essie isn't going."

Sebastian turned his icy gaze on Marcus, and another divine light tear rolled down his cheek then melted into his skin. "You'd be an idiot not to take her. If things get bad, take off the cuffs and point her in the right direction."

That sounded like a terrible idea. "I agree with Marcus. I can't control my blast. It's too dangerous."

"If things get bad for your guys, it's really bad." Sebastian's attention jumped back to Gideon and his expression turned grim. Whatever Sebastian had teleported into when he'd rescued my guys, it had scared him. "You'll need a bomb, not a scalpel."

He had a really good point. My chest squeezed, remembering how near death they'd been when Sebastian had brought them back. Even if my blast incapacitated me, it could be enough for my guys to drag me out of there... if I didn't hit them, as well.

Marcus's eyes narrowed. "She's just about killed herself twice in as many hours trying to save us."

"And she'll lose her mind if you go down and she's not there." The muscles in Sebastian's jaw flexed. "Trust me. That wasn't pretty to watch."

I shifted to look Marcus in the eyes. "I'm getting the charm. We can decide if it's safe for me to go into the field after that. I'd rather not find ourselves wishing we had it."

"Agreed," Gideon said. "What type of payment do we need and what's it going to cost us?"

"Nothing. Essie's already paid, remember?" Sebastian grabbed a marble from the bowl on the coffee table and pressed his free palm to the center of his chest.

Icy blue light blazed beneath his white button-down as he activated a glyph. The divine light flared in his eyes and his body stiffened, the veins in his neck and arms bulging. Light raced along those veins and swept into his hand, then twisted into a miniature vortex in the marble, whirling faster and faster.

My buzz whispered just under my skin, the promise of a biting, searing fire, barely trapped by the containment cuffs. I tried to bite back a groan, but couldn't, and Marcus tightened his grip on me

"Bane?" he growled.

Gideon and Jacob also tensed. Even Kol shifted to the edge of the couch, his hands sliding to his back where he hid his sheathed daggers.

Sebastian ignored them, his attention locked on the marble. His breath grew ragged, sweat beaded on his forehead, and large divine light tears rolled down his cheeks and splattered onto his thighs before sinking back into his body.

The pressure from the vortex grew. Fire crackled under my skin, my buzz no longer just a whisper, and light billowed over my hands. I was going to burst into flames and take my guys down with me.

"Sebastian, stop," I gasped. "I'm going to lose control."

CHAPTER 9

MY BREATH TURNED RAGGED AND MY BUZZ SLICED DEEP, seizing my muscles and threatening to consume me. The power in my hands grew, and I fought to hold it back. *Come on. Control it. Please, God, let me control it.* But the power kept building and my mental grip started to slip. "Please, Sebastian. Stop."

Gideon jerked toward Sebastian as his power surged, making the light in my hands flare, searing my palms. I screamed and yanked the power back under my skin, praying I'd be the only one I'd hurt this time. Then the power snapped off, and my buzz and magic vanished.

Oh, thank God.

Trembling and breathing hard, I leaned into Marcus. I needed his warmth and strength. In just a few seconds, Sebastian had demonstrated why taking me anywhere was a terrible idea.

Marcus rubbed his hands over my arms, trying to help me warm up. He glared at Sebastian, who held out the marble to Gideon, his hands shaking and his breath as ragged as mine.

"Your payment," he said.

Gideon glowered at him. In fact, all my guys looked like they wanted to rip his head off, even Kol. But Gideon took the marble instead and handed it to Kol. "It better be clean."

"My essence would be in there, as well." Sebastian sagged back, his icy gaze meeting mine. A tear of divine light, not as bright as before, trickled down his cheek and melted back into his skin. "It's the light magic you pumped into me, so both our essences are entwined in it. If I didn't strip it down to pure magic when I put it in the marble, a strong enough witch could use that to influence us."

"That's why angels don't sell their divine light," Jacob said. "They don't want to risk leaving a hint of essence behind."

And that had to be why Gideon had told Sebastian he was never getting my magic again.

"Angels also don't usually have access to someone who's magically sensitive that they trust, or who's sensitive enough, who will tell them if the magic is pure." Kol's attention flickered to me then jumped to Gideon, and he handed the marble back. "She's safe."

"Good." Gideon pocketed the marble. "Let's make this quick."

I stood on shaky legs and checked my hands. They were sore but thankfully not burned. So while I might be going out in a bloody shirt with my hands cuffed together, at least I wasn't injured.

"What are we going to do about Essie's cuffs?" Marcus stood, drawing up close behind me and steadying me. "It's dangerous for her to be hampered like this."

Except his tone made it clear he was really saying it was just plain dangerous for me to be doing anything.

"Can you do anything with the containment spell with all that extra magic Essie gave you?" Gideon asked Sebastian.

"I think I can split it if you can cut the links." Sebastian rubbed his face and sat forward. He met my gaze and pointed to the edge of his coffee table. "Sit."

I sat and Gideon created a small blade of divine light. Sebastian activated three small glyphs on his right arm, took a cuff in each hand, and gave Gideon a nod. Gideon sliced the chain holding my hands together, leaving the cuffs around my wrists, and Sebastian's power snapped over them. It curled up my arms, the right side sinking into Gideon's brand and drawing a hiss of pain from both of us.

With a groan, Sebastian closed his eyes. The muscles in his jaw flexed, and he took a slow breath as if to steady himself, but at least this spell didn't look as difficult as putting my magic into the marble and didn't reawaken my buzz.

"There." He sat back. "That'll hold for about a day."

"How long is *about*?" Jacob asked.

Sebastian cocked an eyebrow and gave him a dry, exhausted look. "If I knew exactly, I would have said so. Esther burns through non-personal magic like it's dry tinder, so it could be a day or half a day. Depends on what she's doing."

"So that might not last until we've dealt with the witches," Marcus said.

"Let's hope it does." Gideon headed to the door. "Because we don't have a second set of cuffs and once that spell fails, nothing is containing her magic."

Which meant everyone near me would be in danger.

"This is a terrible idea," Marcus growled.

Hell, yes. In fact, I shouldn't be anywhere near my guys if I wanted to keep them safe.

Except that thought made my pulse stall. So far, not being near them hadn't kept them safe.

"We haven't been hiding our brands, so the witches know we're connected to Essie," Gideon said. "If we disappear from their magic sight, they might start looking for her."

Marcus groaned. "I hate when you make sense. Let's go."

"You should change first," Jacob said to me, grabbing a shirt from a bag on the floor near the hall and tossing it to me. "You'll draw enough attention with the cuffs as it is, even if they are separated."

"Yeah." I looked at everyone in the room. They'd all seen me in my bra, or less, no point in hiding in a room just to change my shirt. I took off the bloody one and pulled on the new one.

We left Sebastian's apartment, stepping into an opulent hall with a marble floor and gilded frescoes, just like the hall outside Victoria's suite.

Sebastian's private stairs were just as upscale, with marble steps and a crystal chandelier that gleamed in more gilded frescoes—these ones of winter scenes—as well as in the polished dark-wood railing. The stairs led up to the roof and directly down to the first floor, with no doors to any of the other floors, and took us to a small patio with a bistro table, two chairs, and four evergreen shrubs in planter boxes. Beyond lay a clean, narrow walking path, cobbled as if we were in an old town in Europe, that led to a side street as far away from Rouge's main entrance as possible.

The sun sat high in the sky, it had to be around noon, and even in the walking path's shadows the air was too warm and muggy. It might have been early summer, but it felt later in the season, and I was sweating by the time we reached the JP SUV sitting at the curb on the street at the end of the path.

We piled into the hot vehicle, everyone except Kol taking their usual seat. He sat in the back with Jacob, leaving me the entire second row. My heart ached at the distance he put between us, making it hard to remind myself that I'd awoken terrible memories for him and healing our friendship was going to take time.

Gideon, sitting in the front passenger seat, showed Marcus the address Sebastian had texted him as he put all the windows down to let what little breeze there was alleviate the heat before the AC could kick in.

"Really? Her? This plan just keeps getting better by the second," Marcus said, his tone thick with sarcasm.

He drove across the Quarter to Squatters' Row, straight to the mouth of Mystic Mavis's back alley, and my heart sank.

Of course Sebastian would send us to Mavis. She was the most powerful non-registered witch in the Quarter.

Jeez, I'd hoped I wouldn't have to remind everyone, especially Kol, that I'd lied to them, but now I didn't have much of a choice.

"So, ah... Just so you're not caught off guard, I've done business with Ma—" Crap. No specifics, in case we were being spied on. "—this witch."

Jacob's vampiric intensity swelled, filling the car and sitting heavy in my chest, and I got out of the SUV, desperate for relief.

"Jeez, Essie. Why would you do business with her?" Marcus asked.

"To hide what she really was," Kol said, his voice soft, making my throat tighten.

I *needed* to make things right. How the hell did I make things right? I wasn't going to apologize for being who I was, and I wasn't sure if apologizing for lying would fix anything.

"The spell that made your essence look human is hers?" Marcus asked. "I didn't think she was that powerful."

"She's not. I just needed to hide my eyes. They never stopped glowing after fighting the archnephilim."

"Blasting all that divine light into your body must have been the first crack in the spell hiding your real essence," Gideon said.

Or at least the first big crack, since I'd already had my buzz for a few years. "I didn't know what to do. I thought I was a nephilim."

"Probably because whoever enspelled you knew that was the best way to ensure you'd keep yourself hidden even after they were gone." Jacob's eyes grew dark and the muscles in his jaw flexed. "To tell that to a child, make them think the world hated them and was after them—" He fisted his hands and strode into the alley, the heat of his anger breaking through the containment cuffs and swirling in my chest, half real emotion and half my weird empathy.

The strength of his reaction shocked me. Yes, my guys accepted who I was and supported me, but I hadn't expected any of them to be furious about how I'd grown up nor to realize so quickly what my life had been like without me even telling them.

"Best way to piss Jacob off," Marcus said, glancing at Kol. "Hurt a child."

Kol jerked away from us and hurried after Jacob.

"So what does she know about you? Does she have leverage we should know about?" Gideon asked, drawing close but not touching me

Please touch me.

His gaze dipped to mine and the angel glow in his eyes flared. For a second I was drowning in a summer-sky, my breath and pulse stalled, hell, my whole essence stalled, focused entirely on him. I needed him, body and soul.

I gritted my teeth, crossed my arms, and shifted closer to Marcus. Maybe being near him would help ease my need to rip my clothes off and beg Gideon to take me.

"What kind of leverage are you talking about?" I forced out. "I bought enspelled contacts to hide my angel glow. I didn't know that every time I used my light strike it ate through her spell, so I had to go to her yesterday for a top-up." I hadn't looked in the mirror—I wasn't sure I wanted to see how stunned I looked this time from every-thing that had happened—but given everyone's reaction to me, I was sure the spell on the contacts was well and truly done. "She wanted more money than I could afford, or my light magic."

The muscles in Gideon's jaw flexed and his pupils dilated, but I got the feeling it wasn't just because I'd bought enspelled contacts from Mavis. "What did you give her?"

"Nothing. I thought I had a day to figure it out, then a building fell on us, and I found out I had wings." A part of me still couldn't believe that. I had wings. And I wasn't a nephilim.

We followed Jacob and Kol toward Mavis's door, the back entrance to a now abandoned building that used to have apartments upstairs and a restaurant on the main floor. A small Eye of Horus, glimmering with a hint of magic, had been drawn in black ink near the top of the solid metal security door. I hadn't noticed the glow before, but that could just mean new powers that weren't completely affected by the containment cuffs were breaking through the spell that had hidden my true essence and abilities all my life.

Jacob opened the door, releasing an impossible gust of cool air—since the building didn't have electricity and could only be air conditioned with magic—and Gideon took the lead. He was the agent in charge. This was his negotiation to handle. Kol went next, and Marcus and I followed, while Jacob took the rear.

The same thick incense filled the air with a purple haze, making it hard to breathe, and the sense of unease that I'd gotten the first two times I'd visited Mavis churned in my gut. The large black glyphs covering the walls also glowed when they hadn't before, and the urge to turn around and get the hell out of there swelled, making me tremble.

"Did you think bringing friends would scare me into changing the price?" Mavis asked, her raspy alto making the hair on the back of my neck stand up.

We stepped into what used to be the restaurant's kitchen. Most of the stainless steel counters had been replaced with dark-wood bookcases, filled with books and boxes and strange things I didn't want to look at too closely. The counters that did remain were crowded with vials and jars and bowls, and stood between a sink filled with dirty dishes and a stove that had a pot of something boiling on a burner that was powered by magic. Dozens of candles illuminated the space, casting dark shadows into all the nooks and crannies, and catching on Mavis's necklaces, bracelets, and multi-chain headpiece.

She sat in a high-backed chair in front of an intricately carved table, still looking like a gypsy from an old movie, wearing a billowy shirt cinched with a corset—this one gold instead of yesterday's black—and a dark red gauzy skirt. Her dark eyes took in every inch of my guys, her perusal slow and sensual, and her blood-red lips curled into a wicked smile. "They are nice to look at, though. All that muscle. My offer might change if one of them is on the table."

"We're taken," Marcus growled.

"The angel and vampire are, that's for sure," Mavis said, tapping her nails up her right arm. "Although I'm surprised the brand is enough to protect you from the angel, given you've been hiding your nephilim nature." She squinted and leaned forward. "Hunh. I was sure your essence said you were human."

Gideon shifted slightly in front of me, but I wasn't sure if he was consciously trying to protect me from Mavis's gaze or not. "My mate's essence isn't your concern. We need five concealment charms to protect against magical spying."

Mavis's eyes narrowed, her expression turning calculating. "A concealment charm will only get you so far and last for so long. If you're going to hide from the JP, you're going to need something more powerful."

"We just need the charms," Gideon said.

"Even if her essence isn't quite human anymore, you know they'll come after her, lover boy." Mavis's grin turned dangerous. "Especially if word so happens to slip out."

"And you'll be the one to tell them if we don't pay you?" Jacob released more of his vampiric intensity. His power wasn't fully revealed, but it was close, since he hadn't pulled anything back after getting pissed about my childhood.

"Something like that." Mavis sat back and crossed her arms, her expression dry. Guess Jacob wasn't powerful enough to scare her, which made me wonder just how powerful she was. I knew from the search I'd done on the dark web that her magic was strong, but she didn't seem at all worried about my guys.

"We're a little short on time," Kol said, "and you really don't want to play this game with us."

Mavis's smile deepened. "Of course I do. They'll do anything to protect her, which means they'll pay anything."

Kol shifted to the stove and took a sniff at whatever was boiling in the pot. "Love potion."

"Didn't think you'd be interested, unless..." Mavis said with a dark chuckle, "you're not powerful enough to break an angelic mating brand." She sat forward, a wicked gleam in her eyes. "You want the girl, too, don't you?"

Kol stiffened, making me ache. He wasn't mine. I wasn't supposed to want him like I did my mates. And he hadn't reacted to Mavis's words because he wanted me.

"I count at least twenty magic violations." He slid his fingers over a jar on the counter. "And this one's serious."

"So *you're* going to call the JP on *me*?" Mavis sneered. "Oh, honey, you shouldn't make a bluff no one's going to believe."

"And you shouldn't try to strong-arm an angel protecting his mate." Gideon pulled his ID from his pocket—I had no idea how he'd managed to keep it in this morning's chaos—and held it up so Mavis could see it. "We are the JP."

Her eyes flashed wide and her face paled.

"Now about those concealment charms," Marcus growled.

"You know it's illegal to make them," she said.

"Which is why we've come to you and not a registered witch." Gideon pulled the glowing marble from his pocket. Her expression jumped from fear to hunger in an instant. "For the charms and your silence."

"They'll still come after her." She held out her hand, her gaze locked on the marble, my divine light reflected in her eyes.

"The charms and your silence," Gideon pressed.

"Yes yes yes." Mavis flicked her fingers, her attention never leaving the marble, and a long metal box with a thick, complicated glyph on the lid floated off the shelf behind her and landed on the table. "Who's first?"

"I'll go," I said. It really didn't matter what order we went in, but I got the feeling the guys would feel better about not being enspelled while I was vulnerable to Mavis. "What do you need?"

"Just your wrist." Mavis pointed to the stool across from her, but Marcus grabbed my arm before I could move.

"I'll go first," he said. "If she fucks with us, better me than you."

"Yeah," Kol said, his back to us and his voice so quiet I wouldn't have been able to hear him without my enhanced hearing. "Marcus can't level a building."

Marcus sat on the stool and placed his hand on the table, palm up, and Kol stepped up beside him.

Mavis ignored Kol and opened the box. Inside, nestled on red silk, was a thin knife, a small jar filled with something dark, a paintbrush, and a half-dozen coins the size of a penny with a complicated glyph etched on them. She opened the jar, dipped in the brush, and drew a simple glyph on Marcus's wrist in black ink. Then she reached for the knife.

"Yeah, I don't think so," Kol said. "We don't know where that's been."

"Well, I need to make a cut," Mavis huffed.

"You can use this." Kol drew the knife from his ankle sheath and set it on the table.

Mavis glared at him, but took the knife, grabbed Marcus's hand, and made an incision through the glyph.

Marcus's shoulders tensed and his wolf darkened his eyes, the only sign he didn't want to just sit there and take it.

A whisper of red mist, demonic magic, curled up from the glyph for a second then vanished. Mavis hissed a word I didn't recognize and set one of the coins on the bloody glyph.

More red mist curled from the glyph. It wrapped around the coin and my buzz tickled under my skin.

Mavis's gaze slid to mine, and she hissed three more words.

The red mist billowed and so did my buzz. She raised an eyebrow as if she could see the effect her magic had on me. Another hissed word, and the coin sank into Marcus's wrist, drawing a grunt of pain. Then the mist vanished and so did my buzz.

"The spell is clean," Kol said.

Marcus stood, rubbing the spot where the cut and glyph should have been, but there wasn't a hint of ink or blood or even a pink line where she'd cut him. Jacob sat on the stool next, and Mavis sank a coin into his wrist, watching me through veiled lashes as she cast the spell.

My buzz blazed a little hotter this time, and the wicked gleam in her eyes that had vanished when Gideon had revealed he was a JP agent returned. She sank a coin into Gideon's wrist, and my buzz flared stronger, reaching a post-nicotine level —at a time when the nicotine patches had actually worked. Her gleam melted into worry as she enspelled Kol and my buzz burned at pre-nicotine levels.

"Last one," she said to me.

I sat, set my hand on the table, and pushed the hand-cuff up to make sure it didn't get in the way of the spell. My pulse beat a little too fast. So far my divine light hadn't flooded my palms, and my buzz had vanished the second the demonic magic had, but I had no idea how I'd react with the spell sinking into my body.

Mavis's worry turned to outright fear when she saw the cuffs. "They're containing your magic."

"Yes." No point in lying. She could probably see or sense the spell on the cuffs, and quite frankly there weren't any other reasons for me to wear handcuffs, even if they were separated.

"They're afraid of you." She painted the glyph on my wrist, my buzz burning without a hint of red mist, and grabbed my fingers with a trembling hand. "They should be."

CHAPTER 10

My buzz burned hotter, snapping under my skin, as Mavis picked up Kol's knife. All she'd done was paint the glyph on my wrist and my magic was already growing past the power of the containment cuffs.

"We're not afraid of her," Jacob said.

"Then you're idiots," Mavis said, and slid the tip of the knife across my wrist.

The blade was so sharp—or my buzz was so strong—I didn't feel anything. For a second I worried Mavis's fear had stopped her from actually cutting me, then blood welled on my wrist. My buzz roared under my skin, and a whisper of red mist curled up from the glyph.

Mavis picked a coin from the box, but it slipped from her trembling fingers and clattered onto the table. Her fear frosted my hand where she held me and curled up my arm. She hadn't reacted this way the last time I'd seen her, so whatever scared her had to have been previously concealed by the now-crumbling spell hiding my true essence. And a part of me feared it had everything to do with how I reacted to demonic magic... which I wasn't sure had anything to do with archangels.

Her grip on my hand tightened. She grabbed the coin, pressed it into my blood, and hissed the first word of her spell. Red mist swept up from the glyph, and my buzz surged.

I gasped, the force of the flare stealing my breath, and Kol tensed, his hands sliding to his hips and closer to the hilts of the daggers on his back. Out of everyone on the team, he was the only one who could see the demonic magic... unless it was powerful enough for them to see... which I doubted, because this wasn't nearly as powerful as Ibizual's magic.

"Kol?" Marcus growled.

"Still good," he said, but he didn't sound certain.

Mavis hissed the next word and the mist surged. My buzz exploded, snapping and slicing under my skin and seizing my muscles. I bit back a groan, and light radiated from my palm. Mavis's fear swept frost to my elbow.

She gasped out the third word and red mist burst from Mavis's necklaces and bracelets, something that hadn't happened with the guys. The magic raced down her arm and over mine, sinking into my skin. My buzz blazed and my divine light swelled to encompass my entire hand.

"What the hell?" Marcus barked.

Mavis gritted her teeth and hissed the final two words of the spell. Agony exploded in my wrist as the coin sank beneath my skin, dragging a stream of demonic magic from Mavis, not just from her jewelry, with it.

With a strangled scream, she jerked close, red mist

pouring from her eyes and mouth. It rushed around her head, spinning into a vortex that whipped up her wild black locks, and ripped off the chain headpiece, tossing it across the room.

Fire and ice, my magic and Mavis's fear, roared through me. My divine light filled the room with stark white illumination. It devoured Mavis's magic, twisting it tight in my chest, threatening to rip me to pieces from the inside out.

Kol seized Mavis's hand, still gripping mine, and yanked us apart. Jacob grabbed me and hauled me off the stool into his arms, while Gideon and Marcus shoved in front of me, ready for a fight.

The stream of magic pouring from Mavis into me snapped. My buzz blazed, and for a second there was a supernova within me on the verge of eruption. Then cold blasted into me, and the power and buzz vanished, once again contained by the cuffs.

I sagged in Jacob's arms, shivering and gasping, while Mavis stared at me, her eyes wide, her face pale.

"What was that?" Gideon demanded.

Her gaze darted over my guys, ready to defend me, then returned to me. "I helped you."

"Did you?" Marcus growled.

"Remember I helped you," she begged.

Gideon glanced at Kol. "Is the concealment spell good?"

Kol stared at my wrist where the coin had sunk under my skin, his gaze slightly unfocused. "It's good."

"Great, let's go," Gideon said.

Marcus stiffened. "I want to know what the fuck just happened."

"We don't have the time." The muscles in Gideon's jaw flexed and he met Marcus's glare, daring him to argue about it. And as much as I was sure everyone wanted to know what had happened, we couldn't risk staying there and being found by the witches.

Marcus snarled and jerked away, heading to the door. "Fine."

Gideon turned to Mavis and set the marble with my divine light on the table. "You say anything about Essie, and I'll bring the full force of the JP down on you."

"The JP is the least of my worries." Mavis jerked back in her chair and stared at the marble like it was going to bite her. "I don't want it. I don't want her essence in my shop."

"Have it your way." Gideon grabbed the marble, not arguing with her that the magic in the marble didn't hold any of my essence. He shoved it in his pocket and headed to the door.

We followed him out, and while I managed to walk on my shaky legs, Jacob kept an arm around me to steady me.

"What the fuck?" Marcus growled as he stormed into the alley.

Gideon glanced up and down the alley, then turned a worried gaze to me. "Are you all right?"

"I'm a little shaky, but fine." And physically I was. Mentally my mind whirled. Once again my magic had sucked in demonic mist. I really needed to read up on archangels... hell, I needed to figure out who my parents

were. I didn't even know if an angel's power was heredi-
tary or not.

"We have to get moving," Jacob said. "If the witches
have a tracking or scrying spell on us, they know where
we are and we've already spent too much time here."

"And now that we've disappeared to their magic, they
know why." Kol drew his daggers and rushed to the
mouth of the alley where the SUV sat.

Jacob moved to pick me up, but I waved him off. "I'm
okay."

He didn't look convinced and neither did Marcus, but
they didn't argue with me.

We hurried to the SUV, quickly checked the street,
and got in. Marcus pulled away from the curb and drove
to the far side of the Quarter.

"I don't know if it's a good thing or not that they didn't
come after us," Marcus said.

Gideon turned in the front passenger seat so he could
see everyone, sweat from the heat in the SUV slicking his
forehead. "They must be busy with whatever they're
planning."

"Which we still need to figure out," Jacob said from
his seat in the back.

Kol shifted beside me. He still had his long daggers
drawn, and he still sat as far away from me as possible,
but at least this time he hadn't made a point of sitting in
the back with Jacob. I wasn't sure if that was an improvement or just because choosing where he sat hadn't been a
priority when we'd hurried to the vehicle. "We're going to
have to go back to City Hall." He raised his gaze to meet

Gideon's. "Unless we know someone who can get us the security tapes."

Marcus barked a bitter laugh. "Assuming the witches haven't destroyed the tapes."

"I'd rather not risk more civilians," Jacob said, "especially human civilians."

"Neither would I, and I don't want to face these witches unarmed again." Gideon's pale gaze met mine, capturing my soul and stealing my breath for a second. I couldn't lose him. I couldn't lose any of them, not even Kol. But I would if we didn't figure out how to deal with these witches.

"Is there anyone else we can go to?" I asked.

"For weapons, yes," Jacob said. "But that still leaves us risking civilians by going to City Hall to follow the only lead we have."

"We have to go to Operations." The muscles in Gideon's jaw tightened. "I took a moment to talk with Bane about the temporal freeze. We can be within the radius of the spell for about five minutes, so if we work fast enough, we can raid the armory as well as use Operations' systems to access and copy City Hall's security footage. The freeze only affects organic material, so the computers and door locks aren't frozen by the spell."

"I'm fast," Jacob said, "but I doubt I can access Summer's computer *and* raid the armory before the spell captures me."

"We'll split into two teams." Gideon jerked his chin at Marcus, who put the SUV in gear.

"Essie's not going in, right?" Marcus asked.

"I'd rather she didn't," Gideon said. "But it isn't safe

for any of us to be by ourselves, even with the concealment spell. Jacob and I will go to Summer's lab. The rest
of you go to the armory."

Marcus turned onto the main street leading through
the center of the Quarter. His nails extended into claws,
his wolf fighting for control. Tension radiated from all my
guys the closer we got to Operations. The light in
Gideon's eyes blazed brighter and Jacob's hold on his
vampiric intensity started to slip. By the time Marcus
parked in front of Operations, their combined power
filled the SUV with a physical, crushing weight.

Kol and I staggered out of the vehicle, while Marcus,
Gideon, and Jacob stormed out, their power rolling off
them in a great wave.

"Jeez, guys," Kol said. "She's not helpless." His gaze
jumped to me for a second, the look in his eyes saying
there wasn't anything helpless about me. Then he yanked
his attention back to Operations' closed garage door.

Jacob squeezed his eyes shut, and the weight of his
power eased. "I know you're not helpless," he said to me.
"I just—"

"It's the brand," Gideon said, his voice strained.

"The soul bonds," Marcus corrected. "I feel it, too, and
I don't have a brand. You've almost died twice today. My
wolf is still losing his shit over that."

I wanted to argue with him, point out that they'd
almost died twice today, too, but my power was unpre-
dictable and dangerous, even with the cuffs on. If something were to go wrong right now, odds are I'd be in the
middle of it.

"It's still safer for her to go with you to the armory."

Gideon pulled out his phone. "Set a timer for five minutes. Jacob, let's use the door closer to Summer's lab."

He and Jacob strode around to the other side of the building, while Marcus pulled out his phone and set a timer as well.

I didn't know the layout of Operations well, but given that Marcus and Kol didn't suggest entering through another door, the garage was the closest entrance to the basement stairs.

Marcus unlocked the heavy metal security door beside the big garage door with his thumbprint and we hurried inside. An invisible weight hit me halfway to the glass door leading into the building. It dragged at my limbs and thoughts, as if I were moving and thinking in molasses.

"How didn't we notice this when we were first fighting the witches?" Marcus gasped, heaving the door open and hurrying into the hall.

"The spell must have taken time to fully form." Kol leaned forward as if he were running into a wind storm.

I struggled to keep a quick pace as my buzz whispered under my skin with the promise of overwhelming fire and power. The hall had never seemed so long before, even during the times I'd been seriously injured and was lying on a gurney headed to triage.

We rounded the corner, and Marcus led us past the elevator and down the few steps into the cafeteria. A guy in dusty overalls stood on the scaffolding at the large decorative rock wall that was being rebuilt after the fight with the archnephilim, while another guy bent over a pallet of small plants. A few feet away, Cassey, one of the doctors who worked with Amiah, half stood and half squatted over a chair, as if she'd been in the middle of standing or sitting when the spell had hit. Another woman in scrubs sat across from her, a mug raised to her lips. Behind them, the squat man who'd served me lunch the day before yesterday held a lid over a tray of food, the steam frozen in the air, curled around his hand.

I shivered. If Sebastian hadn't cast that protection spell, that would have been us.

If we didn't hurry, that *would* be us.

Except each step grew harder and harder, and by the time we took the stairs down to the basement, I was sweating and gasping for breath, my buzz burning hotter.

I staggered around the corner and past the wide wooden table and couch just outside the elevator doors. The fluorescent lights hanging from the ceiling flickered on, filling the cold space with harsh white light, our movement tripping the motion sensor. Beyond the table stood the archives with row upon row of shelves filled with books, while opposite us was the locked armory door.

Marcus pressed his thumb to the keypad and lurched to the locker just inside the door.

"Sixty seconds, no more," he said. "We need time to get back up those stairs."

He tried to toss a duffle bag to Kol, but couldn't move his arm fast enough, and it fell to the floor halfway between them. I grabbed it and another one from Marcus and met Kol at a locker at the back of the narrow room.

Inside the locker were sheathed bladed weapons of all shapes and sizes. Kol dropped in three swords—

thankfully one short enough for me... not that I had any skill in using it—and a dozen knives and daggers of varying lengths. I turned to the shelf beside him and emptied the ones with boxes of 9mm and 5.56mm rounds for the sidearms and M4 into my bag, not wasting time checking to see if any of them were the special enspelled ammunition or not.

"Thirty seconds, then we leave," Marcus gasped.

I heaved around to the sidearms and tossed in a few Glocks and a couple Berettas—since those were Jacob's weapon of choice—then grabbed two M4s from the rack.

"Time."

I wrenched against the spell and my buzz flared. It stole my breath and made my knees give out. Kol reached for me as I fell, but wasn't fast enough to catch me. My knees hit the concrete hard even though I was falling in slow motion.

"Shit, Essie." Marcus took a staggering step toward me.

"I'm fine." I grabbed the narrow work table in the middle of the room and hauled myself to my feet. My muscles screamed with the effort to rise against the spell. God, how the hell were we going to climb the stairs?

Kol groaned and grabbed my arm, helping me steady myself. We staggered out of the armory and back to the plain concrete stairwell. My chest burned, each breath an agony as my lungs fought to move against the spell. Power crackled under my skin, my magic responding to the magic of the spell just like it had when Mavis had cast the concealment spell or when the witches had activated their glyphs, although thankfully not nearly as painfully.

"We need to move faster," Marcus growled, reaching the first floor landing and heaving open the security door.

"Trying," Kol gasped.

I didn't bother saying anything. I barely had enough breath to move, let alone speak. We still had to make it out of the cafeteria and down the hall, and I had no idea how I'd manage it. The spell's pressure kept growing. Each step, each breath, hell, each blink of my eyes, had become an agonizing effort.

Gritting my teeth, I fought my way up the few steps out of the cafeteria, past the elevator, and back into the God-awfully long hall. Marcus's wolf had risen to just under his skin, darkening his eyes, elongating his canines, and even starting to change the shape of his jaw. His claws had fully formed and fur darkened the backs of his hands.

We reached triage's frosted-glass door. Almost there. I could hold out for just a little longer. Please, God. I just needed a little more strength.

My body burned, the agony from my muscles stronger than the burn of my buzz. A part of me hoped my buzz would flare and I'd magically have the strength to fight the final few feet through the spell, but I had no idea if that was what would happen or not.

We reached the end of the hall and the door to the garage. Dark specks and brilliant flashes danced across my vision. I couldn't catch my breath, couldn't breathe deeply enough. I took another step forward, my leg refused to hold me, and I went down again.

Kol grabbed the back of my shirt, not bothering to

help me stand, and dragged me. The darkness swarming my vision thickened. Marcus turned back and grabbed my arm and they ripped me out of the spell.

The pressure vanished, but lightning roared through my mating brands and strength swept out of me into Gideon and Jacob. Ice clenched in my chest and every cell in my body screamed to save them, protect them, get them the hell out of there.

CHAPTER 11

I GASPED AND THE PULL OF STRENGTH TO GIDEON AND Jacob grew stronger, except the desperate screaming need to save them that I'd expected when they'd been fatally wounded didn't overwhelm me. They weren't in dire need, but they were exhausted and low on strength.

I tried to stand, feeling like I should do something, but not sure what. Except my muscles were too weak and my body wouldn't obey my commands. All I could do was sit there and fight to draw breath. Which made me want to scream. My mates, even if they weren't dying, still needed help. I was supposed to be able to help them, supposed to be just as powerful and competent as them. I was tired of being useless, tired of my buzz and fear controlling me, and tired of being the weak link.

My buzz flared and light blazed in my palms, defying the containment cuffs and reminding me that I *was* as powerful as them, more so, dangerously so.

I focused on my magic, drawing it into me, willing it to give me the strength to stand, march around to the door where Gideon and Jacob had entered, and find them, wherever they were. I climbed to my feet, took an unsteady step, and my legs promptly gave out.

"Jeez, just take a moment," Marcus said.

Gideon's lightning crackled into Jacob's brand and the pull of strength swept over me. The garage darkened and spun, and my worry deepened. They might not be dying, but they were still in trouble. If they didn't get out soon, they were going to be trapped.

I tried to stand again, unable to resist the need to protect them, but Kol grabbed me and pulled me back down. "Just stay put. You're going to hurt yourself."

I jerked against his grip but didn't have enough strength to pull free. "They're still in there. I have to help them."

"You can't even walk. Getting caught in the spell won't help," Marcus growled at me.

The pull of strength grew and the black specks now completely devoured my vision. "Please, Marcus. They're pulling strength from the brand. They're in trouble. Maybe they're in the doorway and all we have to do is yank them free." But I knew Marcus was right. Gideon and Jacob weren't dying and no matter how much power I had, it wasn't enough to help me stand, let alone walk around the building.

The lightning crackling up Gideon's brand into Jacob's snapped, an agonizing slice, then the pull of strength vanished, the change so sudden it made me gasp.

They were out. Thank God, they were out. I sagged

against Kol, my breath heavy as if I'd just pulled free of the spell again.

"I think they're free," Kol said, sitting me forward and putting distance between us that made me ache. "I'm mostly recovered. I'll go check on them."

Marcus pulled a small black box from his duffle bag and took out an ear piece. "Take this and let me know when they can walk."

Kol put the com in his ear and staggered out of the garage, while Marcus inserted another one into his ear and crawled to my side. He wrapped his arms around me, and I melted into his embrace. I ached for him and Jacob right now almost as much as I ached for Gideon... and Kol, but my bonds with them were secure and it was easy to just savor Marcus's warmth and strength.

"You're allowed to ask for help, you know," he said.

"I feel like all I do is ask for help." I felt like I'd run a marathon uphill and through water. Every muscle burned and trembled and I couldn't catch my breath. But I also felt as if my world had blown up and I didn't know what I was doing or where I was going, or hell, even who I really was. "I'm a mess right now."

Marcus snorted. "But you're my mess, and once we deal with the witches we'll have time to figure things out."

Except there was a lot to figure out and it seemed like every time we dealt with one thing, something else happened.

I wasn't sure how long I sat there with Marcus just holding me. The exhaustion from the temporal freeze spell eased, but my thoughts continued to whirl. And really, they'd been whirling since I'd fallen from City Hall's roof and my wings had appeared.

Kol told Marcus he, Gideon, and Jacob were on their way to the SUV, so Marcus and I stood, staggered the rest of the way out of the garage, and climbed inside the vehicle to wait for them.

My pulse beat faster as I sat there. Logically I knew they were okay. They weren't pulling strength from the brand, Kol had said they were out of the spell, and yet a part of me was still holding its breath, waiting to see them.

Then they rounded the corner, still gasping and trembling, but safe.

The pressure in my chest released.

They were all safe.

"Let's get back to Bane's and figure out what we're going to do," Gideon said as he got into the front passenger seat.

Jacob got in the back and Kol joined him. Swell.

We returned to Sebastian's and collapsed on his couches. Kol sat on the couch across from me—as far away from me as possible while still staying in the conversation area—while Marcus and Jacob squished in on either side of me. With a groan, Gideon settled in beside Kol and set a USB key on the coffee table, then turned to Marcus.

"What did you get?" he asked, jerking his chin to our duffle bags sitting on the floor a few feet from the couch.

"Coms, containment cuffs, enspelled zip ties," Marcus said, "and various holsters and belts."

"A handful of sidearms, two M4s, some ammunition, and a variety of blades," Kol finished.

Jacob turned on one of the two laptops they'd taken from Operations and inserted the USB key. "This could take a while."

"And even if we do figure out what they're doing, we still have no way to stop them," Marcus said.

"We just have to hope Bane can find us an area containment master ward in time." Gideon rubbed his face.

"Will that be enough?" I wasn't going to go through the pain of feeling them die again. Ever. Except with their job, I wasn't ever going to be able to guarantee their safety.

And God damn it, there wasn't anything I could do to help. Marcus might have said I wasn't useless, that even if I couldn't ever go into the field again I'd still be more than just away to keep them alive, but I'd never felt more useless in my life. If my emotions got out of control or someone used powerful magic, my magic blazed through the containment cuffs and endangered everyone.

Pointing me in the right direction and using my power like a cannon was only useful in certain situations. If the witches' plan involved a populated area, then that was too dangerous. I wasn't going to risk hurting bystanders, be they super or human... which I wasn't anymore... had never been.

I shoved that thought back and stood. "I'm going to help Bane look for answers for... whatever it is he's looking for." My problem, the witches' problem, I didn't care. I just couldn't sit there and do nothing.

"Get something to eat first," Gideon said. "We missed breakfast."

"And you missed dinner yesterday." Jacob frowned. "And lunch."

Marcus's eyes narrowed. "When was the last time you ate?"

I had no idea. A lot had happened in the last couple of days. If I really thought about it...

"I got healing in the hospital after the zip OD." As well as healing after feeding Jacob for the second time that day. That had to be why I wasn't starving now.

"Come on." Marcus stood and headed to the kitchen. "Let's see if Bane has more than orange juice in his fridge."

Sebastian's kitchen was as white and shiny as his living room, with white marble counters, stainless steel appliances, and decorative tin ceiling tiles that reflected the light of yet another crystal chandelier.

"He certainly has a specific style," Marcus said, heading straight to the fridge.

"I feel like I'm in a snow globe. A really expensive snow globe."

"At least his fridge is stocked. How about an omelet?" He set a carton of eggs on the counter, and pulled a red pepper and half a dozen stalks of green onion from the crisper, not waiting for me to answer.

"What if I said no?" I headed to the coffee machine, a complicated, single-serve appliance that made specialty coffees with the press of a button.

"You'd still get an omelet. It's the only thing I can

cook." He flashed me a tired smile, and my heart squeezed.

It hadn't just been a stressful couple of days for me. Sure, I'd ODed on zip, had a building fall on me, fell sixteen stories then was arrested, but Marcus had dealt with that, too.

"When was the last time *you* ate or slept?" I checked the coffee machine's reservoir and hopper. Already filled with water and beans.

He snorted and rolled his eyes at me as he rummaged in the cupboard beside the stove and pulled out a cast iron frying pan. "You would ask that."

"What?" I opened the cupboard above the machine in search of mugs.

"You just had your life turned upside down and you're asking me how I'm doing?" He grabbed my hand and pulled me into a firm embrace. "You're allowed to think about yourself for a minute."

I stiffened in his arms, my throat suddenly tight, my eyes burning with tears. "If I think about myself, I'm going to start crying again, and I'm tired of crying."

"We already know you're tough." He rubbed gentle circles on my back. "Crying won't make you look weak."

"It's not that, it's—" A tear rolled down my cheek. "All my life I was told no one would understand. I was sure no one would. I've seen all the videos. Michael's nephilim were monsters. I thought I was a monster."

I hadn't realized how alone and scared that had made me. I thought I'd compartmentalized it and was able to carry on as if everything was normal. It had been hanging over me all of my life. I was used to it. But just like I'd spent all those years pretending my supernatural nature didn't exist, I'd also pretended my fear didn't, either.

Marcus's grip tightened. "Anyone who's spent more than a minute with you knows you're not a monster. Even if you were a nephilim, you're nothing like them."

"Cassius didn't think so."

"Cassius is an idiot."

Except I couldn't fool myself and think anything would get easier now that my eyes glowed and my essence still didn't say I was an angel. If I was smart, I'd find a way to respell or replace Mavis's contacts and pretend I was—

What? I had no idea. If my essence didn't say I was human, I couldn't pretend to be a human. Maybe I could get away with pretending to be a half demon. That would at least be easier for the world to accept.

Sure, my guys had stood by me, but that was only because of our soul bonds. I didn't have a bond with Kol and he'd tried to kill me. "Cassius reacted like a lot of people would, like Kol did."

"Kol's experience with Michael's nephilim was extreme." Marcus pressed his lips to the top of my head. "I don't know the details, but I heard he'd spent a long time in self-isolation after Gideon and Jacob rescued him. Kind of like you."

"I wasn't isolated."

"Sure you were." He captured my cheeks with his hands and tipped my head up to look me in the eyes. "That's why you never really socialized or became friends with the other officers when you were off duty, or why you never told me anything about yourself. I bet that didn't change in the four and a half years we've been apart." His lips quirked in a smile. "Hell, you didn't have a plant. Still don't."

"I've been meaning to get one in my new place." And by new I meant the one I'd rented two years ago, with the amazing skylight and roof access... for the wings I hadn't realized I had.

"It all makes sense now, why you fought so hard to stay away from the supernatural world, why every time I mentioned it you got a terrified look in your eyes." He brushed his lips against mine, a tender whisper of a kiss. "You're not a monster. You don't have to run anymore. You're not alone."

Which was something I still couldn't wrap my mind around. Marcus hadn't even thought twice about staying with me. Even believing I was a monster, all my guys had fought to protect me.

Except Kol.

Which only made me more heartbroken for the horror he'd experienced at Michael's hands.

Marcus turned back to making our omelets. "So if you were going to buy a plant... what would it be?"

"Are you trying to figure out what to buy me?" I reopened the cupboard above the coffee machine, grabbed a mug, and set it in the machine.

"Maybe. Although we're going to have to figure out where to put it. You can't stay in your room at Operations forever, and there isn't enough room for all of us in any of our apartments." He opened the cupboard in front of him, frowned, and moved to the next one.

My thoughts jumped to all of us trying to squeeze

onto Marcus's bed. Hell, even Jacob's, which was huge, wasn't designed for five... er, four people. And would all of them be interested in that? Sure, Marcus had joined me and Jacob in bed, but that had to have been an extenuating, amazing, sexy, satisfying circumstance.

Marcus chuckled, and I jerked my attention back to him. His piercing green eyes lit up with a smile wicked enough to compete with Kol's. "Wow, that's a look. What are *you* thinking?"

Heat swept over my cheeks. "Nothing."

He pulled out two plates, slid the first omelet onto one of them, and held it out to me. "That didn't look like nothing."

"I... ah..." The memory of being pressed between his and Jacob's hard bodies flashed through me, flooding my face with more heat. I grabbed the plate and started pulling open drawers looking for cutlery.

"She was thinking about sex," Kol said, striding into the kitchen and heading straight to the coffee machine.

Marcus snorted. "Already figured that out from the blush. Need another top-up? I'm sure if I ask nicely, Essie and I could accommodate you." He cracked eggs in the pan to make another omelet.

Kol's gaze jumped to mine. The hellfire in his eyes smoldered, bright red pricks in his dark eyes, and heated desire slid across my senses. My pulse tripped at the memory of his magic pouring into me, bone-melting liquid yearning. Need swelled low within me. I craved more of his magic, of him, and not just on a human-craving-an-incubus level, but deeper. Soul deep.

CHAPTER 12

My breath picked up, and everything within me begged to hold him, kiss him, tell him I'd give my life to protect him. He was family. He belonged. I didn't care if he was a soul mate or not. I didn't want to give him up, and I didn't want him to give up the team. It'd been clear from the tour he'd given me of the Quarter the other day that the team meant everything to him. I couldn't take that away from him.

He blinked, releasing my soul for a second, then recaptured me again. The hellfire burned brighter, but now as well as hunger, I could see exhaustion in his eyes. I didn't know how much sexual energy he needed to properly heal, but it didn't look like he'd gotten enough.

"I'll finish breakfast and see how Jacob is doing. Pretty sure he didn't get enough, either."

"Well, that backfired." Marcus rolled his eyes at me. "I was trying to get you back into my bed, but there you go, thinking about what's best for all your mates again."

"Who said it has to be just me and Jacob?" I asked.

Oh, man. Did I just say that?

Ah, yup. And I'd meant it. When we had a moment, I was going to need a frank conversation with my guys about what I wanted and what they wanted.

"Well, then," Marcus said, his voice husky, indicating the threesome with Jacob wasn't a one-shot deal for him.

The hellfire fully consumed Kol's eyes and he jerked his attention to the counter beside me. "Don't bother," he said, his tone flat as if he'd just remembered who he was talking to. "I'm fine."

He pushed past me, set the first coffee on the counter, and put a new mug in the machine. Even with the cuffs suppressing my empathy, the emotional chill froze all the way to my heart. God, I just wanted to fix this, help him, help all of them.

Except right now the best way I could help Kol was to give him space. No matter how much that hurt. Jeez. Even if taking no action was the best action, it still drove me crazy.

"I'll go see if I can help Sebastian."

Marcus gave me a sad smile. He might not know exactly how I felt about Kol, but he knew everyone on the team was dear to me. Funny how everyone thought Marcus with his possessive wolf was going to be a problem, and he'd been the first to fully embrace all of me.

I found a fork and hurried out of the kitchen.

Gideon was gone but Jacob still sat on the couch, working on the laptop. He looked a little tired, but not nearly as bad as he'd been the last couple of days. A pressure that I hadn't realized had been in my chest eased. The witches might still be more powerful than us, but at least the next time we wouldn't be fighting with serious injuries.

"Where's Gideon?" I didn't need to talk to him, just wanted to see him and reassure myself he was okay, or as okay as he could get with his brother slowly dying, three powerful glyph witches threatening the city, and—if he felt like me, which I was getting the impression he was— the aching urge to solidify our bond.

"He stepped into one of the other rooms to talk to head office, trying to get an ETA on backup." Jacob jerked his chin to a second closed laptop on the coffee table. "But he'll be back in a minute if you want to talk with him."

"I'm fine."

"Okay." His eyes narrowed. "You should eat more than that."

"This is round one. I might as well eat and read at the same time."

"So long as it *is* round one." He released some of his vampiric intensity, making me shiver with desire.

I forced myself to head to the hall before I climbed into his lap and asked him to satisfy me again. We needed to solve problems. My desire could wait, but damn, it was difficult to resist the pull of our bond. It was still so new. All of my bonds were, and all I wanted was to keep them close and strengthen our connection.

I knocked on the first door in the hall and opened it without waiting for a reply.

Sebastian lounged on a couch, a massive book in his lap with more books piled around him. My divine light still radiated from his eyes, although no longer rolling down his cheeks like shimmering tears. Amiah sat behind a desk near the back, framed by a tall, slightly purple window. She was also reading and also surrounded by books. A fireplace—not in use since it was so damned hot out and Sebastian had his air conditioner running—sat against the right-hand wall and, along with the window, was the only other break in the wall-to-wall floor-to-ceiling bookshelves. Sebastian even had a floor-to-ceiling narrow ladder on a track to access the top shelves.

The room smelled of wood smoke and old leather. A heavy rug covered most of the marble floor, and even though the color scheme was still wintery, it felt comfortable and warm. I hadn't thought of Sebastian as a bookworm, but the room made me wonder if buying and selling hard-to-find magical items satisfied a personal need as well as a financial one.

Sebastian glanced up from his book. "Who's making omelets?"

"Marcus."

Amiah's shoulders stiffened.

"Great. I'm starving." He stood and set his book on his seat, leaving it open to the page he'd been reading. "If you're here to help, start on the pile on the floor by the desk. You're looking for anything that might explain what kind of magical poison is killing Cassius."

He left and Amiah raised a chilly glare at me.

I hadn't expected a warm welcome, but this was frigid.

Just great.

Well, no way was I going to let her cold-shoulder me

out of the room, especially since this was the only way I could be useful at the moment.

I grabbed the book at the top of the closest pile. It was big and thick, with a swirling design etched in the leather cover on the front and back, and the edges of the pages were ragged, as if the paper had been handmade.

Power whispered across my senses, not strong enough to make my buzz flare, but enough to remind me that it was still there, contained by the handcuffs. Whatever this book was, it felt old and powerful, and ever so slightly alive.

I fought a shiver, shifted to sit on the floor with the book beside me but not touching me, and balanced my plate in my lap. "Anything specific I should be looking for? Certain words? Symptoms?"

Amiah continued to glare at me, and a heaviness joined the ice in her eyes. I had no idea what that meant, and, funnily enough, was once again wishing I had access to my weird empathy. Although with my luck, the heaviness, whatever it was, would still probably manifest as cold, and then I'd just be cold and slightly tired.

"Fine." I opened the book, ignoring another whisper of magic. The title page was handwritten in faded black ink in big flowing letters, and the paper was thick and stained with age. *Theories on Magical Healing.* That sounded dry.

I turned to the table of contents—a little surprised that a handwritten book would have a table of contents—and ate some of my omelet, which was really good. Although that could have been because I was starving.

Amiah shifted in her chair, her lips pressed tight, the tension in her shoulders growing to encompass her torso.

According to the book, angels weren't the only ones with healing magic. Which surprised me more than the book having a table of contents, since I'd never heard of any other super with the ability to heal others. Yes, Kol had helped me twice now by giving me some of the magic that sustained him, but I hadn't thought of that as healing. Except there it was, chapter fifteen, *Succubi and Incubi Energy Conveyance*.

When I'd been shot and dying, none of the guys had known Kol could help me that way, and Kol had said incubi didn't like anyone knowing that they could. Which only added to the evidence that this book was old and rare.

I scanned the rest of the table of contents. While I was curious to know more about how Kol could just give his life energy to me, I doubted it would help us figure out what kind of poison was killing Cassius or how to save him.

The light in Amiah's eyes grew and her hands curled into fists. Jeez, just sitting in the same room with me made her angry.

I fought to focus my attention on the book and not the rising tension. Aside from the chapter on incubi healing, there were a dozen chapters on angels, two on fae, and one on humans. I flipped to the human chapter. Maybe Amiah and Priam couldn't identify the poison because it wasn't angelic. Since the glyph witches were human, that seemed like the best chapter to start with. But the first few pages were exactly what the book's title claimed, theories on if it was even possible for humans to possess healing magic.

I was barely one book in, but my gut said I was looking for the wrong thing. I shouldn't be searching for healing, but trying to identify the type of magic used to poison Cassius. Glyph witches had a bit of demon blood somewhere in their family tree, either biologically or because of a demon-deal they or an ancestor had made for their power. They had the ability to permanently bind spells in glyphs that had been etched or drawn onto an object or inked onto their bodies and then activate the spells with their magic.

The spiders that had poisoned Cassius had been summoned by a glyph, which meant they had to have been some kind of spell. And that was as far as my magical knowledge went.

I took another bite of my omelet. Sebastian hadn't returned, so I couldn't ask him about spells. What were the odds that Amiah would actually talk to me? Probably zero. She was radiating so much tension, it made me squirm.

Best to go find Sebastian or one of my guys. I moved to stand, and Amiah's icy gaze captured mine.

"The mating brand is supposed to be sacred."

This again? Yeah, I got it. I wasn't worthy, I'd never be worthy, and I was ruining Marcus's life. "You're just going to have to get used to the idea that I'm branded and move on. It's not like I can get rid of them." Which I never would. Funny how just a few weeks ago that was all I wanted. Now the idea of losing my bonds made my heart pound.

"That's what's so terrifying," Amiah said, the heaviness in her gaze shifting, revealing her struggle to contain her fear. "You can't get rid of it. Your fate is controlled by someone else."

"None of the guys control me." Although I could see her point, and given how in control Amiah always was, losing any kind of control probably terrified her. Did little angel girls and boys dream of soul mates just like some little human girls and boys? Had Amiah? Angelkind had the possibility of a rare magical bond, making that dream of destined true love all the more possible. And now she'd seen the truth. An angelic mating brand wasn't as wonderful as it had been made out to be.

"They don't mean to control you, but they do. I hadn't realized how consuming the bond was." Her hands shook, and she clenched them tighter. "You just dropped to the floor the moment they were in danger. Helpless."

"They have to be mortally wounded for that to happen." Something I prayed would never happen again.

"You couldn't stand. You couldn't breathe." A shudder swept over her. "I've treated the angel half of a broken angel-human bond and it was difficult, but that—" Light flared from her eyes. "How could anyone ever think that was beautiful and sacred?"

"That's only one part of it." I didn't know why I was bothering to defend my situation with Amiah, but I just couldn't seem to help myself. My connection with my guys, all my guys, *was* beautiful and sacred. It was also terrifying and dangerous and amazing and nothing I could have ever imagined.

"How can you just accept the control the brands have on you?"

"I don't know. I don't think about it as being controlled. I just know I belong with them." I couldn't fight it if I wanted to. In fact, Gideon and I had fought our bond and that had been a disaster. I still felt broken, my soul cracked in a million pieces because we hadn't fully solidified our bond.

"You're independent to a fault. You'll recklessly do what you think is right." She huffed a bitter laugh. "Just like a lot of angels."

"Except I can't seem to follow the rules." Which, for a second, made me wonder if I really was all angel. Although Gideon and Cassius had demonstrated that when their emotions were strong, the rules didn't matter.

"Not all of us follow the rules to the letter like most humans believe. Yes, we need order, although some of us more than others." She spread her hands over the desk with the messy pile of books. Her office had been messy as well, completely opposite to Gideon's organized-within-an-inch-of-its-life space. "But almost all of us need justice. However we justify it. Michael thought ridding the world of humans and supers was justice for the destruction you'd wrought on the world."

"Any way you look at it, taking billions of lives isn't justice."

"Billions of lives that willfully hurt this planet."

"It sounds like you agreed with Michael."

"Never." The fearful hardness in Amiah's eyes bled into pain. "My magic is the gift of life. I couldn't have watched your slaughter from the Realm of Celestial Light if I'd wanted to. If Michael had attacked the Realm of Celestial Darkness, I would have gone." She ran her hands over the open pages in front of her. "But I at least get to choose how and when. The brand gives you no choice."

Except even if the brand did give me a choice, I'd choose my guys every time.

Someone screamed and the door flew open, revealing a wide-eyed Priam in the doorway. "Amiah. I need help. It's Cassius."

CHAPTER 13

Priam rushed back into the hall, and Amiah bolted from her seat. She ran into the room across from Sebastian's office, not bothering to shut the doors. I hurried after her, but froze at the sight of Cassius on the bed.

Black veins bulged on his neck and arms and he panted as if he couldn't catch his breath. His back arched off the mattress and he screamed, a strangled cry of agony. Priam pressed his palms to Cassius's temples. Light, not the brilliance of divine light, but a gentle healing glow, radiated from his hands, but with another scream, Cassius's back arched again.

Amiah dropped onto the bed beside him and pressed her hands over his heart. The glow from her hands wasn't as strong as Priam's, but I doubted that was because he was more powerful. Amiah had spent all of her magic saving my guys, and she'd barely recovered enough to help Cassius.

Gideon hurried into the room. A whisper of cold swept

around me, his fear so strong it defied the containment cuffs. He hugged himself, staying back in case Amiah or Priam needed to move, but Sebastian, who entered next, didn't hesitate. He shoved past me and slapped his hand against his shoulder. The activated glyph lit up under his shirt, more brilliant than I'd ever seen any of his other glyphs glow.

"Both of you let go for a second," he said.

Amiah and Priam pulled away, and Sebastian pressed his hands over Cassius's heart.

Cassius gasped and his body went limp.

Amiah put her hands back on Cassius, but she stared at Sebastian. "What did you do?"

"Sleep spell." Sebastian shuddered and a weak divine light tear rolled down his cheek. "Hopefully with Esther's extra juice, it'll buy you and Priam more time."

Marcus, Jacob, and Kol crowded into the room behind Gideon.

"Have you found anything?" Gideon asked, his gaze locked on his brother, asleep but still gasping quick shallow breaths.

"Not yet," Sebastian said.

Priam closed his eyes and the light from his hands billowed. "It's getting harder to keep him stable. We're running out of time."

"When did the black veins show up?" Jacob asked. "It looks like blood poisoning, but I know it can't be because he isn't a vampire."

"Could it be something like that, though?" I asked. There had to be a way to figure out what this was and stop it. I couldn't accept that there wasn't anything we could do to save him. Cassius might not have treated me well, but he didn't deserve to die.

"There are a number of spells that behave in a similar manner, but I've searched for them in his body," Sebastian said. "Even with your extra power, I can't identify the poison."

"Do you have to know what it is?" Marcus asked. "Can't you just pull it out?"

"No," Amiah said, her voice soft. "It's in his essence. If we pull it out without dispelling it, we'll end up taking his essence with it."

And if too much of a super's essence was taken, he'd die.

The muscles in Gideon's jaw flexed. "Do what you can. Jacob, do you still need Marcus's and Kol's help reviewing the security footage?"

Jacob glanced at Cassius, his expression pained at the choice he had to make. If he said yes, then some of us weren't searching for a way to save Cassius. If he said no, then the witches could succeed and who knew how many lives could be in danger.

The glow in Gideon's eyes dimmed for a second, and he drew in a ragged breath. "Marcus and Kol, keep helping Jacob," he said, taking Jacob's hesitation as an affirmative. "I'll help Bane."

Marcus frowned. "Gideon—"

"We can't endanger the lives in this city. Not even for Cassius." Gideon pushed past us and strode into Sebastian's office, his eyes, his body, everything about him hard, except his expression. That was tight with fear and desperation.

I hurried after him. "Hey."

His back stiffened and he fisted his hands. "Don't tell me to get everyone on saving my brother. We're JP agents, we have a job to do, and if you ask, I'll do it."

"I wouldn't ask that." I drew close, needing to touch him, comfort him, but knowing if I did the bond would overwhelm me.

"Marcus would," he said.

"Of course he would. His first loyalty is to the ones he loves." He'd shown me that time and again. "He'd sacrifice anything and everyone for them."

"Just like you would," Gideon said.

"I couldn't sacrifice anyone." Not anyone from Union City and certainly not any of my guys. "The only thing I have to offer is myself." And that wasn't an option, because my life was entwined with my guys.

"Don't you dare." Gideon turned on me and grabbed my shoulders, his grip so hard his fingers dug painfully into my biceps. Terror filled his eyes and frost swept over the backs of my hands. "Don't you do that to Jacob or Marcus."

His power crackled through our brand, little bites of electricity, so similar to my buzz and yet so different. It sizzled through my nerves, filling me with strength and yearning.

"Stop putting yourself in danger," he begged. His gaze dipped to my lips, and my pulse picked up.

I had to step back, pull out of his hold before I lost control, but the draw to be with him surged and my nerves thrummed with desire.

"Stop giving more than you have," he said, his voice breaking with need.

I gritted my teeth. "I'm not helpless."

"No, I am." His fingers tangled in my hair, his pupils dilated, and he shook, his struggle to control himself making his angel glow flare. "I need you, Essie. Our bond is too fragile, and I feel like I'm going to fall apart. I can't lose you, I can't see you hurt. I thought I could, thought I could resist the bond a little bit longer, but—" His chest heaved with rapid breaths and the tendons in his neck flexed. "I can't do it. There's just too much. Too many hard choices. Save our bond, risk the city. Save my brother, risk the city. I need to do all of it, but I can't."

His churning emotions sliced through the containment cuffs, and our bond squeezed my chest and tightened my throat.

I tried to focus on anything other than the need to ease the pressure of our bond, because for both of us the lives of others came first. They always did. Gideon would never forgive himself— hell, *I'd* never forgive myself if we let the bond take over and people died. Even just for a quickie. Because it wouldn't be quick. If I released my hold, I'd want all of him, completely. I knew in my heart that for our first time I'd lose myself in him, join with him, body, essence, and soul, and not care about anything else. We couldn't afford to get caught up in that, not when every minute might count.

"Our bond will survive," I said, as the bond within me screamed to draw closer, kiss him, shove him onto Sebastian's couch and take him.

More of his power crackled through his brand, and he

tipped his forehead against mine, his breath ragged, desperate gasps. Warmth radiated around my hand —not with the burn of my divine light just my magical strength —and I pressed my palm over his heart and sent a trickle of power into him. He needed it more than I did. I had Jacob and Marcus helping me resist the bond. He didn't have anyone.

A moan escaped his lips and his breath feathered across my face.

God, kiss me. Please.

No. Focus.

We had to deal with the immediate issues first.

"Let's save your brother," I forced out, really wanting to say *take my clothes off*.

"You can take a few minutes in the guestroom next door," Sebastian said behind me.

"That's the problem." Gideon jerked back, releasing me and squaring his shoulders with a force of will that hurt to watch. "I resisted the bond for too long."

"I thought the brand was all that wonderful sacred angel crap." Sebastian picked up the book he'd set on his couch and sat. "Why would you resist it? Especially since resisting a soul bond like that is akin to losing your mate. It'll drive you crazy or kill you."

"Essie was in love with Marcus first." Gideon's angel glow flared and he took two more steps back, putting more distance between us.

"Ah," Sebastian said, as if that explained everything. And in a way it probably did. No one thought it was possible for Marcus to accept me with other mates, since wolves didn't share well with others.

"Okay." I shoved that thought aside and fought the urge to draw close to Gideon again. "You said you looked for spells in Cassius. Is there a type of magic you're not familiar with?"

"There always is. There are two basic types, light and dark, but there are variations, different ways of manipulating the magic, within both the light and dark spheres. So it's possible the spell on Cassius is in one of the variations I'm not as familiar with, or a whole new variation." His gaze grew unfocused and he frowned. "Some witches can create their own way of casting... And these witches have access to an outside power source, like they'd been saving their power up in a reservoir... but it feels more powerful than that and the spell on Cassius doesn't feel like a regular spell..."

He set his book back on the couch, pulled his ladder in front of the door, and grabbed a thin book from the top shelf.

"What are you thinking?" Gideon asked, his gaze locked on Sebastian.

"That I, of all people, should have looked past the fact that those women were glyph witches."

"But they're witches, aren't they?" I'd felt it every time they'd activated one of their glyphs.

"And so am I. My glyphs are real," Sebastian said, hopping down from the ladder and leaning against it. "I keep power stored in them, but I can also channel raw light magic and shape it to my will without burning up."

"Now it makes sense." Gideon's attention, filled with need, flickered to me for a second then jerked back to

Sebastian. "You didn't just use your fae essence to tele-port us."

"No matter how good Amiah is, I'd still be uncon-scious if I had. That would have drained me too deeply."

"And that means?" I asked.

"Most fae cast spells using their own magical essence." Sebastian pointed to his glowing skin. "Some supers like angels and witches have their own internal battery to power their magic, while others, like fae and vampires, use the magic in their essence. All of which, essence and battery, slowly refill through a passive connection to the primal energy in the realms. Some supers can transfer power from their internal battery to an external one, like what you did with your light magic into me and then I did into the marble."

"But that also gives another person access to the essence of the super who donated the magic to the external battery," Gideon said.

Sebastian raised his hands, his expression fully sincere. "And I have no intention of using Esther's essence against her."

"You better not."

Realization hit me and a small knot of fear tightened in my gut. The guys hadn't made a big deal about it, prob-ably because they recognized there'd been no other option, but if the situation hadn't been so serious I was sure all of them would have given me an earful. Pouring my power into Sebastian had given him access to my essence. And when Jacob had woven his essence in mine, he'd been able to command me even if that command put my life in danger. I didn't want to think about what

Sebastian or someone else could do to me holding my essence.

Sebastian rolled his eyes at Gideon. "There are also a small few of us who can open ourselves to the energy in the realms and shape it into anything we want... if we have the strength of will to do it and our magical channels haven't been burned raw."

"The harder the spell, the more dangerous it is for the sorcerer," Gideon said.

"So you're one of the fae sorcerers who helped with the war?" I couldn't believe I was talking with one of them. Humans and supers talked about them with whispered awe. Few had actually seen them, and they'd always worked behind the scenes. Some people didn't believe they were real, that the fae had locked the portals to their realm until the war was over, and since travelling to a realm other than the human one or your own required extreme amounts of magic, many thought the fae portals were permanently locked. "I thought all of you returned to your realm."

Sebastian shrugged and flipped open the book.

"Thank God you have a teleportation glyph that you keep charged," Gideon said. "We wouldn't have been able to get out of Operations without it."

"Oh, I have the glyph, but it's just to focus my magic. I never keep it charged. It's too big a spell," Sebastian said casually, scanning a page then turning to the next one.

"You don't keep it charged?" Gideon's eyes widened. "How could you not keep it charged? That's the only way you could have cast it without— Even with the glyph to focus—" His gaze leaped to mine, his eyes filled with fear.

"You channeled enough magic to teleport seven people? Do you know how dangerous that is?"

Sebastian's expression snapped to serious. "I'm very aware."

The knot in my gut tightened into a frozen stone. "And you think these witches have that kind of power?"

"I think they're channeling an outside source, but it's not raw magic and it's not theirs saved up in a reservoir." He flipped a few more pages in the book then stopped. "It's worship magic. Followers drain their essences over and over again in worship of a god or idol. Some don't even know that they're doing it. Essence magic is different than light and dark magic. It's usually locked to the person's essence and is difficult, if sometimes impossible, to manipulate by someone else unless they've already been given a way in. With worship magic, the followers' essences go into a reservoir and the god—if it's a living god—and his or her priests or priestess can control it. "

The muscles in Gideon's jaw flexed. "So there are more of them?"

"Possibly. And maybe a god," Sebastian said, scanning the next page.

"I didn't think gods existed." How the hell did I not know gods existed? And why hadn't any of them shown up to help fight Michael?

"There aren't any gods in the sense you humans usually think of them, like all powerful and all seeing. They're supers pumped up on worship magic." Sebastian turned the page. "And as far as anyone knows, there hasn't been a significant god for two, maybe even three thousand years. It takes a pretty strong super to control an essence-draining ritual and remain lucid. Usually it's a powerful priest or priestess who uses a super to power the spell, which puts them in a catatonic state. But whether it's just the priestess or the god or both, they're all bound by the same restrictions I am."

"Too much power, too quickly," Gideon said, "and you burn up."

Jeez, and I thought my power was scary.

My thoughts stuttered. Every time I used my divine light, I burned my hands. Except I was pretty sure there was no such thing as an angel sorcerer, even an archangel one, so my magic had to be something different. Which was something I could worry about once we'd figured out how to safely release it.

"So," I said, shoving aside the thoughts of my power, "now you know what it is. Can you stop it?"

Sebastian's pale gaze rose to meet mine. "I could have all the magic in the world, and I wouldn't be able to unwrap the spell from Cassius's essence. The essence in the worship magic is controlled by the god or the priest. No one else can use it without permission." He glanced back at the page and pursed his lips. "The only positive is that this kind of poison, at least if it's like all the other non-worship magic spells like it, pulls power from the witch who cast it, and will continue weakening her until it's run its course."

"That's not a positive," Gideon said. "The outcome of the spell is Cassius's death."

"There has to be something we can do." I couldn't accept that there wasn't anything we could do.

"Kill the root of the spell. But that could be the witch,

or the god, or both. " Sebastian snapped the book closed. "Or find a sin eater."

"Kill a god, or find a demon Michael made extinct on the slim possibility that they had the power to consume the spell keeping his nephilim alive." The light in Gideon's eyes dimmed, and more of my soul fractured at his grief. "There's no other way?"

"No." Sebastian climbed the ladder and put the book back.

"A shaman could unravel the spell," Amiah said from the doorway, unable to enter the office because of the ladder. Her complexion was gray, and she clung to the doorframe to keep standing. She must have given Cassius everything she had left. "Shamans use a form of worship magic. They take the essence naturally sloughed off by all living things and channel it into spells."

"Maybe." Sebastian pressed the balls of his feet to the ladder's rails and slid to the floor. "They are the only super able to channel someone else's essence for their magic."

"Not maybe," Amiah corrected, making Sebastian scowl at her. "Shamans have the innate ability to manipulate essence no longer within a body. It doesn't matter where it comes from."

"But the essence powering the spell on Cassius is locked with the god or priest." Sebastian pushed the ladder aside. "It can't be done. Besides, there isn't a sane shaman left on the planet."

I glanced at Gideon. "Pretend I'm an idiot and don't know anything."

"You're not an idiot," he said, shifting toward me but

stopping himself before he could make contact. "You've just spent your life avoiding everything super."

"All the shamans went insane from the flood of power of billions of deaths during Michael's war," Sebastian explained, his gaze never leaving Amiah, his expression daring her to argue with him. "Looking for a sane shaman is as much a waste of time as looking for a sin eater."

Amiah huffed. "And here I thought you were the man who could get anything, given enough money."

"If it exists."

"There's a shaman a quarter of a mile past the Pine-brook Forest wall," she said.

Sebastian rolled his eyes at her. "Bull shit. If there was, I'd know about him."

"Her," she corrected, "and she had the misfortune of being a child and infected with lycanthropy at the beginning of the war."

"So her power wasn't fully developed and her DNA was being rewritten when the power flood happened," Sebastian said. "Well, shit, that would do it."

Amiah turned her attention to Gideon. "If you hurry, you can get her here within the hour. Tell her it's for me."

A phone rang. Sebastian pulled his from his pocket and strode to the back of his office. "Yes."

"I'll gather the guys," Gideon said, heading to the door.

Amiah grabbed his arm, stopping him before he passed. "She might not react well to the whole team."

"Nothing happens outside of this apartment without the whole team." His attention jumped to me for a second, the fear still in his eyes along with a hint of his aching need. And by whole team, he meant the guys. Not me.

Well, I was a liability and powerless, and while I could now go out armed to the teeth, that probably wasn't the best idea to pick up this shaman. The woman lived past the wall of Pinebrook Forest. That was the smallest shifter forest at the farthest end of the Quarter on the other side of Squatters' Row. Kol had said during my tour of the Quarter that only a handful of shifters used that forest because it wasn't in a convenient location. If she lived out there, more or less isolated, then it meant at best she preferred her privacy, and at worst, she was afraid of people.

"Then go in gently. Willow is a firebird. Their nature is sensitive enough. And while she's not insane, she's still fragile."

Gideon pressed a hand to Amiah's shoulder. "I'll be gentle," he said, and turned to go.

"Wait." Sebastian pocketed his phone. "I've got your area containment master ward, but you have to go now."

"It can't wait until we've picked up this shaman?" Gideon asked.

"Not if you want it, and you're not going to like all the terms." Sebastian leveled his icy gaze on me.

CHAPTER 14

FROM THE LOOK IN SEBASTIAN'S EYES, I KNEW I WASN'T going to like the terms of the deal, which meant Gideon was going to hate them.

"What are the terms?" Gideon asked, his voice low, dangerous.

"You have to bring Esther along."

"It's a risk to take her out in the field, but not an unreasonable one," Amiah said. "Especially if you're just going to buy a master ward, even if that master ward is rare and powerful."

I had to agree, which meant, given Sebastian's expression, there had to be a catch.

"Bane doesn't always do business with the nicest people," Gideon said.

"I'm aware," Amiah huffed.

Sebastian flashed his wicked smile. "And yet you still do business with me."

Gideon glared at him. "The terms."

"You're meeting Voth at his office right now. The price

is half a million, cash, non-negotiable, and yes, I'm willing to loan you the money until you have time to transfer it back to me. He also wants to see, and I quote, the mated couple for himself. Also non-negotiable." Sebastian looked at me and his smile turned apologetic. "There are disadvantages to being rare. And just wait until people realize you've got two brands."

That made my insides squirm. Even if I no longer needed to fly under the radar, that didn't mean I'd lost the urge to do so. Except we didn't have time for me and Jacob to get long-sleeved shirts—and that would look weird with the summer's heat—so there wasn't any way for me to hide Jacob's brand. But if getting gawked at and talked about meant I could stop those witches, so be it. "So we go, pick up the master ward, and get the shaman. Back within the hour."

"I'm not taking you to a hotel for supers owned by a greater demon. Especially one who reveled in his war assignment to take out as many nephilim as possible. Any way possible. Not with your essence unreadable and your eyes glowing." The room's temperature dropped a few degrees, Gideon's fear strong enough to bleed past the containment cuffs. "They'll think you're a nephilim."

"And tonight he's got that big fight," Sebastian said. "Smaller fights all afternoon leading up to the big bout."

"So even though it's the middle of the afternoon, the hotel will be packed." Gideon shook his head. "No way."

"At least he's banned all media and you won't get caught on TV," Sebastian said.

"No," Gideon snapped, his voice sharp, whatever control he had over his emotions starting to crumble.

"We don't have much choice." If we didn't get the master ward, the witches would win, except— "Will the area containment master ward even shut the witches off from their power?"

"Nothing in or out, not even worship magic. The witches will still have access to their personal magic inside the contained area," Sebastian said, "it's not like the handcuffs, but it does create a barrier impenetrable by magic."

"Essie isn't going. I won't— I can't—" Gideon's breath picked up. "What if we paid double? What if—" Gideon pulled the marble with my light magic out of his pocket. "What if we paid with this?"

"Whoa, Mavis didn't take the marble?" Sebastian asked.

Gideon shoved the marble toward Sebastian. "Will this double the payment?"

"It'll cover the payment and then some, but Voth's terms were clear. No mated couple, no master ward."

Shit. If Gideon feared I'd be mistaken for a nephilim, I really didn't want to leave the apartment, not until I figured out how to deal with that. "What about my contacts? Can you top up the spell?" Perhaps if I just went in with a weird essence, we could claim it was the effect of my brands... although I had no idea how we were going to explain the brand I shared with Jacob. We'd just have to hope no one would think about it until after we were gone.

"I can only top it up if you haven't completely destroyed the spell," Sebastian said.

"Do it," Gideon snapped.

"Only if the spell is still there." Sebastian shot Gideon a hard look, sat on the couch, and pushed the book aside. "Sit. If I can top up the spell, this might make you dizzy."

I sat, and he pressed his palms over my eyes. Heat radiated from his hands and my buzz whispered under my skin. I drew in a deep breath, trying to steady myself and keep my magic under control.

"Are you okay?" Gideon asked, his tone sharp with worry.

"Fine, just trying to contain my magic."

"Even through the cuffs?" Amiah asked.

"I did say she was the most powerful super in the room," Sebastian said.

Which scared me, especially since Gideon's reaction to Sebastian teleporting seven people with raw magic implied he was a big, powerful deal. Sure, I wanted to be able to hold my own with my guys, but I didn't want to be so powerful that people were afraid of me. I didn't want to lose myself to that kind of power. Knowing I could bring justice, instantly punish anyone, would make it too easy to lose perspective. I could fall into the same trap Michael did, thinking that killing billions of people was the right decision.

Except I had my guys. They wouldn't let me get away with any of that. That thought eased my fear. A bit.

"The spell is still there." The heat from Sebastian's hands grew and sank into me, making my buzz bite harder in response. It wasn't close to what it had been after Mavis had cast the concealment spell on all the guys, but it'd be there soon if Sebastian's top-up took much longer.

White light shot past my closed eyelids and drove into my skull. I gasped and Sebastian's hands tensed.

"She's fine, Gideon," he said, a little too quickly.

"She better be."

"Jeez," Sebastian huffed, his power still pouring into me. "Mated angels are a pain in the ass. Just as bad as wolves. How do you put up with it, Esther? Or is he just on edge because he hasn't gotten any?"

"Bane," Gideon growled.

"You'd be on edge too if you'd ignored your bond for weeks," Amiah huffed.

"I'm not stupid enough to ignore a bond like that." The light swelled and I bit back another gasp. "Of course, I'm also not stupid enough to get trapped in a bond like that."

Another brilliant swell and then the light and the heat—and my buzz—vanished with a whoosh. Sebastian drew his hands away and sat back. Another weak divine light tear rolled down his cheek and sank back under his skin.

"How long will that keep happening?"

"No clue. I've never had raw power pumped into me like that before. And you gave me a lot," he said. "I'm surprised you had power left to respond to my top-up."

I was surprised as well and a part of me was afraid to know the reason.

"All right," Gideon said, his body so tense it made me ache to look at him. "Let's go."

Amiah grabbed his wrist, her expression grim. "I think you should take me and Cassius to Operations first."

"Why—?" Realization flashed across his expression. "You want to take him into the temporal freeze."

"And be there with him when the spell ends."

Gideon pressed his hand over Amiah's. "Amiah—"

"Getting Willow here within the hour might have been tight to begin with," she said. "If you have to go to Voth's first, Cassius might not last."

"Will the temporal freeze stop the spell?" I stood and the room tilted.

Sebastian grabbed my arm and steadied me until the dizziness passed. "Yes. Most magic is considered biological, so the freeze will keep him at the state he's at."

"Will it also freeze the drain on the witch?" I wasn't sure how spells worked. Would she know the spell was frozen or would she think Cassius was dead?

"The spell will stay active but stop draining," Sebastian said. "She'll know we put Cassius in the temporal freeze."

"So she could go after him." I hated to think that way, but putting Cassius in the freeze spell made him a helpless target.

"It's a risk we're going to have to take." Gideon gave Amiah's hand a squeeze. "Trapped in the spell, he'll no longer be a threat to their plans. We have to assume they won't do anything about him until after they've completed their goal."

"And we still don't know what that is," I said.

"One thing at a time." Gideon shot me a look filled with yearning, then jerked his attention away and strode into the living room. "Gear up. We're going to Voth's to get the area containment master ward."

"Light weaponry?" Jacob asked Gideon. "They're going to confiscate everything at the door, but it'd be better if we were armed when we're on the move."

"Agreed," Gideon said. "And while I really want Essie in a vest, I'd rather not have JP on her chest making her a bigger target than she already is."

Marcus jerked to a stop mid-step on his way to the duffle bags with our gear. "Essie is *not* going."

"This isn't a democracy," Gideon snapped. "Voth wants to see the mated couple as part of the buy, non-negotiable, and we need that master ward."

"I'm with Marcus. Essie's essence is muddled and her eyes—" Jacob's gaze froze on mine. "What happened to your eyes?"

"Enspelled contacts," Kol said without looking up at me. "Bought them from Mavis, remember?

"Everyone take a com." Gideon glanced back at Amiah. "You too. Jacob, when you're armed, get Cassius. We're taking him and Amiah to Operations to buy him time with the temporal freeze."

Marcus swore. "Still no way to save him?"

"We have a possible solution but we have to get the master ward first." Gideon turned to Sebastian. "Are you coming?"

"No. I'll get working on figuring out Esther's problem." Sebastian looked at me. "Try not to take down a building or anything while you're out."

"Gee, thanks." Except a part of me feared that, even with the cuffs, that could happen. While the rest of me was trying to figure out how to not draw attention to the fact that I wore separated handcuffs while I was being *seen* by Voth.

Everyone got a com, and those of us who needed weapons geared up. I really wanted to bring an M4, but arriving to buy a rare magic item armed to the teeth probably set the wrong mood. I was just going to have to trust that Mavis's concealment spells would keep us hidden, that the witches wouldn't attack while we ran our errands, and be happy with a Glock and two extra magazines.

Priam stayed behind with Sebastian. He'd been supposed to start his shift at Mercy Memorial in a few hours, but Amiah, as chief physician at Operations, commandeered his services for the JP for an indefinite amount of time.

As we got ready, Gideon, his posture tight, his gaze constantly darting back to me and making my pulse trip with need, gave the rundown of what we needed to do: buy the master ward and find Willow. The guys still didn't know what the witches had been doing at City Hall, only that one of them had stopped the mayor's assistant and briefly talked with him. So far the assistant hadn't answered his phone, and as soon as we got back from getting the master ward and picking up Willow, Gideon was going to breakdown and return the mayor's call. That, however, wasn't going to be a short conversation, since the JP had been involved in yet another public fight with supers. And at City Hall.

We hurried out of Sebastian's apartment and down the alley to the SUV. The sun was still pretty high in the sky but was now partially obscured by clouds, as if even the weather was starting to worry. We piled into the blazing hot vehicle with me sitting between Kol and Amiah on the middle bench. Kol leaned as far away from me as possible, while Amiah sat with her back stiff and her attention locked ahead of her—and I wasn't sure if she was staring at Marcus's headrest or out the windshield. Thank God it was a short drive to Operations.

Kol jumped out of the SUV before it had come to a complete stop at the curb, and I resisted the urge to scream at him and demand we work out whatever the hell was wrong. I knew what was wrong. I just needed to stay patient. God damn fucking patient.

We gathered outside the security door beside the garage's big door, everyone tense and worried.

"The spell starts about halfway to the inside door," Marcus said to Amiah. "It'll take about five minutes before the spell captures you, but moving through it is tough."

Amiah nodded.

Marcus's wolf darkened his eyes. "You don't have to go in with him."

She reached to take his hand but stopped and crossed her arms instead. "I need to be at his side the moment the temporal freeze ends."

"We'll have Willow ready and waiting," Gideon said.

"I know." She gave me an icy glare and marched into the garage.

Jacob hefted Cassius on his shoulder and followed her. My stomach churned at the idea that he was going back in there.

"Keep it fast," Gideon said, his voice beside me but

also in my ear over the coms, drawing a shiver of need. "Get him on a bed in triage then get out of there, even if Amiah doesn't make it all the way."

"Copy that," Jacob said.

A whisper of power, perfectly still and intense, crept through his brand. He'd stepped into the spell. I drew in a slow breath. He'd been in the spell before. Putting Cassius on a bed in triage wasn't going to take as much time as going up to Summer's lab and downloading City Hall's security footage.

Marcus shifted closer to me. Gideon started to join him, then forced himself to stay put, which only made my yearning for him stronger.

"You're going to need to deal with that," Marcus said to Gideon.

"It can wait until we've dealt with the witches." The muscles in Gideon's jaw flexed.

Marcus's eyes narrowed and he wrapped his arms around me. "I'm not so sure about that."

I wasn't so sure, either, not on him *or* me being able to focus on the job and resist the brand.

"It's going to have to," Gideon said.

The whisper of intense power in Jacob's brand grew. He'd only been in there a few seconds, and he wasn't drawing strength from me, but I could feel him fighting the spell's pressure. My pulse picked up... or was that Jacob's? I wasn't sure. I didn't think my connection with him was that deep, but then it had started before our brand had formed, when he'd woven his essence into mine and claimed me.

He grunted across the coms, and I drew in another slow breath.

"Hurry up, Amiah," he said.

"Just go," came her strained reply. "I'll make it."

Another grunt. Someone was breathing heavily. Amiah? It didn't sound deep enough for Jacob.

I strained to hear anything past the breathing. Had I sounded that exhausted trying to get to the armory? Amiah wasn't a fighter, but she also wasn't a pushover. She was an angel and that automatically came with more power than the average human.

Come on. Come on. God, was the temporal freeze slowing time around Operations as well? Seconds were ticking away too slowly. Jacob was taking too long.

Marcus pressed his lips to the top of my head, as if adding more physical contact would help steady my nerves. Kol stepped farther away from us and leaned against the SUV, his posture stiff, not his usual sexy, dangerous grace.

"Jacob? Status?" Gideon asked.

The heavy breathing turned into slow gasps.

"Jacob? Amiah?"

"In triage," Amiah said.

"Almost— Out." The power in Jacob's brand melted back into my body.

Oh, thank God.

A few seconds later, Jacob staggered out the door, and I rushed to him, unable to stop myself.

"It was harder this time," he gasped, leaning on me to keep standing. "I think the spell is getting stronger."

"How long will it take you to recover?" Gideon asked.

"You mean, will I be ready by the time we get to Voth's?" Jacob shuffled toward the SUV. I stayed at his side. I couldn't hold his weight, he was just too big, but I could help him keep his balance. "I have no idea."

Jacob and I got in the back and he leaned forward, his chest heaving with deep breaths. "I thought the last time was bad."

"We wait until he's good," Marcus said.

"We could miss our chance to buy the master ward." Gideon turned in his seat to look at Jacob. "We've already pushed our luck by taking this detour."

"Then drive," Jacob gasped. "I'll be fine."

He wasn't, and I didn't know how dangerous Voth—or rather how more dangerous—he was, given that he was already a greater demon. I also didn't know what the situation we were walking into was like, but no way was Jacob going anywhere while still recovering from fighting that spell. I'd given Gideon extra strength even when he wasn't pulling it from the bond. I should be able to give it to Jacob.

My buzz flared at the thought, tickling against the magic of the containment cuffs. I ignored it and concentrated on gathering some of my strength. I didn't need all of it. The situation wasn't dire, but I still needed to be mindful. It wouldn't help anyone if I was out for the count.

The power warmed my palms, and I pressed them over our brand on his biceps.

"Essie," he said, his voice that low rumble that always made me ache with need.

"I've got lots." I let my strength seep into him until his

breath steadied. I didn't even feel weak afterward. His love for me warmed my chest with real emotion, defying the handcuffs, and he dipped in and kissed me.

"Thank you."

Out of the corner of my eye, I saw Kol shift.

"We good?" Gideon asked, his voice and posture tight.

"Jeez, man, *you* aren't," Marcus said. "You've got to finish sealing your bond."

"We've already had this conversation." Gideon pointed down the street. "Drive."

"Fine," Marcus growled, and he put the SUV in gear.

We drove to the other side of the Quarter and through Squatters' Row to a massive, beautifully restored 19th century hotel. It didn't look like it had been touched by the war, and maybe it hadn't. Most of the buildings in Squatter's Row hadn't been touched, merely abandoned.

The ten-story yellow brick building sprawled on a hill at the very back of the Quarter, with a long, circular driveway leading up to a grand front entrance. Only the bottom five stories of windows had the telltale purple hue of UV-blocking glass, indicating that it catered to vampires but they weren't the hotel's only clientele.

Marcus drove to a parking lot at the side of the building, partially hidden by the hill. It was packed with vehicles and we were forced to take a spot at the far end of the lot.

"Do the vampires just stay until dark?" I asked, getting out of the SUV and following the guys across the hot parking lot to a set of double doors that, while not as grand as the front entrance, were still impressive.

"Voth had a subway built connecting the hotel to the vampire section of the Quarter," Jacob said.

"Which we should avoid at all costs," Gideon added. "We still don't know how Victoria is taking you taking Jacob from her, and anyone we run into in that tunnel will be a vampire."

I fought a shiver despite the day's heat. Yeah, that was another problem I didn't want to think about. I hadn't meant to sever her link with Jacob. Hell, I hadn't even meant to bind his soul with mine and brand him. But fate hadn't given me a choice, and if it had, I still would have picked Jacob.

Marcus fell into step beside me. "Don't forget, most supers are more aggressive than humans, and these supers will be riled up by the fights."

"So keep my head down." I rolled my eyes at him. "I was already planning on it. My power is restricted. I'm more vulnerable now than I've ever been."

His pupils slitted as his wolf tried to push to the surface. "Really didn't need that reminder."

"If I can keep it together," Gideon said, his body tight with strain, "you can."

CHAPTER 15

WE REACHED THE DOUBLE DOORS AND STEPPED INTO AN air-conditioned grand vestibule with a wide, sweeping staircase to our right, a long hall leading deeper into the hotel straight ahead, and a coat check, or rather weapons check, to our left. People packed the space, the roar of their voices echoing off the marble floor and walls, and the sense of power squeezed within me. Not just the force of vampiric intensity, although I could feel that in the mix, but the power of witches and demons with an innate ability, even the wild ferocity of shifters. There was so much magic crammed into the space it stole my breath.

"You okay?" Marcus asked.

I fought to make my lungs work against the pressure. This had to be part of what it meant to be a super, how they sensed essences or something. But man— "How long does it take to get used to it?"

Marcus frowned. "Used to what?"

"All the power of so many supers in one place. It's crushing."

"What power?" Gideon asked.

"You can't feel it?" How the hell couldn't they feel it? Except he didn't look affected at all. None of my guys did—

No, that wasn't true. Kol's posture had tightened even more and his expression was edged with pain, although if you didn't know him you probably wouldn't have noticed. I had thought the tension was because he was holding back his power to avoid turning on every woman and gay man in the vestibule, but maybe there was more to it.

"It'll get better in a month or two. Maybe more," Kol said with a shrug, confirming my suspicion. "Depends on how sensitive you are."

"Shit, right, she's a sensitive," Marcus said.

Jacob's gaze slid over the crowd. "Then this isn't the best place for her right now."

"So let's do this quickly." Gideon headed to the weapons check, where a bulky demon stood by the wall and a pretty demon stood behind the counter.

The bulky guy was about as tall as Gideon but twice as wide, with onyx colored skin that looked more like stone than flesh. He wore a white suit, a stark contrast to his black skin, and radiated danger. The pretty demon was his complete opposite. Petite, delicate, pale, with small horns poking through her long golden locks, she wore a barely-there dress, oozed sexual grace, and had a hint of hellfire in her eyes. Without a doubt, she was a succubus.

Her lips curled in a sultry smile and she wiggled her fingers at us. "Hi, guys."

None of my guys reacted to her—which surprised the

shit out of me, because I knew how difficult it was to resist the pull of Kol's magic.

Mr. Muscles beside her counter straightened. Guess if seduction didn't work, then they'd make us check our weapons with force.

"We're here to see Voth," Gideon said.

I handed over my Glock, but kept the magazines in my back pocket. The girl gave me a flirty smile and a chip for my gun, then turned her flirty smile to Marcus and Jacob as they handed over their sidearms. Attempt number two and she still didn't get a reaction from my guys.

Her lower lip curled into a soft pout and the hellfire in her eyes flared. Sensual heat swept over my skin, and Gideon's breath picked up. Her pout shifted into a wicked smile, and she leaned forward, showing off more of her cleavage and trying to get Gideon's attention. But instead of turning from Mr. Muscles to her, he turned to me with aching desperate need in his eyes, a need that fueled my own. God, we needed to solidify our bond before I shattered, and my soul cried for me to do it now, here, to hell with everyone else.

Kol slid up to the counter and flashed her his own wicked smile. "Keep trying." His expression snapped to deadly, the hellfire in his eyes brighter than hers. "I dare you."

The succubus jerked back, her hands raised. "Just having a little fun."

The heat vanished and Gideon drew in a ragged breath.

"Have fun with someone else." Kol drew the matching

daggers hidden on his back and set them on the counter, not bothering to take his shirt off to keep the blades in their sheathes. He turned to leave and Mr. Muscles cleared his throat.

"And the other ones."

For a second it looked like Kol was going to deny having them, but Gideon shot him a hard glare, and with a sigh, he drew a blade from each boot and another hidden in his jeans at his hip.

"Voth is expecting us," Gideon said through clenched teeth.

Mr. Muscles jerked his chin at the succubus, who was back to pouting. She picked up a phone, called her boss, and a few seconds later a wiry man in the same white suit as Mr. Muscles strode down the stairs and wove through the crowd to the weapons check counter. He looked completely human, not a hint of feralness, or vampiric intensity, or hellfire. His brown hair had been buzzed, making him look like a soldier, and if I added the confidence of his stride and the way he carried himself, I'd have guessed he'd been military before the war—and not just a volunteer like the thousands of others who'd signed up when humanity realized we were in the fight of our lives.

He gave us a cursory glance then turned on his heel and marched toward the hall. We fell into step behind him, Gideon leading the way, Marcus at my side, and Kol and Jacob taking up the rear. The hall didn't have as many people as the vestibule, but the crush of power didn't ease up. In fact, the closer we got to the end and an enormous set of gilded doors, the more the pressure squeezed me.

My buzz tingled under my skin, and I gritted my teeth. *I will not lose control. I will not lose control.* I could hold out until we'd gotten the master ward.

Two women giggled and another one fanned herself, but the reaction wasn't as strong as it had been when we'd walked into City Hall. I didn't know if that was because these women weren't human, or if Kol had regained control of his magical shields and wasn't leaking excess magic.

Our escort heaved open one of the doors and a wave of roaring voices and power crashed into me.

I gasped, and Marcus grabbed my arm to steady me.

Inside was a spectacular theater like the big fancy ones in Las Vegas, with a fight ring in the center and stadium seating all around, going down half a story and up at least one. Supers filled the seats, yelling and cheering. One man, or rather demon who looked a lot like Mr. Muscles, stood in the caged ring, wearing nothing but shiny shorts, his hands raised, making the crowd cheer louder.

A deep masculine voice announced someone else, the name flashing on the big screen hanging over the ring, then the image switched to a man with the intensity of a shifter jogging out of a tunnel between the aisles. The roar of voices swelled and so did the power crushing my chest.

People from the hall crowded in behind us and pushed past to take the stairs to their seats. Our escort led us along a wide hall ringing the theater, through more people, around a slight corner, and to a plain, glossy black door. We were led into a luxurious private box, complete with plush carpet, black leather couches, and a fully stocked bar. The noise of the crowd vanished as our escort returned to the hall, closing the door behind him, leaving us alone with a massive demon.

He wore an all-black suit and stood at the front of the box, one enormous hand pressed against the glass, the other holding a glass of amber liquid. Physically he looked human, with the exception that he was taller and broader than Jacob, if not seven feet tall then awfully damn close, with bulky muscular shoulders. But the waves of heat and crushing power radiating from his body, and the delicate tendrils of red mist curling over his skin then sinking back into his body, said in no uncertain terms he was a powerful demon.

"I don't see a bag," he said, his voice low and threatening, like powerful thunder heard in the distance. "The deal was cash. Non-negotiable."

"I don't see an area containment master ward," Gideon replied.

Voth glanced over his shoulder at us. Pricks of red hellfire smoldered in his black eyes and the force of his power swelled. "This isn't a game you want to play, angel."

My buzz grew stronger, and I strained to keep my breath even.

"This isn't a game." Gideon drew the glowing marble from his pocket.

Voth's eyes narrowed. "Put that on the bar and step away."

"Show me the master ward." Gideon squeezed the marble and the light in his eyes blazed brighter.

"Put that on the bar," Voth snarled. His red mist swept around him, his canines extended into fangs and horns grew from his forehead. The hellfire in his eyes didn't surge, but the crush of his power did.

Holy hell. I bit back a groan and grabbed Marcus's arm to keep standing. Light stuttered from my hands and he winced, but didn't pull away. Thank God, because I would have dropped to my knees if he did.

Voth's lips curled into a sneer. "Your brand has made her sensitive, and the spell on those containment cuffs isn't enough to prevent her from sensing my power."

"It's not," I gasped. We didn't have a lot of time to begin with and, God, if I didn't get out of there soon, I was going to collapse. Maybe if I stroked his ego, we'd move past the posturing. "I've never felt anyone as powerful as you." Which actually was the truth. Even Victoria with her enormous power hadn't affected me like this. "Just put the marble on the bar, Gideon. If he's going to break his word, there isn't much we can do."

Voth's sneer deepened. "Except he can't put it on the bar, because that would leave you defenseless."

Marcus snorted. "She's hardly defenseless."

"You don't count, puppy. I could crush you with a thought."

Except I was pretty sure that hadn't been what Marcus was thinking.

"None of you count." His power surged and my knees gave out.

Marcus grabbed me before I hit the floor and light

blazed around Gideon's hand. Jacob and Kol stepped ahead of me, and Voth howled with laughter.

"Careful, angel. Looks like you've got some competition from your team for your mate." The misty magic twisted around Voth's fingers and over his hands. "Is your mating brand strong enough to survive that?" His gaze landed on Jacob and he frowned.

"It's not really a competition." Jacob shrugged his branded shoulder. "You've seen our brands, you know we've got the money, so are we doing this deal or not?"

"But I haven't really *seen* the brands."

"That's it," Gideon said. "We're leaving."

Kol grabbed the door handle but the door wouldn't open.

"What makes angels so special?" Voth set his glass on the bar and stalked toward Gideon, his power growing, stealing my breath and making the room darken.

My focus narrowed to Gideon, with his light blazing around his hands and from his eyes.

"How can your souls bond and a demon's can't?" Voth asked.

Marcus swept me into his arms, his body tight and trembling. "Kol?"

"It won't open."

"I'm going to fucking kill Bane," Marcus growled.

"Tell me," Voth hissed.

Red mist exploded from Voth's back and he released enormous leathery wings in the same way angels released their wings. He lunged at Gideon, who jerked back and shot him with a blast of light. It scorched Voth's chest, burning fabric and flesh, filling the room with a coppery acrid scent, but Voth didn't even stumble. He seized Gideon's arm and red mist poured into the brand.

Gideon screamed and dropped to his knees. Jacob leaped toward them, but red mist shot out of his brand, and he howled and collapsed.

"What's so different about your souls?" Voth knelt before Gideon and grabbed his chin, forcing Gideon to look at him. "What makes you so special?"

Fire and pressure whirled inside me. The misty demonic magic wept from my brands, curled around my arm, and sank back into my skin. My buzz snapped, making my muscles seize and my power gather in my palms.

"Tell me," Voth growled.

Gideon groaned. "I don't know."

"She has an angel and a vampire. Even a vampire's soul is worthy, but mine—" Voth howled, the sound filled with rage and pain.

With a moan, Marcus sagged to the floor. He struggled to keep hold of me, but couldn't and I rolled out of his arms into a heap on the floor.

"She has the puppy, too. What makes her so special?" Voth shoved Gideon out of the way and grabbed my head with one big too-hot hand. His mist swept down his arm and into me, whirling into a supernova in my chest.

I squeezed my hands into fists and clutched them to my chest, desperate to hold my magic back. The containment cuffs heated, turned red, and burned my skin and the front of my T-shirt, but I kept my hands closed. There was too much power inside me, like there'd been too much power when I'd fought Ibizual. The hellfire prince had tried to flood me with magic until I exploded, but we'd managed to stop him in time. I had no idea how we were going to stop Voth. All my guys, even Kol, were prone and gasping. I could blast him, but who knew how many people could be hurt?

Voth lifted me to my knees, the hellfire consuming his eyes, the heat radiating from him like a sauna. "Why you? Why them?"

He blinked and for a second his eyes were filled with heartache. What he was really asking was 'Why not me?'

"I don't know."

"You must. You bound them to you with your power." He pressed his palm over my heart. "You're strong, but I'm stronger."

I seized his wrist. I had to do something. Maybe if I focused my blast, I could get him to let go and not hurt anyone else.

But his grief crashed into me. So much pain. So much heartache. So much loneliness. My concentration slipped and my power roared from my palms. But instead of a fiery blast, it surged into Voth and wrapped, warm and tender, around his heart with my love for my guys.

It glowed golden like the swirling threads of our brands, a pure connection of souls with a magic more powerful than all other magics. It wasn't light or dark or essence-based. It was primal, the core of everything within the universe. I hadn't believed true love or destined mates was real, but I couldn't deny the truth. I belonged with them and they with me, and nothing could change that.

Voth gasped and a red misty tear rolled down his

cheek. The demonic magic whooshed out of my chest into Voth, and his crushing power vanished. He released me and sagged back, clutching his hands over his heart, his expression stunned and sad. "So that's the truth."

"Yes," I gasped, even though I wasn't entirely sure what truth Voth had seen.

Gideon groaned and rose unsteadily to his feet. He clutched the marble in his fist and pointed it at Voth. "Let. Us. Go."

I wasn't sure what Gideon was going to do, since his first blast had barely affected Voth, but I knew he'd fight until his last breath to save me.

Voth stared at him, his expression still stunned.

The marble's light glowed brighter, and Gideon's body trembled.

Voth blinked away his shock, straightened, and with a billow of misty magic, pulled his wings back into his body. "You came for a master ward and you've more than paid for it." He pulled a phone from his pocket and sent a text, then leveled his dark gaze on me, only a hint of hell-fire in his eyes. "People won't understand you. But I've seen your truth. You're nothing like them. If you call, I will come."

What the—? I had no idea what he was talking about or what the hell had just happened. The ferocity of his attack, the depth of his heartache... none of it made sense.

The door opened, bumping into Kol, who crawled out of the way, and the guy who'd escorted us to Voth's private box entered with a briefcase. He set it on the bar, opened it, and left. Inside was a small silver plate etched with glyphs. *Please, God, let this be the area containment master ward.*

"The master ward activates with a drop of blood and the word *vade*. Stay as long as you'd like. Watch the fights. Have a few drinks on me," Voth said, as if he hadn't just flattened us with his power and there wasn't a hole burned in the front of his suit. "And leave the marble on the bar."

He strode out of the room and Gideon sagged onto the arm of the closest couch.

"What the fuck just happened?" Marcus growled, sitting back on his heels. "I didn't think a greater demon was that powerful?"

"He used our soul bond with Essie against us," Jacob said, his palm pressed to his brand as if it hurt.

Kol crawled to the bar, used it to help him stand, and looked in the briefcase. "It's got power, and it could be the real deal, but the spell's too complicated for me to properly identify. You'd have to ask Summer to be sure."

"Except we can't ask Summer," Gideon said, "and we're running out of time."

"We're in no condition to move." Jacob squeezed his eyes shut. He didn't look hungry or hurt, just exhausted. They all did.

I considered standing but thought better of it. I was still shaky from all the power and pressure. At least my buzz was gone, not even a whisper like when I'd first entered the hotel. Maybe I was getting used to the power. And maybe I was just too magically worn out. The containment cuffs, however, looked like they'd barely survived Voth's attack and had melted painfully into my wrists. I could only hope I wouldn't face anything like that again, or that Sebastian would be able to figure out how to help me, before they melted off.

And since there wasn't a damned thing I could do about it, or my burned wrists, I wasn't going to think about it. "I think I can help everyone but Marcus."

"Even if all I do is shift and shift back, it'll help." Marcus reached for his right boot and started unlacing it.

"It's not helpful if you exhaust yourself," Gideon said to me.

"Better me than all of you."

"I'm not going to bite you," Jacob said. "I'm not that weak."

"That wasn't what I was thinking." And while I craved my guys, I wasn't interested in having exhausted sex with them in a greater demon's private theater box. "Let me use the brands to give you a little strength." I pointed to the floor in front of me. "Come here. I think it'll be easier if I can touch you."

Gideon glanced at Jacob, who sighed and eased within arm's reach.

Marcus pulled off his T-shirt, and my pulse tripped at the sight of him. I forced myself to turn my back on him so I could concentrate, and laid my hand on Jacob's arm on top of his brand. I drew in a steadying breath and imagined my strength seeping into him. My buzz didn't even flare like it had in the SUV, making me wonder even more if I was finally out of juice. For a second, I feared I wouldn't be able to give my guys some of my strength, but then heat swept over my palm, and the quiet intensity that always came from Jacob's bond strengthened and grounded me. Thank goodness my soul bond with my guys wasn't completely connected with my personal magic.

Jacob leaned closer to me, his eyes dark with desire. He pressed his cool hand over mine and brushed his lips across my temple, then pulled my hand away. "Just enough to keep us going."

He placed my hand on Gideon's arm, and my strength slid from him to Gideon.

The light in his eyes flared, his pupils dilated, and his breath picked up. "This is a bad idea."

"Just give it a minute," Jacob said. "Then we'll get this shaman and get back to Bane's."

Gideon's jaw flexed and his body started to tremble. With a groan, he fisted his hands and bowed his head.

Kol hesitated for a second then staggered from the bar, eased to the floor behind Gideon, and grabbed his other arm. His eyes rolled back and he drew in a deep, shuddering breath, his reaction the complete opposite to Gideon's.

Gideon groaned again and lifted his gaze to mine, capturing me in his clear, perfect summer-sky eyes. My breath hitched. I ached to close the distance between us. No, *needed* to close it. Now.

"Aaaand that's where we should stop," Kol said as he yanked Gideon away from me.

Gideon panted, his expression hungry and desperate. He squeezed his eyes shut and his whole body tensed.

"Okay," he said, his voice husky. "Jacob, Kol, are you good?"

"Yeah." Kol glanced at me, a strange look in his eyes before he jerked away and strode to the door.

"I'm good." Jacob stood and helped me to my feet. The world swayed a bit, but not any worse than when I'd fed Jacob.

Marcus secured the fly on his pants and pulled his T-shirt back on. He still looked tired, but not nearly as exhausted as a moment ago.

"Okay. Protect Essie and the master ward." Gideon set the marble on the bar, closed the briefcase, and handed it to me. "Let's get out of here."

With Jacob steadying me, we hurried into the hall. The crush of power of all the supers in the theater squeezed inside me. It wasn't nearly as painful as Voth's fully released power, but it wasn't pleasant, either. At least my buzz didn't tingle under my skin. There wasn't any threat of me hurting anyone or doing serious property damage.

We rounded the slight corner in the hall ringing the theater, and a group of vampires peeled away from the walls, blocking our way.

"Victoria is pissed with you, Jacob Lockwood," a rake-thin man said. He had sallow skin, stringy brown hair, and wore jeans ripped on both thighs along with a T-shirt fraying at the neck. Gus. The vampire who'd tried to claim me the first time I'd been to Victoria's nightclub.

Marcus groaned. "You got to be fucking kidding me."

CHAPTER 16

My mind raced through our options, which were pretty much fight or run since no one was letting Gus take Jacob to Victoria.

The vampires released their intensity and the other supers in the hall either hurried away or drew to the side to watch. Only a few of the vampires had the weight of Jacob's power, but we were outnumbered three to one and we were tired.

"So you're her messenger now?" Jacob asked. "Tell her thanks for the invite but no thanks."

"This isn't a request," Gus said, flashing his fangs. "And I'm not Victoria's messenger, but I will be her new favorite once I bring her you and the bitch."

Gus jerked forward and the hall erupted into chaos. Gideon barreled toward Gus and slammed his fist, glowing with divine light, into Gus's chest. In a flash, Jacob had grabbed the vampire who'd been beside Gus and tossed him into the two vampires behind him, while

Kol pounced on another vampire. He dodged that vampire's punch, seized his extended arm, and broke his elbow.

I met Marcus's gaze to confirm we were thinking the same thing. Yep. Make a run for it.

We bolted through the opening in the center of the pack the others had made for us, and had almost made it through when a vampire lunged at me. I wrenched the briefcase up and smacked his hand away just before he grabbed me. His eyes flashed wide with surprise that I'd moved that fast—I was surprised, too—and I clocked him across the face with the briefcase.

Marcus punched another vampire in the chest, shoving him into a naga with scaly red skin standing by the wall watching. The naga hissed and shoved the vampire back toward Marcus, who punched him again in the chest.

Another vampire seized my arm and wrenched me around. I swung the briefcase at her head, but she jerked back and I missed. With a snarl, she reached for my throat, and I heaved the briefcase up, smacking her hand away and buying myself time to scramble back.

A flicker of buzz whispered over me. I didn't know how I still had power left after everything that had happened, but I sure as hell couldn't let it blaze out of control.

The vampire lunged at me, and a blast of divine light shot from across the hall and hit her in the head. She howled, the side of her face burned, but it was nothing a vampire couldn't heal with a feeding. Gideon met my gaze for a second, the look in his eyes wild, before he wrenched his attention back to the fight.

Beside him, Jacob punched another vampire, but a bulky demon took his place, ramming his shoulder into Jacob's chest and shoving him into the wall. Behind them, more supers had joined the brawl. Kol fought with a shifter and another vampire, while two of the vampires who'd stopped us fought with a group of twisted-horned demons.

"We have to get out of here," Marcus gasped over the coms. "People are just joining in for the hell of it."

A shifter punched out a wiry demon and wrenched around to find another target. His gaze locked on me. *Shit.* I tensed, ready to fight, but Marcus shoved the guy aside into a squat demon, who seized the wiry demon and tossed him into another group of shifters.

"Get to that maintenance door," Gideon said. "Fifty feet up the hall."

I twisted out of reach of another demon, my buzz crackling stronger, and squeezed between two separate fights between vampires and demons, determined to get to the maintenance door. Marcus followed, but a green-skinned demon wrenched him back and the vampire/demon fights shifted, closing the path between us.

Jacob rammed his elbow into the chin of the bulky demon who'd pinned him to the wall, knocking him back, while Kol bounded off that demon's back to gain height and gravity to strengthen his punch into a vampire's face. Gideon slammed another divine-light enhanced strike into a demon's chest and shoved closer to me.

A vampire stumbled out of a fight with a shifter and bumped into me. She turned, her lips curling into a wicked smile as she recognized me.

Oh, shit.

My buzz flickered again. I gritted my teeth and jerked back, running into someone behind me. The someone, a bulky demon with onyx skin in a slinky gold dress, wrenched around and snarled. I ducked down, praying the demon would focus on the vampire. She did, and I scrambled to the side as the two women went at it.

Only a few more feet to the door.

Except Gideon had been pushed farther away again, and Jacob and Kol had only managed to move about five feet forward. God, even moving fifty feet was impossible. Where the hell was security? I would have thought Voth wouldn't have wanted fighting in his hotel's halls, but then I had no idea what amused a greater demon. Maybe all this chaos was exactly what he liked.

The guys grunted and panted and yelled over the coms. My breath burned my lungs and my body trembled. I was too tired for this kind of a fight. Hell, even if I'd been at full strength and hadn't been dealing with the pressure of everyone's power, I wouldn't have wanted to find myself in a brawl with supers. And my buzz—my God damn buzz—was at it again with tiny bites under my skin. Post-nicotine levels, so it was manageable, but that didn't mean it couldn't blaze out of control at any minute.

A few feet away, Marcus snarled and dug his claws into the gut of a vampire. She screamed and seized his throat. Her eyes gleamed with wicked cruelty as she squeezed. Marcus gasped, yanked his claws out of her gut, and drove them back in, but she didn't let go.

I lurched toward them. I didn't know how I could stop her without my magic. All I knew was that I had to try. But someone grabbed the briefcase and jerked me back. I stumbled, not letting go of the case, and the woman, a vampire in biker leathers, grabbed my ponytail and wrenched my head back.

"You really pissed off Victoria." She grabbed my chin with her other hand, taking full control of my head.

I heaved the briefcase back, but didn't have a good angle. The case skimmed her side and didn't even draw a grunt, let alone loosen her grip, and none of the guys were close enough to help.

Gideon punched a thin demon in the chest, knocking him back, his chest burned and oozing from Gideon's divine light. Kol kicked out the knee of the demon attacking him and rammed his elbow in her temple, while Jacob fought against the two vampires who'd had the strongest intensity among the original group who'd attacked us. Their movements were fast, almost a blur, and I couldn't tell if Jacob was winning or just holding his own.

Marcus growled and clawed at the wrist of the vampire choking him, but she held tight even though blood poured from her arm. With a snarl, she heaved him around and slammed him against the wall. His head snapped back and he gasped.

I wrenched against the vampire holding me, my buzz biting stronger. Marcus couldn't die. Not today. Not if I could help it. Except I couldn't break free. Not without using my magic and endangering everyone.

"They say you're delicious," the vampire hissed in my ear, her breath hot against my neck.

I rammed my elbow back, drawing an *oomph*, but she didn't let go.

Marcus gurgled and his movements grew weaker.

"Jacob, Kol," Gideon barked. "Protect Marcus and Essie."

But the guys, like Gideon, were caught fighting multiple people and could barely shove forward, let alone move the thirty feet to us.

"They say that's why Jacob left Victoria for you." She raked her fangs across my throat, not hard enough to pierce skin, but enough to let me know what she planned —as if I hadn't already figured it out.

Fuck no. Panic seized my chest and my buzz exploded out of my control into a fiery inferno, blazing from my whole body, not just my hands.

Oh fuck oh fuck oh fuck. I scrambled to hold my power back, but it roared through my mental grip and filled the hall with blinding white light, forcing me to squeeze my eyes shut. The vampire screamed and collapsed at my feet, panting and moaning, and thank God, not dead. The roar of the fight snapped to silence, and for a second I feared I'd killed everyone. Except if I hadn't killed the vampire who'd been holding me, surely those farther away had taken a weaker blow. Then screaming and yelling filled the hall, and my vision returned.

The vampire holding Marcus looked at me with

horror. Everyone who wasn't running looked at me with horror.

My whole body shook and I fought to breathe. The buzz was gone and so was the fire, replaced with a bone-deep chill.

"You wanted a fight," Jacob said, his voice low, dangerous.

The vampire released Marcus and bolted. So did everyone else.

Marcus grabbed the wall, steadying himself and leaving a bloody smear. "Your eyes are glowing," he said, his voice raspy.

"We need to get the hell out of here before someone comes to the wrong conclusion." Gideon glanced down the hall behind him. "Jacob, help Marcus. Kol, take Essie."

Kol opened his mouth as if he were going to argue, then snapped it shut. Save for Marcus, none of my guys looked too hurt, but Gideon had a edge in his eyes and a tension in his body and we all knew it was because our not-yet-solidified bond, when he'd seen me in danger, had filled him with fear.

Jacob threw Marcus over his shoulder, and Kol swept me into his arms without giving me warning.

"Keep your eyes hidden," he said without looking at me. "That fight was bad enough. I don't want to deal with the rest of the hotel."

I wrapped my arms around his neck and buried my face in his shoulder, savoring the warmth radiating from his body. I wasn't freezing, not like I'd been when my brands had formed, but I was still cold, hollow.

He held me as if I didn't weigh anything, but his body was too stiff, his discomfort at carrying me clear. I ached to go back to the time before my wings had appeared, to the time when cuddling with him was safe and comforting.

We hurried down the hall and rounded a corner—best guess was we'd left the theater and were back in the main hall leading to the vestibule, but I wasn't going to risk someone seeing my eyes to take a peek. The rumble of voices returned, filled with excitement and fear and curiosity.

"Go straight to the SUV," Gideon said over the coms. "I'll grab our weapons."

Kol hurried out of the hotel, and sunlight and muggy summer heat wrapped around me. Sweat beaded on my forehead and between my breasts, but I didn't care. We were out of there and all my guys were safe.

"Can you walk?" he asked, shifting to set me on my feet without waiting for an answer, even though we were only halfway across the parking lot and not at the SUV.

"Yeah." I didn't know if I could, but I didn't want to make Kol more uncomfortable than he already was.

He put me down, but surprisingly held my shoulders to steady me. Hellfire and pain blazed in his eyes, breaking my heart.

I pulled my com out of my ear and swallowed against the lump in my throat. "When this is over, I'll take a break from the team," I whispered. And the break wasn't just for him. I needed a moment to catch my breath and figure out how to deal with my magic.

He took out his com. "You know none of them will

accept that." He pulled his gaze from mine. "I can manage. Be a professional."

Gideon hurried out of the hotel and caught up to us. Kol put his com back in, took his blades, and strode toward the SUV.

I holstered my Glock, frustrated at my disappointment. *He just needs time. And he isn't mine.* No matter how much I wanted him to be.

"You okay?" Gideon asked, his voice husky, sending a shiver of need through me.

"Are you?"

He reached to cup my cheek, his breath a little too fast.

Please touch me. Please kiss me.

But if he did I wouldn't be able to stop myself, and we'd end up having sex in the parking lot.

He jerked his hand away. "I can still work."

Marcus grunted over the coms but didn't argue.

We headed to the SUV. Jacob had set Marcus on the middle bench behind the driver's seat and had started the engine, while Kol had climbed into the back. Gideon took his usual seat and I climbed in beside Marcus.

"How are you?" I asked him.

"I'll shift when we get to Pinebrook. That'll help." He threaded his fingers between mine and I leaned into him.

Jacob drove to a major cross street in the middle of Squatters' Row, and turned away from the rest of the Quarter and the human part of Union City, heading to the outskirts of town.

This part of the city had been expropriated by the plan for population growth of the supernatural community, and Pinebrook had been a part of that multi-year development. So while it wasn't near much of anything at the moment, that didn't mean it'd always be that way.

It sat on the other side of a small, abandoned single-story public school. Weeds grew out of cracks around the foundation, and all the windows were either broken or boarded up. Those boarded up had been tagged with graffiti, and so had every inch of the school's dirty-gray siding. Jacob drove around back and parked near the rusted shell of a portable building, as close as the SUV could get to the forest without off-roading.

Marcus had already taken off his boots and T-shirt, and he climbed out of the back and shed his jeans. God, he was gorgeous. Ripped muscles, a tight ass, and those piercing green eyes. His neck was red with little runnels of blood that had trickled down his throat from where the vampire had punctured his skin with her nails, and a massive bruise was forming on his chest.

He flashed me a tired smile, took a step forward, and his body turned to liquid flesh, morphing in one fluid movement from human to wolf.

I'll run ahead and see if I can find a break in the wall, he said in my head.

"Go. We're right behind." Gideon gathered Marcus's clothes as Marcus bounded off, then Kol and Gideon hurried after him, while Jacob offered me his arm.

"Thanks." I was still weak and unsteady, and didn't know how well I'd manage running through the forest. Especially since we still didn't know when the witches were going to do whatever they were going to do and had no idea how much time we actually had.

The hollowness in my chest hadn't eased in the five-minute ride from the hotel, and while a part of me was worried I didn't have any magic to defend the guys if we ran into trouble, another part of me was relieved. There wasn't any chance I'd accidently hurt someone if things got stressful.

I took Jacob's arm and he drew in a sharp breath, his gaze on my wrist. "We need to get these cuffs off you."

The metal containment cuff had melted, not just in a circlet into my skin, but had dripped runnels down my forearm, and my skin was raw and blistered.

"Not until we figure out how to control my magic," I said, pushing through the tall grass and weeds that used to be the school's football field. "It's too dangerous. I think I'm out of power now, but for how long?"

"Every super recovers their magic differently. Archangels have a deeper connection to the Realm of Celestial Light, so they tend to recover pretty fast," he said.

"So I'm going to return to being a bomb sooner rather than later. Just great."

We reached the edge of the forest. Gideon and Kol were already inside, jogging down a narrow path, and Marcus was out of sight.

"You'll get control," Jacob said. "You just need time to get used to it."

"It's all just so overwhelming." I'd been running on adrenaline, trying—and failing—to keep hold of my emotions. But the adrenaline was about to run out and I was afraid what my reaction would be. "I keep trying to tell myself it's fine. I'm fine. But I'm scared of what I can do, of all the people I can hurt. Of hurting all of you."

"You won't hurt us."

"I burned Gideon to a crisp a few days ago." My throat tightened at the memory of Gideon screaming as he sucked in all my power, stopping me from killing myself. "The power within me now feels stronger than that. The cuffs can barely contain it." I bit back a bitter laugh. "They can't contain it. Not when I'm scared."

"And you'll get control. You're one of the strongest people I know." He grabbed me, making me yelp in surprise, and swept me into his arms. "Give yourself a break."

"I can walk, you know."

He tightened his grip on me. "Break, remember?"

Fine. I leaned into him, resting my cheek against his massive chest. As a vampire he didn't have a heartbeat, but I could feel something gently pulsing inside him. It pulsed inside me, too, through our brand. A thrumming certainty that we belonged together, that we'd have each other's back.

"You might not be in transition like a shifter," he said, his low voice rumbling through me, "but you're changing. And any supernatural change is hard." A whisper of sadness crept into his certainty.

Had he had trouble? He'd once been human. I didn't know how difficult it was to become a vampire, although it didn't strike me as easy since one of the steps was dying. Marcus had also had trouble. He'd said it had taken him over a year to feel right in his own skin again. But my transformation wasn't anything like that. My

DNA wasn't being rewritten, turning me into something else. It felt wrong to compare my struggle with theirs.

"Except I'm not actually changing, not like you or Marcus did. I've always been this. I just didn't know it."

"You thought you were a powerless nephilim. Your body felt like a powerless nephilim's. Now you have power you can't control. You're afraid of hurting people. You're scared," Jacob said. "Sounds like you're changing to me."

"How did you deal with it?"

"You should probably ask Marcus. I didn't handle my death well." Jacob's eyes darkened, his control on his intensity slipping. "I wasn't exactly willing, but Logan wanted more power and Victoria wouldn't turn him without turning me as well."

"So your brother coerced you?" That was horrible. Even though we'd had to kill Logan to prevent the hellfire prince Ibizual from escaping his cage, that didn't mean Jacob hadn't loved him. Logan's family had taken Jacob in, and the two had grown up together like brothers.

"Back then I would have done anything for Logan," he said. "I let him convince me that I could accept being a vampire. That a life of darkness and blood was an acceptable price for vengeance. It took me a long time of fighting my new nature, starving myself, feeling sorry for myself to come to terms with the new me. I fought my transition every step of the way, drew out the torture." He stopped walking and met my gaze, his quiet stillness radiating from the brand. "Don't fight it. It won't be easy, but you can get through it."

My emotions swelled and I turned my gaze to a large

break in the canopy above as I fought back irrational tears. The clouds were starting to thicken and the wind was picking up. A storm was building, just like the one that was building within me.

"We'll help you," he said.

"I know you will." And that was part of what scared me. They weren't going to leave me alone, and I was an explosion waiting to happen.

CHAPTER 17

WE JOGGED FOR ABOUT FIFTEEN MINUTES AND REACHED A six-foot brick wall half covered in moss and vines, with trees and bushes growing against it. It marked the edge of the Quarter's limit and had been magically put there, along with all the other features that had been magically added to the Quarter, when it had first been created. Not all the walls in all the forests were this tall, but, by request from the shifter community, there was always something to let a shifter caught up in the excitement of a chase know where the Quarter ended.

Thankfully this was the narrowest part of Pinebrook, although while this was the easiest way to get to it, it didn't mean that Willow lived close by. Gideon was looking along the wall off to the right, while Kol leaned against it, his posture relaxed and languid until he saw me.

Marcus loped toward us, bounding over a fallen log and skirting a thick bush. He reached us and shifted, one step as a wolf, the next as a human.

"There's a gate in the wall about ten yards that way." He pointed the way he'd come and took his jeans from Gideon. "It opens to a path leading to a cabin on a hill."

"All right." Kol pushed away from the wall, heading in the direction Marcus had pointed. "Let's do this."

"Amiah said to be gentle." Gideon dropped Marcus's boots in front of him and Marcus shoved in his feet. "Kol, I want her to see you first."

"And I should be the last," Jacob said.

"You know we already know this, Gideon," Kol said over the coms, not stopping or looking back at us.

"Give the man a break. He's not at his best right now." Marcus laced up his boots and pulled on his T-shirt. "And you and Essie are fixing that the moment we get back to Bane's." Gideon opened his mouth and Marcus glared at him. "The *moment* we get back. I'll get you two once we know what the witches are up to."

"Don't I get a say in this?" I asked.

"Would you prefer the SUV? I didn't think that was your style, but then—" Marcus glanced at Jacob and offered me a wry smile, making me instantly think of being in bed with both of them. "You did surprise me."

"I surprised you?" I asked as he hurried after Kol. "You surprised the hell out of me."

Jacob chuckled and easily fell into step beside Marcus with his enhanced speed. "I think we can agree the most surprised was Kol."

"Can we *please* stop talking about sex," Gideon begged, the tendons in his neck straining.

We reached a tall wrought-iron gate in the wall that swung on well-oiled hinges, and followed a gravel path through a field of flowering weeds to a log cabin. The sun fought to slice through clouds that did little to alleviate the summer's heat, and while the guys had to be exhausted even with the extra strength I'd given them, they didn't slow their pace. Yes, we didn't need Willow right away because Cassius was in the temporal freeze, but we did need to confirm her help and get back to stopping the witches. Because once we'd dealt with the witches—and we sure as hell were going to deal with them—Cassius would need immediate help.

The one-story log cabin wasn't very big, probably just a single room. Overgrown bushes with big dark leaves and bright red flowers crowded the front door and the single window and carried around the side of the building. Beside it, ten feet away, sat a shed made up of a patchwork of siding and a tin roof with a large, healthy vegetable garden stretching behind it. A single, massive maple offered shade behind the house and just about every possible flower bloomed in a chaotic jumble around the tree, edging the garden, curling past the shed, and even trailing back to an outhouse.

"Do you think she's out here because she's a shaman and wants to be with nature or because she's a firebird and fragile?" Although I wasn't quite sure what exactly a firebird shifter was.

We reached a front door that, while weathered, looked solid and secure. Jacob set me on my feet and moved back, while Gideon and Marcus took up position behind Kol. Even with Kol's sexy smile they were still going to be intimidating. I slipped past Marcus and stood beside Kol. I didn't know if this made us look any less intimidating, but at least she wasn't opening the door to a wall of muscular men.

Kol knocked.

A sparrow on the shed's roof chirped and took off.

Kol knocked again.

A gust of wind caught a loose strand from my ponytail and tickled my cheek.

"How long do we wait?" he asked. "We've only got about six hours left until the witches' temporal freeze ends."

"We take five minutes. Search the area," Gideon said, his voice icy and hard, even though the idea that we couldn't get Cassius help had to be eating him up. "Then we have to head back."

"I'll call in a favor with the pack. Get someone to sit on the house." Marcus headed to the shed.

"Thanks." Gideon pushed through the thick bush to peer in the windows.

Someone screamed, and a small, pale, feminine face appeared on the other side of the window directly in front of Gideon, making him jerk back. She had yellow, orange, and pink spiky hair and a small mouth and nose. Sparks danced off all of her exposed skin, and her eyes were blue... no, brown... no, green... no, purple?

"No no no no," she said, her words fast, her voice high-pitched and soft, softer than it should have been with how angry she looked and how thin the glass appeared. "You've ruined my bush!"

"Willow?" Gideon asked.

"Get out of my bush! I'm not talking to you," she

snapped. "I didn't answer the door and that means I don't want to talk to you."

"We need your help," Gideon said.

"Did I open the door? No, I didn't," she said, without giving Gideon a chance to answer, more sparks bursting around her. "That means I'm not talking to you."

Kol bit back a snort. "Except she *is* talking with us," he said under his breath.

"We don't have time for this." Marcus shouldered Kol aside, and tried the door. It opened without him forcing it and he stepped inside. "Now, listen—"

"Get out! Get out!" Willow squawked, her voice rising an octave and gaining a little more volume.

I hurried in after Marcus. "Amiah sent us."

Willow froze, tilted her head to the side, making a lock of pink hair sweep over her shoulder, and blinked her green, yes, green— blue?— something eyes. She didn't have any of the feral intensity I recognized as a shifter's magic, but she did have power. It half fluttered and half unfurled in my chest, as if it couldn't decide what it was. It wasn't crushing like Victoria's or Voth's, but it wasn't weak, either. Just... different.

Kind of like the rest of her. She looked to be about my age, was thin, five foot nothing, and had multi-colored hair of a variety of lengths and kaleidoscope eyes. She wore men's boardshorts with a yellow and red Hawaiian pattern on them that came halfway down her calves, and her top was a billowy, short-sleeved blouse with fringe and sequins and dotted with snowflakes and stars.

I took a tentative step toward her. "Our friend has

been enspelled with worship magic and Amiah thinks you're the only one who can help him."

"We really need your help," Kol said from the doorway.

She narrowed her eyes and glared at him. A single spark jumped from her cheek and vanished in a small puff of smoke. "The angel ruined my bush."

"I'm sorry about your bush." Gideon stepped past Kol and drew close to me. "My brother is dying. Please."

"My bush could have died."

"Willow," Kol said, his voice sliding across my senses, soft and sensual. A whisper of heat unfurled within me, but I knew the sliver of power wasn't for me.

"It. Could. Have. Died." She crossed her arms and raised her chin, not even a flicker of desire for him in her now yellow eyes.

"For fuck's sake. We're on a bit of a time limit. He said he's sorry." Marcus took a step toward her, and her defiance vanished. With a squeak and flurry of sparks, she scrambled to the far side of the cabin, heaved open the back door, and bolted outside.

"Wait." I ran after her, but she'd only gotten ten feet away when she skidded to a halt, her attention locked on Jacob on the other side of her vegetable garden.

"He won't hurt you," I said. *Please, calm down so we can talk to you.* I tried to will her to listen to us, to help us, but her gaze never left Jacob. "None of them will hurt you."

She extended a hand to Jacob and wove her way through the garden, slow and careful, as if she were afraid *she'd* spook him. He crouched so he wasn't towering over her, and waited for her to come to him.

I followed a few feet behind her and Gideon stayed back, motioning to Marcus and Kol to do the same.

"I've never seen one in the daylight before," she said, as if Jacob were a rare animal or bird that she was finally getting a glimpse of. She glanced back at me, a flicker of eye contact before returning to Jacob. "I don't know why you bother with the others when you have him. So still. So calm. How can you be in the sun?"

"I have a special charm." Jacob sat in the grass and raised his wrist, showing the thick silver bracelet with prongs every eighth of an inch digging into his skin.

Willow shifted closer to him and reached out with a tentative hand. She brushed her finger over the charm then jerked her hand back, her expression filled with wonder.

"Amiah said you might be able to help us," he said, his deep voice soft, filled with a tenderness that made my heart swell. "Our friend has a worship magic— an essence-based spell on him."

She drew a little closer and sat, her hand darting out again to touch his charm. "The turbulent angel's brother. But that isn't why he's breaking."

"No." Jacob's gaze rose to mine, filled with love and worry.

Willow followed his gaze to me. "But you're not breaking because you have him. So much stillness."

I knelt in the soft grass near her, but out of reach, hoping she wouldn't feel threatened. "We were confused and now—"

"Now the angel is breaking." She frowned, blinked,

and did another bird-like tilt of her head. "You're broken, too, but not *breaking* and not because of him."

I wasn't sure what to say to that. A part of me was broken because I hadn't solidified my bond with Gideon, but I had a feeling she was talking about my magic and not my love life.

"And not because of all that—" She waved at my guys and scrunched her nose. "So much activity, noise. So so loud."

"Is that why you live out here?" I asked.

"People have too much life." She tentatively pressed a finger to the back of Jacob's hand. When he didn't move, she took his hand between her tiny ones and turned it palm up. "It vibrates too fast, charged with emotion." She traced a line in Jacob's hand. "You have emotions. Deep emotions. But you're so still. The angel and wolf and demon are blinding, grating."

"Am I grating?" I asked Willow. "I'll move back." I didn't want to jeopardize getting her help because I was grating to her magical senses.

"You burn brighter than all of them." Her frown returned. "But there's something I need to tell you."

"What?"

Her eyes flashed through the rainbow with gold and silver thrown in. "I can't remember. You should leave."

I glanced at Jacob, who shrugged.

"Can you help us? Can you break an essence-based spell? Will you come into the Quarter and remove the spell on Gideon's brother?" I asked as I stood.

Jacob started to rise, but she tightened her grip on his hand. "No."

"No you won't come to the Quarter?" Jacob asked. "Or no I shouldn't leave?"

"Correct."

"What the fuck?" Marcus growled.

She looked up at me. "Yes, yes, no, yes, and yes."

Ah...?

"Did she just answer your questions?" Kol asked.

"So you can break an essence-based spell and you will help us, but you won't go into the Quarter?" Except once Cassius was out of the temporal freeze, I doubted he had the time to be hauled through the forest. "Cassius can't be moved."

"If I'm with you, can you handle being in the Quarter?" Jacob asked.

She turned a brilliant, adoring smile to Jacob. "Can I have him? Please? So still and calm and kind. He's perfect."

"I belong with Essie," Jacob said.

She stroked his hand as if petting an animal. "She can visit."

"Is this the price for saving Cassius?" I wasn't sure I wanted to know. So far every super I'd come across traded in something other than money.

She blinked at me. "Should it be?"

"No," Jacob said quickly. His gaze rose to mine and captured me with its dark intensity. My pulse picked up with need and awe for the love in his eyes. "I'd start breaking if I stayed with you. Just like the angel."

"That's why she can visit," Willow huffed.

"It he stays, we all stay," Marcus said, raising his voice so she could hear him.

"Marcus—" Gideon hissed.

Marcus shot him a dark look. "We'll be crammed in your little cabin. All the time. Killing your bushes. Being emotional."

Her eyes widened in horror and a spark jumped off her cheek. "You'd let him do that?" she asked Jacob.

"Essie wouldn't be able to leave me, and Marcus and Gideon can't leave her," he said.

"Then you *can't* stay." She jerked to her feet and stormed farther from the cabin with a trail of sparks and smoke. "No no no. You can't stay."

"Damn, Marcus," Gideon snapped. "We need her."

I scrambled to my feet. "Please. You're the only one who can help."

"But you have to promise not to stay." She whipped around to face me, her body tense and vibrating as if she needed to fight, her eyes deep purple. Sparks snapped and popped around her. "None of you stay. Promise."

"Promise." Jeez, so much for Willow being the last sane shaman on the planet.

She stomped her foot. "And I'm not leaving my cabin."

"But we need you to remove the spell." The conversation was going around in circles and we really didn't have the time. How the hell did I convince her to come into the Quarter?

"I don't need to leave to do that." She rolled her now blue eyes at me as if I should have known that and held out her hand to Jacob. "I can give you a door and a bell. Just ring and open and I'll work through you."

Jacob took her hand. "Thank you."

She closed her eyes and the strength of her power swelled.

"Wait—"

Her eyes flew open and the power dimmed. "What?"

"Is it permanent?" The answer wouldn't change Jacob's decision. Even if it was permanent, he'd say yes—I would have, too—but I wanted to know everything we were getting ourselves into. We'd already walked blindly into Voth's attack, thinking we were just there to buy a master ward. I wasn't sure why I'd thought it'd be a simple deal, nothing so far with the supernatural world had been simple, but I wasn't going to be caught off guard twice in one day.

"Permanent? No." Horror flooded her face again. "Permanent means you'll stay and you can't stay. You'll kill my bush." Her eyes snapped closed and her power swept over me like a giant wave.

I dropped to one knee and Jacob tensed, but I waved him off. I was fine. Willow's power wasn't nearly as crushing as Voth's.

"I can handle it," I said, hoping the others would stay back as well.

Her strange fluttering power beat against my ribs as if trying to escape, and heat swelled in Jacob's brand.

Willow clicked her tongue and did another bird-like tilt of her head. Golden light blazed from our brands, both my arm and his, and the fluttering grew faster. My buzz stayed quiet, making my stomach queasy. I really was out of magic and defenseless, and my fear of not being able to protect myself and my guys grew beyond my fear of accidentally hurting someone.

"You can't be in here," Willow said, the fluttering pounding harder in my chest. "The door is just his. Only his."

"How do I get out?" I gasped.

"Just get out," she snapped.

Sure. Just like that. I tried to open myself up and release the flutter, but it turned into desperate slamming strokes inside me. Maybe I needed to imagine distance between me and Jacob. I thought about drawing away from him, imagined a great void between us.

The heat and light in my brand blazed stronger and Jacob's power, calm and intense, swelled around my heart.

Willow scrunched her face in concentration, and a piece of the fluttering, still smashing inside me, snapped off. Jacob gasped and Willow fell back onto her butt.

"Is it done?" Gideon asked.

"No thanks to you." She whirled around and glared at me, sparks bursting off her. "You shouldn't have been in there. You—"

Her head snapped back and the fluttering exploded inside me. Her power burned along every nerve and seared into every cell, stealing my breath.

Jacob leaped to my side and caught me as I toppled over. Willow grabbed my hand, her eyes no color and every color, wide with fear, her sparks showering around us, stinging my skin.

"Hide. You have to hide. You must hide." Her tiny nails dug into my palm. "She's looking for you!"

"Who's looking for her?" Marcus asked, his voice right beside me and in my ear.

"Mommy," she said.

My mom? How could my mom be looking for me? She's dead. But the moment I thought that, I knew Willow hadn't meant the woman who'd raised me. "My birth mother. She's looking for me? She's still alive?"

Willow's hand trembled... or was that me trembling? My thoughts stuttered at that. I hadn't realized until now that I'd assumed if both of my biological parents were angels, then they'd died in the war. If they'd lived, surely they would have come for me by now.

"What do you know about Essie's mother?" Gideon asked, his voice also close.

The fire of Willow's power sputtered, with sparks that stung my skin as well as inside me jerking my essence. On off. On off. On—

"Too much power. Too much emotion." Sparks flashed off her cheeks and hands. "It's in everything. Woven into the heart of every flake of essence. You have to hide. You must hide. She lost the war but she's not dead, and when she finds you, she'll take you."

CHAPTER 18

ICE SWEPT INTO ME AS WILLOW'S HEATED MAGIC sputtered off and stayed off. My mom— my biological mom was looking for me. She wasn't dead. And she'd lost the war.

She'd fought with Michael against humanity and the Angelic Defense.

"You can't stay here! Hide!" Willow hissed at me and bolted into her cabin with a flurry of sparks.

I dragged my gaze from Jacob's intense stare, to Marcus's piercing green gaze, to Gideon's summer sky, to Kol's hellfire. They looked as scared as I felt, and Willow's fear had shaken me to my core. I hadn't thought I had enough magic for my empathy to work, especially with the containment cuffs on, but her fear terrified me.

"What just happened?" Marcus asked, his wolf slitting his pupils. "Who the hell is your mother?"

"We'll figure that out later." Gideon straightened. "Did we get what we needed to save Cassius?"

"Yes." Jacob adjusted his grip to carry me, his hold a little too tight, his body trembling.

"Then let's move." Gideon hurried back toward the forest and we followed.

I didn't know if we were running to get away from the threat of my biological mother or because we needed to get back on track with figuring out what the witches were doing. I couldn't get my mind to work enough to think straight. I had to hide. I couldn't let her find me. I—

Jacob climbed into the back of the SUV, still holding me, while the rest of the guys piled in. I hadn't even noticed us running into the forest or leaving it.

If my mother had fought for Michael, did that mean he was my father? God, could I be the child of the angel who'd slaughtered billions of people? Sure, I'd had nothing to do with that, but— Maybe I was still a monster, just not a nephilim.

Except maybe Michael wasn't my dad. Rafael and Lucifer had also fought for him. But that thought didn't make me feel any better. Rafael had been Michael's right hand during the war, and Lucifer was... well, Lucifer.

"Who the hell am I?"

Jacob pressed his lips to the top of my head. "You're Esther Shaw."

"Am I? My mom fought for Michael. My dad—" I tried to focus on the calm within Jacob's brand, let it seep into me, ease my panic, but couldn't still my whirling thoughts enough to draw in his stillness.

"Your dad could have fought for the Angelic Defense," Gideon said. "If your mom chose Michael's side and your father didn't, it'd make sense he'd want to hide you until the war was done."

"But he didn't come back for me." My throat tightened with all the hurt that I'd spent years pushing deep inside me. It was like I was nine again and realizing for the first time that no matter what my mom said, he was never coming back for me.

And now my mom wasn't my mom. But of course, I already knew that. If I was a full angel, the woman I loved, who'd given everything for me, was just some woman. Except she wasn't *just* some woman. She was the only parent I'd ever known. The only one who'd known my secret— although maybe she hadn't known. Maybe my father had lied and told her I was a nephilim.

But then why would she have lied to me about being my biological mother? Why lie about loving my father?

It was all a lie. My whole life had been a lie.

Marcus parked in the alley near Sebastian's private door and we got out of the SUV. Jacob reached to pick me up again but I pushed his hands away. I couldn't let him carry me. I had to take action. Do something. Anything. Hide. Cry. Scream.

Pull your shit together.

Gideon needed me. The whole team needed me. Even if I physically couldn't help with the fight against the witches, they wouldn't be able to focus if they were worrying about me.

We climbed the stairs, but even knowing that freaking out wasn't helping them, I couldn't push it all down.

It was all a lie.

The words kept whirling around and around in my head.

A lie, and my mother was powerful and terrifying and looking for me.

We reached the top floor, but I couldn't bring myself to step into the hall and head to Sebastian's apartment. It was too much. I had to think, draw breath, do— God, I didn't know what.

"Essie?" Jacob asked.

I glanced up the stairs leading to the roof. "I just need a minute."

Marcus shot a look at Gideon. He didn't look well and we needed to solidify our bond, but—

A minute, that was all I needed. Sky. Quiet. A moment to mourn a life that had all been a lie.

"Take as much time as you need," Gideon said.

I pulled out my com, not wanting to hear the guys, shoved it in my pocket, and fled up the stairs. Tears burned my eyes and tightened my throat. Fear, hard and cold, squeezed my chest.

The door at the top of the stairs opened onto a barren rooftop with a tall metal HVAC unit. The UV-blocking canopy angled down and attached to the far side of the roof, marking the edge of the vampires' part of the Quarter. It tinted the brilliant sunlight purple, making it feel off. Just like I felt off. Add a lack of breezes, particularly with the clouds above racing by, and the roof didn't feel freeing or comforting.

A tear broke free and rolled down my cheek. Standing on a rooftop had always made me feel safe. Which was crazy, since Mom had always told me angels attacked from above. But now I knew why. I was an angel. And my mom wasn't my mom.

And I was trapped on this roof. The glass canopy was less than seven feet above me. Even if I could release my wings and knew how to fly, it'd be a challenge to take off. I'd have to go to the other side and jump.

Maybe I should. Run. Get the hell out of there. Hide like Willow had told me to do.

But that was the panic talking. When things got bad, I'd been taught to run. And I didn't want to run anymore.

I wanted to be with my guys. They'd stood by me even when they'd thought I was a nephilim. Which I wasn't. Because I was an angel and—

Come on. Pull it together. I could do this. I'd dealt with lots in the last couple of weeks. This was just one more thing. I could handle it. They'd said I was an angel and at least half archangel. I knew my father could have been on the wrong side of the war. I knew my mother could have been, as well. Deep down I had to have known Mom had lied to me. And really, did any of that change who I was? What kind of person I wanted to be?

Another tear rolled down my cheek, and I drew in a ragged breath.

I couldn't give in to my fear and grief. There'd be time after we'd dealt with the witches for that. Perhaps then I'd have calmed down and would be able to think straight.

I squared my shoulders and wiped my cheeks.

Right now my first priority was Gideon.

I drew another breath to steady myself. My guys had

my back. They loved me regardless. With them, I could deal with anything.

My attention slid to my brands. Gideon's lightning gently crackled over my arm, and Jacob's powerful stillness seeped into me. I was stronger than I'd ever been before, and that had nothing to do with my growing magical power. I'd faced monsters and survived. I'd faced monsters and saved my guys. Even exhausted and fighting to contain my dangerous magic, I could handle whatever came next.

"I've been looking for you," a familiar sultry alto said behind me.

I jerked around, and Victoria rushed toward me with her enhanced vampiric speed, faster than humanly possible. I turned to run, and she clamped a hand around my neck and squeezed.

"You took what's mine." Her gaze jumped to my eyes. A hint of hesitation flickered over her expression, but then she released her power with an intensity that stole what little breath I had left. "And now you have the nerve to enter *my* house."

I clawed at her hand, my lungs screaming for air. Her lips, painted blood red, curled into a sneer, revealing the tips of her fangs. She was horrifying and beautiful, with her hunger filling her gaze and her voluptuous curves barely covered in a tight black dress.

"Thought you could sneak in?" She raised me up with her enhanced strength.

My toes skimmed the rooftop. I clutched her wrist with both hands, and darkness swarmed the edge of my vision. My thoughts jumped to my light strike, but my buzz didn't even whisper under my skin.

"You think you can do anything," she snarled.

The words of the light strike spell rushed in my head, something I hadn't needed for a while now. But still no buzz. Not even a glimmer of light in my palms.

Come on. Please. I had to get free, but I was too physically weak to make her let go and I didn't have any power to blast her with light.

"You think the mark on your arm protects you." She slammed me into the side of an HVAC unit, cracking my head and shooting stars across my vision.

Her grip eased, and I drew in a ragged breath before she tightened it again.

"He was mine." With her free hand she grabbed my hair and dug her nails into my scalp. "Mine." Her fangs extended in full and her intensity swelled, the pressure of her power crushing inside my chest.

Fear pounded through me. Still no light, no buzz. The words of the light strike spell muddled. My thoughts muddled.

"No one takes what's mine." She released my throat, and I gasped in another ragged breath as she sank her fangs into my neck with slicing pain.

With a snarl, she dug the nails of her now free hand into my chest and pinned me to the HVAC unit. She took a long pull, not using her magic, sending screaming pain through my neck.

No. Please, God, no.

I yanked my leg up to knee her in the groin, but she pressed close, her body tight against mine, making it impossible to land a good blow with knees or hands, not that I had the strength to move her. But I couldn't just stand there and let her kill me.

"Now I know why they want you," she said against my neck. "All this power. You're delicious. Should I drink you dry or save you for later?"

"The angels will come after you." I wrenched against her grip. "I'm sacred."

Her nails dug deeper into my chest and she took another agonizing pull. "Then I guess I can't drink too deep."

She ripped open my shirt and bit down hard. I screamed, making her purr with pleasure, and she pressed her palm over my heart, just like Jacob had done when he'd claimed me.

My pulse stuttered. I couldn't let her entwine her essence with mine. I might have been able to resist Jacob's claim after only a few weeks, but Victoria was a master vampire and so much more powerful than him.

I wrenched harder, but couldn't break free. My buzz sparked under my skin. *Yes!* And vanished. *No, please.*

"When you're mine, I'll make them watch you fuck me."

"Never," I gasped. *No. Please, no.*

My buzz sparked again and I mentally clutched at it. I couldn't draw enough breath to scream. It was the only thing that could save me. But it sputtered out, dying in my mental grasp.

"With my claim on you, you'll be begging for it."

Please, God. Help. "I don't consent."

"I don't care." Her crushing intensity slid into my

veins, forcing my cells to thrum to her desires, just like they'd aligned with Jacob's when he'd claimed me.

She took another long pull on my vein and her palm heated. My soul screamed. I'd fought possession by the archnephilim and a hellfire prince. I had to be able to fight Victoria.

"The more I take, the stronger the claim." Another long pull.

The rooftop darkened and spun and a weight swept through my limbs. I strained to stay conscious. If I passed out, I became hers, and no way in hell was I becoming hers.

"Touch me," she purred.

My hand slid from her arm to her ribs.

God, no.

She moaned against my neck, the sound vibrating through me like Jacob's voice did, and my hand plunged into the front of her dress.

Get out of my soul. Get the fuck out.

My buzz sparked and I seized it, willing it to stay alive and grow stronger. I needed to release it. All of it. To hell with having any kind of control. I needed to get her away from me and force out her essence.

"I didn't say you could stop." She took another agonizing pull and her essence sank deeper into me.

I had to get it out. Even if I managed to blast her back, she'd still have control.

My hands started to move back to her breasts, but I yanked them away and slapped them against my chest. I released my buzz and fire erupted in my body, burning from my hands, through my skin, and into my cells. It surged against Victoria's essence, but with a snarl, her power grew stronger. The force of her magic stole my breath with its crushing weight and her essence roared, stronger than ever inside me.

I strained to hold onto my power, burn her out of me, but it wasn't enough. I barely had any magic left and I was fighting the containment cuffs on top of that. She was going to take control of me and there wasn't anything I could do. I just didn't have enough power.

My hands dipped under her skirt and skimmed her thighs.

No please. I didn't want to do this. *Fight. Flee. Please. Help!* But I couldn't draw breath, couldn't make my mouth work to yell.

Except I didn't have to yell. I had a connection with my guys. The cuffs didn't affect the brands.

Which meant I also had access to Gideon's power.

I concentrated on the lightning crackling over my right forearm, barely noticeable against Victoria's crushing power. I seized it and yanked it into me, letting it surge into my body.

Victoria tensed, her teeth digging deeper into my neck. I whimpered against the pain and gave in to Gideon's power. It seared every cell in my body with screaming agony and consumed Victoria's essence.

She howled and heaved away from me, her eyes wide with shock. "How did you do that?"

My knees gave out and I sagged to the rooftop.

"How did you—?"

The light in my palms stuttered and went out. My buzz vanished again and so, too, did Gideon's power.

Her shock snapped to rage. "You'll still pay for taking him. Even if I can't have you, you'll still pay."

She lunged at me. I tried to get out of the way, hit her, block her attack, anything. But she was too fast and I was too weak, and she sank her teeth back into my neck.

CHAPTER 19

I FOUGHT AGAINST VICTORIA'S GRIP, BUT I HAD NO MORE strength and no more power. Her claws dug into my scalp and shoulder, pinning me against the HVAC unit, and sharp pain cut through my neck where she bit me.

I screamed to Gideon and Jacob in my head, begging for help over and over again, but had no idea if they could hear me. We hadn't communicated telepathically before. It might not even be a power we'd develop with our bonds. But it was the only thing I could do. Surely Gideon had felt me take his magic. Surely he knew I was in trouble.

The world darkened and spun, and I wondered how many times a person could be drained by a vampire in one day and survive. I tried to raise my arms but couldn't, and my breath slowed.

A faraway part of me realized I was sucking strength from my brands, but Victoria was consuming it as fast as I got it. It wasn't going to be enough to save me.

"Step away from her, Victoria," Gideon said from somewhere far away... or was I far away?

Victoria snarled, bit down harder and tore her teeth out of my throat. Hot blood gushed over my neck and down my chest. I gurgled and tried to clamp my hands over the wound but I was too weak to raise them.

"Oops," Victoria said with feigned innocence.

Someone yelled.

A blast of divine light slammed into Victoria and knocked her away from me.

Then Jacob appeared before me.

I hadn't seen him move, but I didn't think that had anything to do with his enhanced speed. He was fast. But not that fast.

"Get Priam," he yelled as he clamped a hand over my neck. "My magic isn't powerful enough to heal this."

I fought to breathe, each gasp an agony while blood raced down my chest, seeping into the lacy white bra Kol had gotten me.

"On your knees," Gideon said, his tone frigid. His divine light sword blazed in his hand brighter than I'd ever seen it before.

"She took what's mine. So I took payment in blood," Victoria hissed. "This is my house. My rules."

"Not for murder." The light in his eyes flared.

"Where's Priam?" Jacob's voice cracked. "Come on, Essie. Hold on."

I dragged my attention to Jacob, who swam in and out of focus. I wanted to tell him I loved him, I loved them all, but I was trapped in a body that wouldn't obey me, every thought and moment slow, stuttering, and heavy.

"Payment in blood is permitted," she said. "She took Jacob. It's not my fault she's not strong enough to pay the price."

"You tore open her throat," Marcus growled.

"Prove I did it on purpose." She cocked a sculpted eyebrow. "You surprised me. My fangs slipped."

"I'll fucking surprise you," Marcus snarled, prowling into my line of sight to stand beside Gideon, his fingers extended into claws and his eyes dark, his wolf on the verge of taking over.

She threw her head back and laughed. "I'm a master vampire, little wolf. None of you can take me."

"Sure, separately," Kol said. He was somewhere out of sight.

Priam dropped to his knees beside me, his face white, his expression tight with concern.

"You attacked a JP agent." Gideon pointed to the rooftop. "On your knees."

"There are no human agents." Victoria wiped a trickle of blood from her chin with her thumb and sucked it clean.

"Head office would beg to differ," Gideon said.

Priam captured my cheeks in his palms, forcing me to look at him. "You're losing too much blood too quickly. I have to heal you fast. This will hurt."

Lightning exploded through me. I screamed and the rooftop vanished into darkness. Jacob's grip on my neck tensed, Victoria released her crushing power, and I fought to breathe.

"My house. My rules. Your delicate sensibilities don't matter. It doesn't even matter if she's really an agent. The

JP will have your head if you illegally kill this master vampire."

"Maybe I don't care," Marcus said. "You tried to kill her."

"Prove it."

Light blazed from Gideon's eyes and he drew in a ragged breath, visibly trying to regain control of himself. "Her house. Her rules."

"Gideon—" Marcus snarled.

"We can't prove anything. She's in her right to claim a blood price for Jacob."

"Which has been paid in full," Jacob said, his hold on his vampiric intensity releasing, adding to the crush inside me.

She raised her chin. "You're worth more than what she can offer."

Marcus snarled. "Paid in full."

She huffed, her dark gaze sliding over my guys.

Jacob stood, murder in his eyes. "In. Full."

A hint of fear tightened her expression.

"Fine. Consider it paid." She squared her shoulders, pushing out her breasts, and sauntered past them with a seductive sway of her hips as if she hadn't just tried to kill me or they were ready to kill her.

Priam's magic turned into a blazing heat. Darkness enveloped me for a second then I dragged my eyes back open. My guys now crouched around me, bodies tense, eyes filled with fear. Sebastian muscled his way between Marcus and Priam, and dropped to his knees beside me. He activated the sleep glyph on his shoulder and pressed his hand over my heart.

Exhaustion swept over me, and I couldn't keep my eyes open.

Feet and bodies moved on the rooftop around me. Jacob wrapped me in his massive arms and lifted me while Priam's hands left my cheeks.

The guys argued as more heat blazed through me, and I drifted in and out of the dark nothingness. The not-water embraced me, but my father didn't appear. My guys drew close, stroking and caressing me, but the dream didn't fully form, leaving me aching with want. Then Kol's magic whispered through me, and the heat of his body pressed against me.

"We can't leave you for a minute," he said.

"This wasn't my fault." Pain crept into my body.

A curl of his magic unfurled in my chest. "You broke her link with Jacob."

"She was hurting him." There hadn't been anything else I could have done. Whether she'd wanted to or not, she'd almost killed Jacob and I'd had to protect him.

"So she hurt you back." His voice slid soft and sensual across my senses and his magic sank low within me. "They can't live without you."

"I can't live without them." I ached for more of his magic, for him to touch me. "Without any of you."

The magic in my chest swept away like fog in a sudden wind. "I'm not yours."

"But I want you to be." Jeez, sexy dream Kol wasn't being very sexy. He'd never been so hesitant before, but I guess even my subconscious realized what I had with him was broken.

"It's just my nature influencing you," he said, and his body heat drew away from me, leaving me cold.

The pain taunted me, promising to scream back to life when I woke, and the soft darkness and the not-water no longer wrapped around me. I was suspended between everything and nothing. The guys said things. The world whirled by. Kol's magic unfurled in me for a moment, but my dream-Kol didn't visit again. More heat sank into my body, vanquishing the pain, and then I heard voices, far off, arguing.

No, not far off, whispering... and I could only hear them because Jacob's claim enhanced my hearing.

"You can't put her to sleep again." That sounded like Marcus.

"She's in no condition to solidify our bond." Gideon. "She's still pulling strength from the brand."

"She's going to have to be. We need you when we face those witches." Marcus again.

"Marcus—" That was Jacob's low rumble.

"I've recovered a bit of magic." For a second I didn't recognize that voice then remembered it was Priam's. "I can give her a little more strength."

"Let her rest." Gideon.

"The temporal freeze ends within the hour. We've run out of time," Marcus said. "Give her as much as you can."

"This isn't the way it's supposed to happen," Gideon replied.

"It's okay." I tried to open my eyes but my lids were too heavy.

"Do it," Marcus said. "You go into a fight like that, you're going to get killed, and that will be worse for her."

A door opened with a soft shushing as if it brushed against carpet, and a weight settled beside me. A warm hand—although not as warm as Kol's—cupped my cheek. Heat and strength seeped into my body. It wasn't much, but it was enough for me to open my eyes.

I lay under a light downy comforter with a big burgundy and green pattern on it. Priam sat on the bed beside me, pouring his healing magic into me, but his complexion was gray and his body shook. He'd already helped heal all of us this morning and had been working to stabilize Cassius. I doubted he had much left, especially since he'd just saved me from Victoria.

The light in his eyes stuttered and darkened and he pulled his hand away. "That's the best I can do. How do you feel?"

Achy and exhausted and dizzy. "Okay."

Marcus snorted. "You're not okay. But you're alive."

I dragged my gaze past Priam. Marcus and Gideon stood in the doorway, but the door was wrong. The doors on Sebastian's rooms had been white, this was dark brown. The walls were also cream and the carpet was burgundy, a match to the comforter. Not at all Sebastian's color scheme.

Marcus's hair was mussed as if he'd kept running his hands through it. His wolf looked like he would take over at any moment and he was keeping himself together by willpower alone. Gideon was gray and trembling. He looked worse than Priam and the glow in his eyes was barely there.

"How long was I out?" How long had Gideon been

trying to hold it together while his soul was shattering because we hadn't solidified our bond?

"Over four hours," Marcus said, his expression grim.

"And Victoria?" I wanted to believe that it was over, that she was satisfied with almost killing me, but I doubted her anger was so easily quelled.

"Still fucking alive." Marcus shot a hard glare at Gideon. "But we're about as far from Rouge as we can get."

"We're in a suite in the Addington Inn," Priam added. "Courtesy of Mr. Bane."

Well, that was about as far away from Rouge as we could get. The Addington was on the opposite side of town from the Quarter, and I wasn't going to ask how many strange looks we'd gotten walking into the most expensive hotel in the city.

"We'll catch you up after." Marcus jerked his chin at Priam and nudged Gideon into the room, his expression turning apologetic. "We're short on time and I know this isn't what either of you want, but—"

"It's okay." I reached out my hand to Gideon, my heart breaking for him. I needed him so much it hurt, my soul just as splintered as his. I had my bonds with Marcus and Jacob helping me, but Gideon didn't have anything. I couldn't imagine how much he hurt.

Marcus and Priam left, and Gideon stared at my hand. "You're still pulling strength from the brand. You're too weak."

"And you're about to fall over. If we wait much longer, neither of us will be able to do anything."

"This isn't how I wanted our first time together to be." He eased onto the bed where Priam had sat.

"Neither of us are dying, so it's already better than my first time with Jacob." I traced my finger over his forearm along the gold thread of his brand, drawing a soft sigh from him. "And we're not having sex in Victoria's bed. Another plus."

"Your first time with Jacob was in her bed?"

"And I kicked her out of her own room."

He captured my hand, his palm pressing mine to his brand, making heat and power flutter in my forearm. "Marcus was right. You don't have any sense of self-preservation."

Not when it came to my mates. "I'd do anything for you, for all of you."

It was crazy that I'd fallen in love with them so quickly. Perhaps it was the soul bonds, but I didn't think so. The bonds were merely a representation of what was fated to be. Even if they hadn't formed, I would have fallen in love with them. Even Gideon. Most of all Gideon. He was the one whose soul best fit mine. We were both willing to do anything and sacrifice it all to do what was right and protect innocent lives.

Marcus I needed for his ferocity, his wild passion that made me feel alive. Jacob grounded me, strong and steady. And Kol—

My throat tightened. Even if Kol wasn't my mate, he was my joy. Playful, mischievous, a reminder to enjoy life. And I'd taken that away from him, reminded him of the horrors he'd experienced during the war.

"Hey." Gideon brushed my hair away from my temple. "We don't have to do this."

I cupped his cheek, my body and soul aching for him to hold me, kiss me, fill me. "But I want to."

He closed his eyes and leaned into my hand. The tension melted from his body, and the fear I'd been holding that we'd never figure things out, that I'd always have a broken part of my soul, released from my chest. We still hadn't figured anything out yet, but we were making the first step.

He pressed his lips to the inside of my wrist. The kiss was tender, soft and sensual at the same time. It reached something deep within me, and my ache for him swelled, my heart and soul overflowing with a love so deep there was no beginning or end. It was all-encompassing, unconditional, warm. There'd never be another lonely, cold night. I would never be alone again. I'd never need to hide or fear for my life. It was comfortable, secure, and sure.

He raised his gaze to mine and sizzling desire swept into the comfortable warmth. His summer-sky eyes were perfect and clear, radiating a brilliant white angel glow. Need as intense as Jacob's and as ferocious as Marcus's dilated his pupils. I'd thought I'd already seen the full intensity of his emotion, his desperation when the zip OD had made me try to kill myself, his anger, his determination, but this desire was consuming. It sucked all the air from my lungs, from the room, and crackled, teasing licks of electricity through his brand on my arm. In this moment the world outside this room, hell, beyond his perfect blue eyes, didn't exist. There was only him and his desire, an aching, throbbing match to mine.

"Kiss me," I breathed.

Groaning, he leaned in and pressed his lips to mine. The kiss was soft, as if he was afraid to release the passion I'd seen in his eyes. And given that I was still weak, that didn't surprise me. For a second I feared my buzz would return. It had the last time we'd kissed. My power had threatened to overwhelm me and hurt him. But I was exhausted and magically spent. The hollowness in my chest where my power blazed was still there. And if Sebastian couldn't figure out how to keep me from exploding, this might be the only chance I'd get with Gideon.

God, please, don't let this be it. I wanted time to explore his body, savor the feel of him pressed against me, and we didn't have the time for that now.

I ran my palms over his buzz cut and drew him closer. He teased the seam of my lips. I opened, and he deep-ened the kiss, stroking his tongue against mine, building the desire already blazing within me. My breath picked up. So did his and his body trembled with restraint. My head spun, dizzy with blood loss and need.

He tugged the comforter away from me and shifted to lie beside me. Someone had cleaned me up and I wore a baggy T-shirt and the white lacey thong Kol had gotten me. My bloody T-shirt and cargo pants were gone.

Gideon slid his hand inside my shirt and skimmed his fingers along the side of my breast. I gasped into his mouth and arched into his hand, shifting his thumb to brush my nipple. My bra was gone as well.

He groaned, a low sound rich with masculine desire that thrummed through me to my core. The electricity in his brand curled over my elbow and danced over Jacob's brand. The pull of strength from Jacob to me increased, granting me the strength to fully embrace being with Gideon.

"Now there's a trick," he said against my lips.

"I hope Jacob doesn't mind." I grabbed the bottom of Gideon's T-shirt and drew it up.

He leaned back, shrugging out of his shirt, and my breath caught, all thoughts of taking strength from Jacob gone. I'd seen Gideon with his shirt off before, but now I could run my hands and lips all over that sculpted muscle. I traced my fingers down his washboard abs to his waistband.

He moaned and captured my mouth again with a demanding kiss, his restraint crumbling. Heat unfurled in my chest and licked blazing desire over my skin, his yearning so strong it defied the containment cuffs and could be sensed with what little magic I had left.

His need and love filled me, and his power danced over my arm, through Jacob's brand, and across my chest. I clung to his waistband, overwhelmed by sensation. He tugged off my shirt and drew my nipple into his mouth, rolling it with his tongue. *Oh, God, yes.* Even with Jacob's extra strength, I was dizzy again, my breath too fast.

He skimmed his hand down my belly, pushing his fingers inside my underwear and brushing through my curls. My breath hitched in anticipation. He captured my mouth again with his and grazed my clit with his thumb.

I gasped and he plunged into me, his tongue in my

mouth and his finger between my folds. My hips bucked, drawing him deeper into me. His breath picked up, matching mine. I grabbed his waistband again, but all I could do was hold on. He added a second and third finger, stretching me, and ground his thumb against my clit, while his lips, still locked on mine, breathed in every gasp and moan.

My desire spiraled tight, need thrumming through me, racing me to climax. The electricity from his brand danced over my skin, so much like my buzz, and yet I knew the power wasn't mine. But even with Jacob's extra strength, darkness danced at the edge of my vision, and I struggled to steady my breath. I needed Gideon inside me, needed to seal our bond, before I passed out.

I opened his fly and pushed his pants off his hips. He released me long enough to pull off his pants and my thong, then settled between my legs, his full erection brushing my folds. His summer-sky gaze captured mine, filled with desire and certainty, and he pushed into me with a steady, firm stroke.

Sensation rolled over me, my muscles contracting around him, a whisper of climax rippling through me. He withdrew and drove back in, again and again, slowly building his pace and my need. The fractures in my soul where Gideon's bond belonged warmed and melded together. I rocked my hips into his, matching his rhythm, taking all of him inside me. His soul filled mine and mine filled his, our essences woven together in a blazing bond, now a match to the bonds I had with Marcus and Jacob.

Gideon's gaze never left mine, connecting us completely. My pulse picked up, our breaths grew ragged, and my desire swelled. It wasn't the wild ferocity of Marcus's passion, or the twisting need of Jacob's magic. It was a rising wave, seeping into every cell in my body with sensation and light, building and building until I was alight with it, unable to contain it all.

It swept me over the edge, my orgasm rushing through me with glorious, breathtaking pleasure, sending stars sparking across my vision and racing through my body. He cried my name with his release, and his electric magic seared my skin.

My buzz roared in response, merging with his magic, suddenly fierce, powerful, out of control, and exploding out of me with a terrible blast.

CHAPTER 20

MY BACK ARCHED AND I SCREAMED, THE POWER TEARING through me. I couldn't control it, couldn't hold it back, couldn't even breathe. It made my pulse stall, and fear seized my chest.

Not again. Please, no. I couldn't burn Gideon again, and my magic was stronger than ever before. I didn't know where this blast had come from, but it exploded out of me like a super nova. He'd never survive. And God, the last time my power had exploded after sex, I'd branded Jacob, severed his bond with Victoria, and incapacitated myself.

But I couldn't stop it. It ripped at my soul, burning through my cells and blazing out of me. My wings burst from my back and my head jerked back. Power poured from my mouth, my eyes, my skin. My heart pounded. I couldn't catch my breath, and every muscle in my body clenched.

Someone screamed. The world shook and twisted. I

was trapped in blinding white agony for a second... an eternity... I had no idea how long.

Then the power released me and I collapsed onto my back, my wings flattened against the mattress and bumping the bedside tables on either side of me. Gideon grasped my shoulders, divine light radiating from his thankfully not-burned skin, but his expression was stunned and his breath too fast. The door crashed open and the rest of my guys, along with Priam and Sebastian, rushed in.

"What the—" Marcus's gaze landed on me, his eyes wide with fear, his fingers extended into claws.

Jacob held his biceps, his brand pulsing with golden light. He'd lost hold of his power and radiated dangerous intensity, his fangs fully extended, while Kol clung to the doorframe, panting, the hellfire in his eyes so strong it licked across his cheeks.

"Esther, your hands," Sebastian said, his voice sharp with warning, his eyes as wide as Marcus's. "Control your power."

"My power?" I couldn't figure out what he was saying, couldn't drag my thoughts past the explosion.

Gideon reached for my hand, and I dragged my gaze to follow his movement. A whisper of light radiated from my palm and—

My pulse skipped a beat. The containment cuff was gone. My wrist was still raw and burned, with the nasty red trail where the metal had melted down my forearm, but all trace of the cuff was gone.

I glanced at my other wrist. That cuff was gone as well.

Panic stole my breath and clenched cold in my chest. "You have to— I'm going to—" I squeezed my hands into fists. The hollow feeling in my chest was still there... sort of. As if I had some power, but not a lot. I had no idea where that blast with my climax had come from, but I needed those cuffs. I was dangerous. I was—

Gently pulsing with power.

A soft thrum, halfway between Gideon's electricity and Jacob's intense stillness, pulsed within me. And no grating buzz.

"Esther, can I touch your hand?" Sebastian asked, dragging my attention back to him, but I got the impression he was really asking my guys, since I was naked with Gideon still inside me.

Well, this was embarrassing. "Can I... we... ah... cover up?"

"Is anyone hurt?" Priam asked, his face pale and stunned on top of his gray exhaustion from before.

I met Gideon's gaze, his angel glow so bright I couldn't see his blue irises.

"You didn't burn me," he said. "I'm okay."

Oh, thank God. And in fact he looked good, better than when he'd entered the room. His complexion had returned to a healthy hue and he no longer trembled.

"Then I'll just step back into the hall." Priam eased past Kol and shut the door.

Marcus grabbed the comforter and tugged it over me and Gideon, while Gideon slid out of me and helped me sit up, making sure I stayed covered. My wings twitched, brushing the headboard, and I shifted to try and find a comfortable position with them.

The room looked like the center of a tornado, with the window blown out and the heavy curtains ripped from their rod. They lay half crumpled on the floor by the window and half hanging out of it. A sharp wind yanked at a scrap of the window sheer, caught in a shard of glass, whipping and twisting it with the promise of a wild summer storm. The TV, its screen cracked, and the bedside lamps, also broken, were on the floor, while the burgundy reading chair by the window lay on its side. A chunk of something metal—the containment cuffs? — had lodged in the ceiling... and in the wall across from me... and the wall by Kol's head.

Jeez. Sex with my guys was getting dangerous and expensive.

Sebastian knelt beside the bed and held out his hand. I extended mine and he took it.

Still no buzz. I didn't know if I should be thrilled or terrified. At least my buzz had given me some warning when my new, powerful magic was about to erupt.

"Gideon, can you give her a little power?" Sebastian asked.

My heart skipped a beat and I tried to yank my hand back, but Sebastian held tight. "Are you sure that's safe?"

"Just a little," he said. "In the very least, you need it to pull your wings in."

Gideon took my other hand and closed his eyes. The electricity in his brand swelled for a second and warm light filled me. I held my breath, waiting for my buzz to roar to life, but my skin didn't even tingle.

"Try pulling in your wings," Sebastian said.

Gideon ran his thumb over the sensitive skin between

my shoulder blades. I gasped, desire heating me again, and concentrated on pulling my wings into my body, not straddling Gideon and taking him deep inside me like I wanted to.

Light flared and my wings sank under my skin with a strange overly full sensation in my chest. I didn't think I'd ever get used to that. And my buzz was gone. No stinging or biting or miniature muscle seizures. I didn't ache or itch or anything. My buzz hadn't even been reduced to post-nicotine levels—not even those early days when the nicotine patches had worked really well. I wasn't wearing the containment cuffs and it was gone. "I don't feel like I'm holding an electric fence anymore."

I couldn't get past that. How could it just be gone? I'd had it for years.

"So what does that mean?" The muscles in Jacob's jaw flexed and some of his vampiric intensity eased away. The glow in his brand had vanished and it no longer looked like it hurt him.

Sebastian's lips curled into a wicked smile. "What do you see?"

"What do you mean, what do we see?" Marcus said with a huff of frustration.

"What do you *see*," Sebastian pressed.

Marcus glared at him. "My mate."

"An angel," Kol said, his gaze unfocused, his expression still stunned, high on the sexual energy Gideon and I had just released. "Her essence now says she's an angel."

"You've broken the spell hiding your essence and power." Sebastian squeezed my fingers then released my hand. "Your magic is no longer trying to break free, so you're no longer going to explode. Although you still have no control and you're dangerous."

Gideon wrapped his arms around me. "Oh, thank God."

"I'll send you my bill if you survive the witches," Sebastian said.

"Of course you will." Marcus rolled his eyes at Sebastian.

"Didn't I already pay with all that extra magic?" I couldn't believe my buzz was gone and—

I mentally reached inside myself, searching for the fractured part of my soul where Gideon's bond had been. I couldn't find it. The ache of our unfulfilled bond was gone, and my connection to Gideon was strong and sure and flooding me with love.

In fact, I could feel love from Marcus and Jacob as well. Kol was still dazed, and Sebastian... I had no idea what Sebastian was feeling. His emotions were a strange, sliding mix that raced through me too quickly to figure out what they meant. But the emotions from my guys were real, not the weird temperature changes I'd been used to. And while the room's temperature was on the warm side, I couldn't tell if that was just the way it was or my unusual empathy.

Gideon captured my lips in a quick kiss that stole my breath, and pressed his forehead to mine. "I really want to stay, but—"

"You have to stop the witches." I ached for him to stay, as well. I hadn't gotten nearly enough of him, or any of them, but my desires could wait.

"We think we might have figured out what they're after," Marcus said.

"The mayor's close personal friend Ambassador Hollaway is stopping in town for a private dinner with him and quick refueling for her jet before she continues on to Rome," Jacob said. "Her plane is landing in twenty minutes at Landry Airport."

"Have you called to warn her?" Gideon asked.

"We were about to when—" Marcus slid his gaze over the room.

"We'll call on the way." Gideon captured my soul with his summer-sky gaze. "Essie, I—"

"Go," I said, my voice breathy. If he didn't leave, I was going to lose what little restraint I had.

"I'll keep an eye on her," Sebastian said, his wicked smile gleaming in his eyes.

Marcus huffed. "That doesn't make me feel better."

"Ah... guys?" Kol staggered closer to me, his eyes still unfocused as he pointed at my arm. "Her wrist."

Jacob steadied him and shot Gideon a worried glance. "We know, her cuffs are gone."

"You need to bleed that excess off before we go," Gideon said to Kol.

"No— Well, yes, but—" Kol shook his head. "It's not that, it's—"

Seductive heat swept through me, filling me with sudden, desperate desire. I ached for my guys. All of them. In bed with me. I moaned and leaned into Gideon. He was the closest. I'd start with him. I needed his hands and lips on me. I needed him in me. Now.

Kol squeezed his eyes shut, and the heat vanished but

not all of my yearning for satisfaction. I drew in a ragged breath, trying to focus. The guys needed to leave. Sex could wait.

"Sorry." He tipped a bit and Jacob caught him before he fell over. "Just... Essie's concealment charm is dead."

"You must have burned out Mavis's spell when you broke the one concealing your true nature," Sebastian said.

Kol dragged his gaze to his wrist with exaggerated concentration. "My charm's dead, too." He grabbed Jacob's wrist. "So is yours."

"Shit," Marcus said. "The witches can find us."

"And you're not going to stop us!"

The witch with the deadly spider tattoo and the bat wings flew through the broken window. Her wings vanished with a billow of black shadow laced with red demonic magic, and she rammed her shoulder into Marcus, shoving him back into Jacob.

Fear licked cold around me, but I couldn't tell who it came from.

Kol lurched toward her. "Stop." A wave of his seductive magic exploded within me with a full-body climax that seized every muscle with glorious contractions and shot stars across my vision. *Oh, my God. That was— Oh. My. God.*

I sagged into Gideon's arms, dizzy and gasping, boneless with bliss and unable to move.

The witch, the real target of Kol's magic, moaned with pleasure. Sebastian grabbed her arm and Marcus grabbed the other so she couldn't activate any of her glyphs, but she jerked her head back and screamed.

Power crashed into me. Kol and Sebastian gasped and dropped to their knees, also sensitive to the witch's magic. Then a physical, invisible force exploded from her and slammed into us. My head and shoulder smacked the headboard, slicing pain through my temple and my collarbone.

Gideon's cheek slammed into the wall beside me, and his eyes rolled back. Sebastian hit the bedside table, arm-first, with a sickening crack, and screamed in agony, and Kol smashed his face into the wall, breaking his nose. Marcus's head snapped back with enough force to crack the wallboard, while Jacob's big body indented it before he sagged to his knees.

The fear swelled, clenched in my chest as a real emotion, and curling over my forearms with frost.

The witch teetered, barely able to stand. She drew in ragged wet gasps, as if casting a spell with so much power had hurt her more than it had hurt my guys. I couldn't figure out her plan. In a few seconds, at least a few of my guys would regain their bearings and they'd have her again. I didn't think she had any power left, and didn't know if she could channel magic from her outside source in her condition. But she dropped to her knees and pressed one palm over her heart and the other to a web tattoo on her biceps. She gasped two words in a language I didn't understand.

"Shit. No." Sebastian, his expression still dazed, heaved toward her, but another wave of power crushed my chest as Sebastian's fear frosted past my elbows, stung my cheeks, and misted my breath.

The blast wasn't as powerful as the first one, and it

didn't pound any of us into the walls, but it shot thick, heavy spider webs out of the witch's body.

The door jerked open. "What was that?" Priam asked, taking a step into the room. His eyes flashed wide as thick strands of web seized him, capturing him in the doorway.

Sebastian was caught mid-grasp, his hand outstretched, only a few inches away from the witch, straining to reach her. Jacob was halfway to his feet, while Marcus had crawled to his hands and knees. Kol tried to turn his head, but the webs had trapped him with his cheek against the wall. Gideon wrenched against the strands, pulling against the ones stuck to my face and shoulders and jerking me toward him.

My mind raced and my teeth chattered. Most of me was under the comforter and not stuck, but without a weapon and almost no magic, there wasn't anything I could do.

The witch's eyes rolled back, and the webs twisted around her body and lifted her off the floor. Blue lightning crackled from her and raced along the strands. It sliced into me, and all my muscles seized as if I'd been hit with a Taser, then released, leaving me twitching and gasping.

Holy crap. If that was what the spell did, I needed to figure out something fast. I wasn't sure how many more of those I could take.

"What the hell is this?" Marcus growled.

"Give it a second," the witch said, her voice ragged and wet, a wild gleam in her eyes.

Sebastian strained to reach her. "If you stop the spell now, you'll still live."

The witch jerked her head to face him. Billowing shadow and demonic mist wept from her eyes, like the magical tears Sebastian had cried when I'd given him too much magic, except hers were made of darkness instead of light. "I'm willing to die for my cause. Are you willing to die for theirs?"

Come on. Think of a way out.

But another blast of lightning swept through the web, stronger than the last, stealing my thoughts. It poured into my body, raced along my nerves, and sliced into my heart. The witch's body seized with ours, and the spell, when it released us, left her panting as well.

Except the spell didn't fully leave me. It crackled in my chest and wrapped tight around my heart. I couldn't draw a full breath and still had no idea how to use the fact that I wasn't fully restrained.

"You think you'll be a martyr, but you won't." A divine light tear rolled down Sebastian's cheek, but before it could sink back into his skin a strand of web curled over his face and the tear sank into it.

"My sisters... will remember me," the witch gasped with a sneer. "Are you... going to tell your friends... their fate?"

Pressure imploded inside me, the power sucking in tight around my heart then rushing into the spell. I gasped, my limbs suddenly weak, my head spinning as if I'd let Jacob feed and then stood up too fast. My magic poured out of me through the web, with little crackles of blue lightning that raced along the strands and into the witch.

"It's a draining spell," Gideon said, slicing a blade of

light through the comforter. He wrenched his hand up and slashed through the web holding him, but the webs reformed, captured his hands, and pinned it above his head to the wall.

Kol moaned, his face tight with pain. He'd managed to get his hand a few inches from his boot, but didn't draw his knife. If the webs could reform, we needed to get smart with cutting them. But how the hell were we going to do that? I was getting weaker by the second and it looked like the guys were as well.

CHAPTER 21

ANOTHER MINIATURE IMPLOSION POUNDED IN MY CHEST and the stream of strength from me into the web turned into a flood. Fear frosted my body and made my pulse race, the emotions inside me so strong it was hard to think straight.

Light flared in Gideon's eyes and his palms glowed with a divine light strike, but the witch glanced at him and the webs encased his hands.

"It's not just a draining spell. It's a full leach," Sebastian said, the web gathering more divine light tears as they welled in his eyes and slid down his cheeks. "It's going to take everything. Magic, essence, and soul. Hers as well."

"And it's going... straight to my sisters," the witch said, her body trembling.

"So killing her won't stop the spell," Jacob said.

The witch laughed a weak, manic laugh. "My sisters have control now. They'll carry on our mission to kill the ambassador. We will win the war."

"What war?" Gideon asked.

The witch's head lolled to the side as if it was too heavy for her to hold up. The billowing shadow and demonic mist leaking from her eyes twisted around her neck and down her body. "Did you honestly think killing Michael and Rafael would stop us?"

"But you're human." At least I thought she was human. The guys hadn't said the witches were anything other than glyph witches with a connection to worship magic. And God damn it, the fear inside me, which I knew was a combination of everyone in the room, was overwhelming.

I clenched my jaw and concentrated on locking the guys' emotions deep within me. I had to get control, do something. There had to be a way out of this. It didn't matter that I knew next to nothing about magic. I couldn't give up.

"If we win... I'll be more than human. My goddess... will transform me," she said.

A whisper of my own fear swept through me, and I prayed her *goddess* wasn't actually alive and was, like Sebastian had said, a super in a catatonic state used to power the worship magic spell.

"You'll be dead," Marcus growled.

"I'll be alive... in my sisters and my goddess." Her eyes rolled back and her head dropped forward, but her chest still rose and fell with quick, desperate breaths.

"Sebastian, is there a way to break the spell?" Gideon asked.

Sebastian strained to get closer to the witch. "If I could touch her—"

The witch gasped and her head jerked up as the webs yanked Sebastian back, pinning him to the bedside table beside me. "I can feel what you are, sorcerer."

Lightning shot over the web, and we all jerked taut, our muscles painfully contracted for an agonizing... second? Minute? God, it felt like forever. It released me and I lay limp, my head and shoulders still caught in the web, every muscle twitching. More of my magic and strength were sucked from me and even the guys' frosty fear started to melt. My empathy was fading and so was I.

"You think by touching me you can break this spell?"

"You seem to think so," Sebastian said.

Weak electricity flickered through Gideon's brand, but it didn't pull strength and I didn't pull strength from him or Jacob. We were all too weak.

The webs jerked Sebastian forward, capturing his hands behind his back and bringing him nose to nose with the witch.

"I'll drain you... first. Your touch doesn't scare me." She planted her lips on his and inhaled.

Sebastian screamed and brilliant white light poured out of his mouth into the witch. Her body shook and the lightning in the web crackled and snapped, slicing agony through me.

Marcus growled and wrenched against the strands, his fingers turning to claws, fur covering the backs of his hands, but he couldn't get enough movement to slice through the web.

Sebastian's complexion turned gray, and he gasped and choked on his power. But the witch also was choking. Her body wracked with strangled coughs, desperate for air, and her muscles clenched and unclenched. The webs tried to jerk her away, but she grabbed Sebastian's head and clung to him.

"I'll have all... of your magic. I'll take every last drop."

The strands holding me trembled, the biting lightning and the sucking pressure sputtering and flaring with painful jerks to my body and soul.

Jacob heaved against his strands, but even with his enhanced strength he couldn't break free. Kol slid out the knife from his boot and flicked the blade so fast I almost didn't see it move, slicing through one of the strands on his arm. The strand didn't reform.

Tears of divine light poured from Sebastian's eyes. The webs sucked it up, and the sputtering and flaring grew jagged.

"Essie, flood the spell with your magic," Sebastian gasped, light blazing from his mouth into the witch. "Burn the spell from the inside out."

"No," the witch screamed, and the pull inside me wrenched at my essence.

Another snap of agonizing lightning, and Kol flicked his blade through another strand of web that didn't reform.

"More power and it'll be too much for the spell to transfer," Sebastian said.

I strained to reach my power, but even my empathy was gone. "I'm out. Gideon?"

"I can't transfer like you can. I can only—" He squeezed his eyes shut and his brand on my arm blazed as his power flooded me, drowning me with magic. "Take it."

I fought to catch my breath. It was too much, too quickly. My body was on fire, but my buzz still didn't make an appearance. The room turned frigid, frost covering every exposed inch of my skin, and the guys' fear and determination crushed around my heart.

"Pour it into the web," Sebastian said.

"It won't be enough," the witch screamed, and she opened her mouth wider, the stream pouring out of Sebastian swelling.

The web's lightning sliced into my body and the pull reached into my soul, hollowing me out. I fought to focus Gideon's power on the web around my head and shoulders, send it pouring through those strands, but the magic raced to my palms caught under the comforter instead.

Shit. Refocus it. Come on. Move to the strands.

"Essie—" Sebastian gasped. The glow in his skin was gone and he looked fragile, like he was made from tissue paper. "Now. Do it now."

I fought hard to move the power to the strands, then realized that was stupid, shoved my hands from under the comforter, and seized the closest strands on my shoulders. Power surged from my palms into the webs. Lightning roared through me and all my muscles seized again. The suck from the spell sputtered and surged.

The witch howled and her manic laughter returned. "That's all you've got?"

"No," Gideon said, and more power blazed through me into the web.

Kol sliced through one last strand of web and lunged, driving his knife into the witch's heart. She screamed, and light erupted under Sebastian's skin. He lit up like the sun, too bright to look at. Magic roared from him and blazed along each strand of the web. It merged with mine, stealing all breath and thought with its force, and together it was enough to ignite the web.

Fire raced through the strands and engulfed the witch, burning her and the spell into ash.

Sebastian fell to the floor and didn't move, and Priam took a staggering step from the doorway toward him, but sagged against the wall before he could take another step. Marcus, already closer to Sebastian than Priam, crawled over to him and checked his pulse.

"He's alive."

Gideon wrapped his arms around me and I leaned against him, shaking, my skin blazing with fiery agony. I was afraid to look at my hands to see how badly they were burned, and couldn't tell if they were because all of me hurt. Maybe all of me was burned, but Gideon wasn't reacting like I was so I just had to trust that I wasn't. Jacob didn't try moving, just slid down the wall, gasping, and Kol collapsed to his knees beside the witch's big pile of ash.

The wind whipped through the window, tossing the ash around us.

Kol coughed, turned away from the pile, and covered his mouth and nose. "That's just gross."

"Who can move?" Gideon asked.

"Give me a minute," Jacob said, his head between his knees and massive chest heaving with deep breaths.

"I need more than a minute," Priam said.

Marcus sat back on his heels and pressed his hands to his chest. "I don't think I can shift this away."

"You can't," Sebastian said, still lying face down on the floor. "It's your essence and soul that's been injured, not your body."

"If one of you could hold my hand and make out with Essie, that would be great," Kol groaned.

"All you, Gideon," Marcus said. "You're the closest."

Jacob grunted his agreement.

Sebastian half raised his hand—still face first in the floor. "I'm close, too."

"Really?" Jacob lifted his gaze, his eyes dark with warning. "You want to make out with Essie?"

Sebastian snorted. "Jeez, you guys are so easy. You honestly think I would with all her mates in the room?"

Marcus rolled his eyes at him. "You can't even raise your head and you're already fucking with us. You sure you're not part demon?"

"Not the last time I checked," Sebastian said.

Gideon held out his hand to Kol. "Come on. We were already short of time before that witch arrived."

Kol climbed onto the bed, knelt beside Gideon, as far away from me as he could get, and took his hand.

Gideon shifted so I wouldn't have to strain my neck to kiss him. "Not sure how much you'll get out of this with our current... mood."

"It'd be better if Jacob bit you," Kol said to me, a whisper of hellfire in his eyes, "but we don't have time for that."

Yeah, and I didn't think I was up for that. And yet the thought of Jacob's bite still sent a shiver of need racing through me. A whisper of heat, one of my guy's desire, licked across my skin.

Kol raised his eyes. "Okay, maybe just thinking about Jacob's bite will help."

Well, hey. Bonus for Kol. Just thinking about sex with any of my guys turned me on. I was still exhausted and sore, but that didn't mean I didn't desire them... and that included Kol.

I shoved that thought away and slid my naked body against Gideon's, drawing a low moan of desire. He tangled his free hand into my hair and kissed me. For a second the kiss was tender, uncertain, then he groaned and released his desire, sending a wave of heat over me. His tongue stroked mine and his fingers dug into my scalp with delicious pressure. I rubbed my hands up his muscular chest and slid my leg over his to get closer, brushing my already slick core against his thigh.

His breath picked up and his erection pressed against my hip, taunting me, begging me to straddle him. God, even sore and exhausted I still wanted to have sex with him. But we didn't have the time. Jeez, why was that so hard to remember?

"Tonight," I gasped against his lips. "After the witches."

He tipped his head back and drew in a ragged breath. "After the witches."

"Are we good?" Marcus asked.

"Yeah," Kol said, but he was curled forward, his forehead pressed to the mattress, his breath fast and body trembling.

"You sure?" I asked. He should have looked satisfied

and relaxed, like he had in Voth's theater box, not... whatever the hell this was.

"Un hunh. Just. Need. A minute." He shuddered, and a whisper of mist filled the air.

"Kol—" Instinct made me reach for him before common sense kicked in

He jerked back, the hellfire in his eyes doing nothing to hide the pain. "Please. Don't."

"Jeez, man, she's not going to hurt you," Marcus said.

"I know." But the look in Kol's eyes and the gathering mist said I was already hurting him. Except, for a second, it didn't feel as if the hurt came from reminding him of the war, but from somewhere else. A desire, maybe? A yearning? Mist usually meant grief or regret.

I had no idea, and then he blinked and that vulnerability vanished.

"It's okay." I drew away from him, now more confused than ever, and turned to Gideon. "Go get dressed and stop those witches. We can deal with everything else when you get back."

"You're coming, too." Gideon pushed the comforter aside and climbed out of bed, not seeming to care that the room was crowded and he was naked and turned on. "Everyone is coming. No one is left alone."

"I'm in no condition to fight," Sebastian said.

"And even if I was in good condition," Priam added, "I'd be useless in a fight."

"I don't care." Gideon grabbed his boxer briefs and shook out the ash. "We're all going. You can wait in the SUV. If you're targeted, then at least someone will be close by to help."

"I'll go get Essie's new clothes." Kol hurried off the bed and into the hall, taking his mist with him. Physically he looked the best out of everyone. Guess there was a lot more sexual energy with my kiss with Gideon than he'd expected.

Gideon pulled on his briefs and shook out his pants. "Priam, have you got anything to bolster our strength?"

"You're kidding, right?" Priam said.

"Do angels actually kid?" Sebastian asked as he struggled to sit up.

"No," the guys said in unison, Priam with a sigh, Gideon as if it were a matter of pride, Jacob like it was fact, and Marcus with an eye roll.

If I hadn't been so exhausted, it would have been hilarious.

"Anything you can give us," Gideon said. "I'd like everyone to survive this fight."

Kol reentered with a bag of clothes. "I'm not one of Essie's mates, but I can still give Jacob a bit of a top-up, so you only have to worry about Gideon and Marcus," he said to Priam.

Priam glowered at him, shuffled over to Marcus, and grabbed his shoulder. Light radiated from his hand and Marcus drew in a deep, relaxed breath.

"That's all you're getting," Priam said.

"It's better than before. Thanks."

Gideon moved to him, his pants still in his hand, and Priam gave him an infusion of energy. I could feel it starting to seep into me through the brand and mentally clamped down on that. I was good enough to sit in the

SUV. Gideon needed every ounce of strength he could get.

He leveled his pale gaze on me. "Take half."

"You need it more than I do."

"Take. Half." Strength surged into me, breaking through my will to hold it back, and evened the imbalance between us so the brand no longer wanted to pull strength.

Priam stared at us wide-eyed for a second, then shook his head. "So it's true. The brand lets you share vitality."

"And takes it from the other if things get bad," I said. "You better not need it back."

"Love you, too," Gideon said, shocking the hell out of me, and he strode from the room.

"Did he just say—?" Sure, we'd had sex, but that didn't mean we knew each other yet. And while I knew in my soul that I loved him, it hadn't occurred to me that he'd come to that realization as well.

"We all do," Marcus said, brushing his lips across my forehead and leaving as well.

Kol set the bag of clothes on the bed without making eye contact with me, and everyone filed out—Priam helping Sebastian to stay upright. The clothes were a repeat of what he'd gotten me before. White lacy bra and matching thong, a T-shirt, and cargo pants. I changed, strode down a short hall with three other doors, and met them in a living room as opulent as Sebastian's, although this color scheme was gold and burgundy.

Wide patio doors led to a large balcony, complete with built-in barbeque and lounges that looked more like inside

furniture than patio furniture. Beyond my haggard glow-
ing-eyed reflection, dusk tried desperately to shine through
dark storm clouds with thin weak bands of pink light. We
were high enough to have a spectacular view of downtown
and Unity Park, where I'd been shot in the chest.

I fought back a shiver and forced my attention away
from the place where I'd almost died, as Jacob slid his
teeth from Kol's wrist and the incubus sucked in a shuddering breath. I caught a glimpse of blazing hellfire in his
eyes before he turned away, and could only assume Jacob
had used his full magic to feed.

Marcus set aside an empty duffle bag that had held
the gear we'd gotten from Operations and started
unloading the other one, adding to the lineup of equip-
ment and weapons on the floor.

Gideon ran a hand over his buzz cut and tossed a
phone onto the couch behind him. "Yours is dead, too,"
he said to Marcus.

"They're all dead?" Marcus asked.

"The leach spell drains every bit of energy. Even
batteries. If all of our phones were in that room, all of our
phones are dead." Sebastian, who sat on the couch with
his head between his knees, glanced up at us. "Did
anyone think to grab a charger when you raided Operations? I didn't think to grab mine when we left Rouge."

"Just great," Marcus growled, picking up the room's
phone. "Do you know how hard it's going to be
contacting the ambassador or mayor from a number that
hasn't been approved?"

"Just try," Gideon said.

"At least we can call for backup," Priam said.

Kol shook his head. "JP backup isn't close. They'll never arrive in time."

"Essie, take a Glock, an M4, and a sword." Gideon selected the weapons from Marcus's rows and set them aside.

"I should stay in the SUV with Sebastian and Priam."

"You should still be armed," Marcus said.

"Actually, she's in as good a condition as you and me, and she's not going to magically explode," Gideon said.

Marcus's back stiffened. "She's not going toe to toe with these witches."

"No, but she can ensure the mayor's bodyguard gets the mayor to safety, and with the M4 she can help keep the witches within the radius of the area containment master ward."

He had a point. Even though I was completely drained of magic, I still had combat training. So long as I kept my distance and stuck to using my firearms, I'd be helpful. And with these witches, my guys were going to need all the help they could get.

I knelt beside Gideon and accepted the sword, the sheath already secured to a belt. "Not sure how useful a sword will be, though."

"It's just a precaution," Gideon said.

Jacob secured two sidearm holsters to his belt and picked two of the Berettas from the row of guns. "The sword will be more effective against the vines than the Glock or the M4."

I was outfitted with my assigned weapons, extra magazines, and a bulletproof vest, along with one set of containment cuffs and a pocketful of zip ties with the one-hour containment spell on them.

The rest of my guys geared up with sidearms, extra magazines, and swords. Even Gideon took a sword, which worried me. It meant his magic was low enough that he feared he'd run out and wouldn't be able to manifest his divine light sword in the middle of the fight.

All the guys took a pair of containment cuffs and a handful of zip ties, and Jacob took the area containment master ward. He was the quickest of the group and would be able to run into the center of the fight and activate it. Then it was a matter of subduing the witches long enough to secure the cuffs or zip ties or both... if we could subdue them.

Gideon made it clear that subduing them was second to stopping them, since they were too powerful for us to not match their lethal force with our own. We couldn't afford to pull our strikes. That could get the ambassador, a civilian, or one of us killed.

Given how our last fight with the witches had gone, I had a feeling we were going to need everything we had just to keep them inside the master ward's radius, let alone subdue them long enough to cuff them.

CHAPTER 22

KOL HAD NO LUCK REACHING THE AMBASSADOR'S OFFICE OR the mayor's, so we left, taking the stairs down to the SUV in the hotel's parking lot. There wasn't anything else we could do.

Wind yanked on my ponytail and the clouds above rushed across the sky, the storm on the horizon growing larger by the minute.

My nerves thrummed with fear. The last time my guys had faced these witches, they'd almost died—and even knowing they were down one witch didn't ease my worries. It didn't help that I had just enough power for my empathy to curl a whisper of my guys' fear over my skin, chilling me despite the evening's humid temperature, nor the fact that none of us were at perfect health.

Kol and Jacob, who sat in the back, looked the best, while Priam looked gray and Sebastian kept flitting in and out of consciousness. Marcus and Gideon, sitting up front, looked like how I felt, tired and achy. I still had some fight in me, but I didn't know how much I could take.

Marcus flipped down the SUV's JP credentials and gunned it out of the parking lot. Rush hour was long past, but there was still a fair amount of traffic on the road.

"Okay." Gideon turned in his seat to look at me. "What do we know?"

Marcus swerved around a slower-moving sedan, jerking us in our seats. The driver stared at us wide-eyed as we sped past, and I didn't want to imagine the conversation we were going to have with the mayor when this was all over.

"Ambassador Hollaway's private jet is supposed to land at Landry Airport," Jacob said as he took a com from the com box and handed it to Kol.

"Which is about all we know." Kol took a com and handed the box to Priam.

Priam took a com, turned to Sebastian, who was unconscious, then passed the box over to me. "At least that witch confirmed they're after the ambassador."

With a squeal of tires, we made a sharp turn to the right, got off one of the busiest streets in the downtown core, and took a narrower, less busy street to get out of downtown. There were still streetlights to slow us down and vehicles to swerve around, but a fraction of the number on the other street.

"We also know that this isn't a public meeting," I said, taking a com and passing the box to Gideon. "That means no media and likely low security, even though she's an ambassador. The mayor probably didn't even request a bigger UCPD detail, since dinner and refueling can happen at the airport."

"Exactly." Gideon handed Marcus a com, took one for himself, and set the box on the floor by his feet. "So we need to get to the airport before Ambassador Hollaway's plane lands and subdue those witches."

"And all we'll have to worry about is the mayor's safety." Marcus slowed at a red light, glanced both ways, then gunned it through the intersection.

Kol huffed. "Given how he feels about us right now, he's going to *love* that."

"Let's just make sure he lives to yell at us another day," Gideon said.

We left the tall high rises of the city core, sped past strip malls and big box stores and car dealerships to the outskirts of town, and turned onto the airport's well-maintained country road. Even though the private airport didn't see a lot of traffic, that traffic usually had a lot of money, some of which the city hoped would be reinvested locally, hence the road's pristine condition.

Tall, wide hangars lined the left side of the road, and the light beacon on top of the control tower strobed across the dark clouds. We turned onto the airport's main drive, then took a quick right to go around the main building and head straight to the tarmac, but skidded to a stop in front of a closed gate with a small guard station.

A young man with freckles dusting his cheeks, wearing a security uniform that was a little too big for him, stared at us, his gaze locked across Marcus on Gideon—the most obvious super in the SUV with his glowing eyes, since Kol with his horns and hellfire was sitting all the way in the back and hard to notice with the low light.

Marcus lowered the window, and Gideon leaned across him and showed his credentials.

"JP," Gideon said. "I need you to call to the tower or your boss or whoever, and divert the ambassador's plane that's about to land."

The man frowned, but I couldn't tell if it was a frown of concentration or confusion.

"If the plane can't be diverted, the pilot needs to be told to stay at the end of the runway and keep the ambassador secure until it's safe. Do you understand?"

"Divert the ambassador's plane or secure the ambassador on the runway," the guy said as he raised the gate and reached for his radio. "Is UCPD coming?"

"Yes," Marcus lied, and he put the SUV in gear and drove away before the guy could ask anymore questions.

"But UCPD isn't on their way," Priam said, thankfully out of earshot of the security guard. "We didn't call them."

"You saw what it was like fighting one of those witches," I said. Someone's fear, probably Priam's by the size of his eyes, swelled for a second, just enough to give me goosebumps. "UCPD is all human. They'll get slaughtered if they show up." Hell, we were all supers and our chances weren't good.

Priam pursed his lips. For a second it looked like he was going to argue. Most angels didn't lie and they didn't disregard protocol, and even though I wasn't familiar with JP protocol, I was pretty sure calling in the local police for a situation of this size was required.

"I don't know how you do it, Gideon," he said. "Just the idea of disregarding protocol makes me uncomfortable."

"Me, too." The light in Gideon's eyes flared. "But the idea of slaughtered cops is worse."

We sped to the side of a large hangar and stopped in the shadows between the lights in front and behind it. With the spider-witch dead and her leach spell overpowered, the other witches had to know we were on our way. We had no element of surprise. But with Priam and Sebastian staying in the SUV, we couldn't just drive onto the tarmac.

"Priam, get in front," Gideon said as he got out. "If things go sideways, get Sebastian out of here."

Marcus shut off the engine but left the keys. Priam took the seat behind the wheel, and the fearful chill swelled again. Yep, definitely Priam's fear.

I got out, chambered a round in my Glock, and reholstered it, then shrugged my M4's sling over my head.

"You good?" Marcus's piercing green gaze darkened with his wolf's ferocious intensity, and he drew his Glock.

A gust of wind whipped my ponytail into my face and stole my breath for a second. "As ready as I'll ever be."

Jacob drew both of his Berettas, and Kol unsheathed the long daggers hidden on his back under his shirt. Another swell of chilly fear made me shiver. It looked like Priam wasn't the only one who was scared. In fact, if I concentrated, I could feel, ever so slightly, real anxiety from all my guys. I could even feel it from Kol, even though we weren't connected with a soul bond. The worry bled into my own fear and churned in my gut.

A thin streak of lightning sliced through the clouds and a few seconds later thunder rolled, low and ominous.

Swell. I gritted my teeth and locked down my emotions. I wasn't as good at doing it as an angel—although maybe I was, since I was an angel—but I could at least do it well enough to focus on the job at hand. I was a cop— no, I was a JP agent. This was my job and I could handle this. *Please, God, let me be able to handle this in my condition. Let all of us.*

Gideon and Marcus took point while Jacob and Kol took the rear, securing me in the center of our formation. A part of me, the part of my soul bound to them, wanted to argue that they were in just as much danger as I was, but they also had soul bonds compelling them to protect me and it was three against one.

We hurried around the edge of the hangar. The tarmac stretched ahead of us, a wide expanse of concrete. Two more hangars sat beside the one where we'd parked. The farthest one had an open bay door and light splashed out the wide entrance in a stark white rectangle stretching over the concrete ground. Beside that hangar sat the main building with most of the lights on and more hangars beyond creating a gentle arc embracing the tarmac.

A black sedan was parked about a hundred feet from the main building's glass back doors. A squat man with a large bald spot that caught the light leaned against the sedan's door, while a tall lanky man in a dark suit stood beside him. A few feet away, standing at the nose of the car to easily get to the mayor or hop back into the driver's seat, stood a bulky guy with a buzz cut. The mayor, his assistant, and his UCPD bodyguard Officer Brant Keels.

My stomach flip-flopped. It was just my luck the UCPD officer assigned as the mayor's bodyguard tonight would be someone who knew me and knew I'd gotten two partners seriously injured. He'd seen my partner Hank bleeding to death after the feral vampire attack, and had been there four and a half years ago for the aftermath of the fight with the werewolves that had made Marcus a super.

And now he was going to see me with glowing eyes. Would he think I was a nephilim? God, would everyone who knew me before I'd broken the spell on me think I was a nephilim?

I shoved that thought aside. Brant was a professional. No matter what he thought about me, he'd do his duty to protect the mayor.

"The mayor is still waiting," Kol said. "Looks like the ambassador's plane wasn't early and has yet to arrive."

I scanned the area around them. No sign of the witches. But there were a lot of places to hide: inside one of the hangars, in the shadows between the hangars, hell, even in the main building.

"Eyes open, everyone," Gideon said as we left the relative safety of the hangar's shadow and hurried across the tarmac.

The mayor jerked away from the sedan before we were halfway to him. He stormed toward us, and his assistant—clutching his jacket to keep it from flying open —hurried after him. Brant followed as well, using his longer stride to catch up, and dropped his hand to the grip of his sidearm, but didn't draw. His eyes, however, widened with surprise when he saw me and cold snapped over my skin, then vanished. Shit. He was afraid of me.

"What the hell are you doing?" the mayor demanded.

"Mr. Mayor, there's a situation," Gideon said calmly, no indication of the tension that radiated from him through our brand.

Brant's posture stiffened, but I didn't know if it was because Gideon had said the mayor was in danger or because of me.

"Of course there's a situation. There's always a situation." The mayor threw his hands up in frustration.

"You need to leave. Agent Shaw will escort you to your car." Gideon gestured to the sedan.

The surprise in Brant's eyes grew. Guess the chief hadn't told anyone I'd been reassigned to the JP, or perhaps his surprise was because Gideon had referred to me as agent, not officer. He, like everyone else, had probably figured I'd already been fired.

"What's it this time? More feral vampires? Zombies? A wild wolf pack?"

The muscles in Marcus's jaw clenched, but he kept his attention on the shadows between the hangars, letting Gideon deal with the mayor.

Brant yanked his gaze away from me to the mayor, and his surprise vanished behind a cool professional mask. "Mr. Mayor—"

"Ambassador Hollaway will arrive in a few minutes and I have every intention of telling her what kind of disaster you are." He turned to his assistant. "In fact,

Allen, make this an official memo to the Joined Parliament."

The assistant, Allen, glanced at Brant, who shook his head no, but Allen pulled out his phone anyway. "Recording."

"Can you please make your official memo in your car, as you leave," Gideon said, the light in his eyes growing brighter.

The mayor raised his chin in defiance. "I cannot."

"You should listen to the JP agents." Brant shifted to scan the area to his right and behind him.

"You need to get into your car," Marcus growled. "Now."

I forced my attention across the tarmac. Most of my guys had the hangars and the main building, so I joined Jacob watching the runway.

The wind yanked on my ponytail and tugged at my T-shirt and cargo pants. Small snaps of electricity crackled through Gideon's brand, while tense stillness radiated from Jacob's, and I fought to keep my grip on my M4 relaxed.

Lightning flashed, illuminating the dark sky and revealing a small jet coming in for a landing.

"The ambassador wasn't diverted," Jacob said.

Marcus swore.

Thunder rumbled in the distance, louder and closer than before. My pulse picked up. The tension of the team was palpable, chilling my skin and squeezing around my heart.

We knew the witches were out there. We knew they knew we'd killed their sister. Their attacks would be more ferocious now than before, and we had no idea which direction they were going to strike.

"Sir." Gideon grabbed the mayor's elbow and jerked him around to face the sedan. "You need to leave. Your life and the ambassador's life are in danger."

"Because you can't do your job," the mayor huffed.

"I can't believe I voted for this asshole," Marcus said. He jerked his attention to the mayor, his wolf threatening to break free. "Get. In. Your. Car."

The mayor yelped and Allen's face went white. Gideon yanked the mayor's elbow, getting him moving, and marched him back to the sedan, with Allen hurrying to keep up but keeping his distance from Marcus. I fell into step behind Gideon and Marcus, and Brant fell into step beside me.

"Shaw?" he asked, his voice low, his attention like my guys' on the area, searching for trouble.

Cold whispered across my skin, and I was grateful I was so low on power. I didn't doubt that Brant's fear and my guys' worry would have already formed ice on my hands and cheeks despite the humidity.

"It's complicated," I said, straining to see anything in the shadows. God, they were here. They were going to attack. Just where?

Something flickered at the edge of my vision. I tensed and jerked my gaze to it. The wind gusted and a plastic bag tumbled across the concrete.

"Are you a—?"

"She isn't," Jacob said. "We're dealing with two extremely powerful glyph witches. Get the mayor and his assistant out of here."

"We don't care how you do it," Kol added.

Another shift of shadow, but I couldn't see anyone or anything by the far hangar. Jeez, now I was jumping at shadows. I had better control of my emotions than this. But it was my fear for my guys and the memory of how they'd looked the last time they'd fought the witches that made my emotions so hard to control.

Lightning flashed again and a heavy raindrop splattered on my cheek.

The mayor jerked against Gideon's grip, but he held tight. "I'll have you written up! You'll be fired before you even get back to the Joined Parliament Operations Building."

"You go ahead and do that," Marcus growled.

Allen's face grew paler and he dropped back from the mayor to walk with me, taking Brant's place as he hurried to the sedan and opened the back door.

"Reckless risk of *human* life—" the mayor said.

"Ah, guys?" Kol said.

"What do you see?" Gideon asked, reaching the car and releasing the mayor.

"I sense—" Kol frowned. "I thought— Essie, do you sense anything?"

The mayor turned to Gideon, his finger raised. "Reckless destruction of city property—"

"I don't sense anything," I said, but then I wasn't concentrating.

"Do you know how much it cost to clean up Unity Park?" the mayor demanded.

Thunder cracked, explosive and sharp, making Allen jump with a yelp, and the clouds released rain that pelted me, instantly soaking my clothes and leaking into my eyes.

"Get in the car," Brant said.

The mayor didn't look away from Gideon. "Do you know how much it cost to clean up the cemetery?"

"Essie? Kol?" Gideon asked.

I closed my eyes and focused on how I felt. The witches' magic had been a pressure that had crushed me from the inside out and sent my buzz blazing. Except my buzz was gone. And the crush—?

A weight slammed into my chest, stealing my breath.

"And don't get me started on City Hall!" the mayor said, grabbing the car door. "Do you know how much—"

A massive pillar of ice dropped from the sky. It slammed onto the hood of the car with a crunching, squealing boom, and the mayor started shrieking.

CHAPTER 23

I JERKED MY GAZE AROUND, TRYING TO FIND THE WITCHES. Another weight crashed into me and shards of ice shot from the shadows between the two closest hangars. With a yell, the red-haired witch barreled toward us, ice blasting from her palms.

Brant yanked the shrieking mayor down and hurried him around the crushed front of the car. I grabbed Allen and did the same. My guys took cover behind the car as well, and Jacob fired two quick shots, but they slammed against an invisible shield protecting her.

"Jeez, she can have two spells going at the same time," Marcus said. "We need to get the area containment master ward out."

"Not until we've got eyes on the other one," Gideon said. "Essie, get the mayor into the main building. Jacob and I will lay down cover fire."

"She's protecting herself with a force field," I said. She wasn't going to care if the guys were shooting at her or not.

"She's not protecting her ice," Gideon said, sending a blast of divine light into a volley of ice shards and destroying them. "Go."

I met Brant's gaze, who gave a tight nod, and we hauled our civilians to their feet. The mayor's shrieking grew louder and Allen's fear made him trip over his feet.

Allen went down.

I grabbed the back of his suit jacket and wrenched him up as another weight slammed into me.

Holy crap. I forced my legs to keep moving, praying that whatever was being cast, my guys could deal with it, but a flurry of vines exploded from the concrete in front of the main building's doors.

The mayor screamed. Brant yanked him out of the way of a thick vine and fired one-handed, point blank, but the shot didn't destroy the vine and it kept surging toward them.

I drew my sword and hacked at it with all my strength. The blade sliced through and it burst into dust, but more vines were surging toward us.

"Gideon, do you see the other one?" I shoved Allen away from a vine and sliced another one in half.

Gideon leaped up beside me, cutting and hacking with his divine light sword. Rain pasted his T-shirt to his muscular chest and torso and made his cargo pants cling to his thighs. "No."

There had to be some place we could go, but without knowing where the other witch was, we couldn't make a run for it or we risked running straight to her.

Another crash of magic.

I gasped, stumbled, but managed to catch my balance.

Red's volley of ice stopped and another massive pillar of ice crashed from the sky.

Gideon yanked me back. Allen dove to the side, while Brant wrenched the mayor, whose shrieking rose in pitch and volume, out of the way. The ice exploded as it hit the concrete, shards slicing my right cheek and arm.

Lightning lanced overhead and thunder roared around us. The mayor gasped shallow, desperate breaths. If he didn't get himself under control soon, he was going to hyperventilate. His eyes were wide and his fear, mixed with everyone else's, tipped my empathy over the top and turned the water slicking my body into a thin layer of ice.

"Second witch at four o'clock," Jacob said over the coms as Kol leaped past me, slicing vine after vine, his blades a water-spraying whirl of steel.

Gideon wiped watery blood out of his eye from a gash in his forehead and glanced to his four o'clock. I hacked my sword through another vine and scrambled around a piece of ice to get to Brant and the others.

"To the hangar," I said to Brant, jerking my chin to the open one in the opposite direction from the vine witch.

More vines surged toward us. One grabbed Brant's arm and I sliced through it, somehow managing to keep my grip on my sword with my wet, icy hands. The mayor had his arms over his head and was sobbing, and Allen looked frozen with fear.

"Get moving," Gideon said.

But we couldn't, the vines surrounded us, blocking our escape, and no matter how much Gideon and Kol sliced at them, we weren't breaking through. The only way to stop the vines was to take out the witch.

"Jacob, target the vine witch." I hacked at a vine about to wrap around Allen's leg.

He fired at Vines, two quick shots, but Red jerked her hand up and her invisible shield sprang up in front of her sister, deflecting the rounds.

Shit—

Except the shield had shimmered on the second shot. Had it weakened?

Jacob fired again. The first shot deflected like the other first one and the second and third shots made the shield shimmer again.

"It's going to take more than a few shots to break through." I fumbled to shove my sword back into its sheath without cutting myself. "Jacob, save your ammo. I've got the larger magazine."

A vine swept toward me and I sliced it with my blade. No way was I going to be able to sheathe the damned thing. "Brant."

He turned to me, and I tossed him the blade, sliding it over the concrete for fear if I actually threw it, I'd hurt someone. He caught the weapon and hacked through a vine wrapping around the mayor.

I wrenched my attention back to Vines, flipped the M4 to fully automatic, and fired.

The rounds slammed into the shield. It shimmered and flashed. Red yelled a word I didn't understand, and another knee-weakening *thu-thud* of power slammed into my chest. Her shield in front of Vines flared, suddenly visible, and the rounds clattered to the ground.

I fought to keep standing and hold my finger on the

trigger. A vine seized my ankle. Gideon sliced it, while Brant severed another one racing toward my arm.

The shield shimmered again and a round broke through, driving through Vine's shoulder. She screamed and grabbed a tattoo on her forearm. The ground shook and another *thu-thud* of magic hit me.

I dropped to one knee and struggled to breathe and keep firing. But a stone pillar shot up from the ground, giving her protection, and her vines surged toward me. The mayor shrieked and Brant rescued him from a vine, while Gideon sliced through the vines coming after me.

But he wasn't fast enough and a thin vine slipped past his guard and seized my arm. I wrenched against it, but without a blade, I couldn't break free. Another vine twisted around the M4. Shit. If it pulled me down, I was done for.

I hit the sling release on the M4, but the vine had also wrapped around the sling and heaved me forward.

Shit shit shit.

"Essie—" Gideon gasped. His blade of light flashed at the edge of my vision, but wasn't close enough to save me.

I twisted, sliding the sling off over my head and arm. It caught on the vine around my arm, but Brant freed me, and I scrambled to my feet, abandoning the rifle.

Red, now almost at the car, raised her hands and hissed words I didn't understand. Another crush of power stole my breath, and lightning lanced through the clouds above us. It filled the air with electricity, and my pulse stalled. Back in City Hall, she'd used a lightning strike to temporarily immobilize the guys. That strike had been invisible and not overly powerful, but this—

"Lightning strike! Move! Move now!" I yelled.

Allen stared at me, still wide-eyed and frozen in fear. It was a miracle none of the vines had taken him down, while the mayor was the complete opposite, flailing and screaming.

I shoved Allen to get him moving—*please God, move*—and a surge of power swept from Jacob's brand down my hand and into Allen. He jolted and the frozen panic vanished. I had no idea what I'd done and there wasn't any time to think about it. We had to get out of the way.

A blast of lightning exploded from the sky. Jacob and Kol bounded away, Gideon released his wings and leaped into the air, and Marcus gritted his teeth and took it—thankfully he wasn't as close to the epicenter and had been twisting and slashing through the mess of vines to get to Vines.

Red took in ragged gasping breaths and Kol bolted toward her. My pulse stuttered, everything within me screaming to call out to him, to stop him. If Red had another lightning strike ready, Kol was dead. But this was the job and my guys had to stop the witches.

And my job was to get the mayor and his assistant out of there.

Marcus reached Vines and slashed at her, and Gideon shot a massive blast of divine light, burning a path through the vines and giving me, Brant, Allen, and the mayor an escape route.

"Get to the hangar." We bolted toward it while Marcus thankfully distracted Vines long enough for us to run through the path.

"Jacob, the master ward," Gideon said over the coms.

Another crush of power. One of my guys grunted. All of their breaths were heavy.

"*Vade*," Jacob said, and a swell of magic, not the same crushing power from the witches, washed over me.

One of the women screamed. Something small thudded in my chest and I realized it was one of the witches casting a spell. But without being able to access their worship magic, the spell wasn't nearly as powerful. *Thank God.*

"Keep them in the containment area," Gideon said over the coms.

I reached the edge of the hangar, drew my Glock, and wiped water out of my eyes. The mayor, Brant, and Allen, all panting, took cover behind the wall, with growing puddles of water forming around their feet.

"What the hell was that?" Brant gasped. "Are glyph witches really that powerful? They didn't say anything about falling pillars of ice or lightning from the sky in the advanced training for supers."

"They had access to extra magic." I glanced out the hangar door to cover our backs, but both of the witches were busy fighting my guys.

"Nine one one," a quiet voice said— no, not quiet, on the other end of a phone call.

Crap. I wrenched around to stop whoever was calling. If UCPD showed up, there'd be serious human casualties.

"Supers—!" the mayor said, his voice pinched and desperate.

"Don't—"

"Landry airport. Send everyone. I'm the mayor!"

"We need backup," Brant said to me.

"No." I shot him a glare and he flinched, afraid of me. That stung, but if it got people to listen to me, so be it. "You honestly think UCPD can help? A human fighting against supers is a death sentence. Trust me."

"Is that why you're now a super?"

The mayor gasped. "You're the human officer—?"

"Officer Esther Shaw," Allen provided.

"Are you her? The one who was assigned to the JP team?" He wrenched away from me, his fear freezing the water on my body, making my pants and T-shirt stiff and my teeth chatter. "Your eyes are glowing."

"I'm not a nephilim. It's complicated." We didn't have time for this. The guys were still battling the witches, and while they were holding their own, it was by the skin of their teeth.

But first I had to get the mayor to safety. Then I could go back and help.

I scanned the hangar. A metal security door sat at the back, past a stack of large plastic shipping crates and a small office area with three desks and half a dozen filing cabinets. "Brant. Take the mayor out the back. Priam?"

Please let him be paying attention to the coms.

"Yeah?" he asked.

Thank God. "We're in the first hangar beside the main building. Come around and get the mayor, his assistant, and bodyguard."

"Okay."

One of my guys screamed and fear clenched my chest. I didn't sense anything from the brands so it had to have been Marcus or Kol. I glanced out, looking for a shot that could help them, but Gideon was in hand-to-hand combat with Red, Marcus and Kol were fighting with Vines too far away for a good shot, and I had no idea where Jacob was.

Crushing pressure exploded in my chest. What the hell? Had the master ward lost power?

"What are you doing?" the mayor yelped.

"Brant. Move the mayor to the back of—" I wrenched my attention to Brant and my words stalled.

Allen had dropped his soaked suit jacket to the concrete floor and shoved up the sleeve of his button-down, revealing a colorful tattoo curling over his right arm that was far too similar to Red's. He clutched his wrist, covering whatever tattoo he'd activated, but whatever it was, it wasn't good. Brant, his body trembling, his eyes wide, had the sword raised and pointed at the mayor, while the mayor stood shaking in a puddle of water with his hands up.

"Drop your gun or I make Officer Keels here kill the mayor," Allen said.

"If I drop my gun, you'll still make Brand kill the mayor."

Allen's grip on his wrist tightened, his knuckles turning white, and I realized his tattoo wasn't exactly like Red's. It wasn't as complicated. There were blank spots where his skin showed through. Did that mean he wasn't as powerful? It probably meant he didn't have as many spells, but that didn't necessarily mean he wasn't just as strong as the women.

Another chest-crushing *thu-thud* weakened my knees, but they locked, keeping me up, and my body wrenched my Glock up and pointed it at Brant.

Panic stole my breath. *My body. No one else's. Please.* I couldn't have someone control me again. I couldn't be forced to hurt someone again. The memory of blasting my divine light into Kol's face made bile burn my throat. *No. Please God, no.*

I wrenched against Allen's magical hold, but all I did was tremble.

"Better yet, I'll make you and Keels kill each other, and then *I'll* kill the mayor."

Brant dropped the sword, drew his Glock, and pointed it at me, his eyes wide with terror.

"Stop. What are you doing?" the mayor cried.

"They say you're a deadly incident waiting to happen, Officer Shaw," Allen said with a dark chuckle. "What would everyone think if you killed Brant?"

My trigger finger flexed, and I mentally heaved at Allen's control, stopping myself from shooting Brant.

Brant's breath picked up, his chest heaving with desperate gasps.

Allen glared at me. "I said kill him."

His magic surged, squeezing around my heart. My trembling grew, my muscles painfully contracting as I fought him. But I wasn't going to hold out much longer, and I didn't have my buzz to help me this time. God, the last time the archnephilim or Ibizual had tried to control me, my buzz had saved me, burning through their magic.

Now, I had nothing.

Water in my hair trickled over my temple and dripped from my jaw. Brant's gasps turned to shallow pants. Another trickle of water slid down my temple and froze.

The mayor's gaze leaped over the three of us and he jerked to bolt to the back of the hangar. But Allen's power thudded into me and the mayor froze as well.

The power seizing my muscles shuddered for just a second, relaxing them then jerking them taut again.

"Shoot him," Allen snarled.

"No," I forced out.

No.

No. No. No.

I wouldn't and he couldn't make me.

Even if I didn't have my buzz, I still had some magic, and I was God damned going to use it to break Allen's control of me instead of freezing water on my face. I knew what my magic felt like. It was a thrumming electricity. Like Gideon's. It always blazed through my body and curled tight around my heart and in my back where my wings—my wings!—were.

"Shoot him." Fire erupted inside me, threatening to burn up what little control I had. "Shoot. Him."

I ground my teeth—me, I did—and mentally dove into the core of my being where my magic curled tight within me. With a scream, I seized it and wrenched my aim to Allen.

Shock flashed across his expression and the fire in my body surged. My hands trembled and shifted away from Allen. I heaved them the fraction back to aim at the center of his chest.

"Fine. If you won't kill him, he'll kill you." Another powerful *thu-thump* pounded in my chest. My fingers went numb and my Glock clattered to the ground.

Brant whimpered and fired. I fought to move, to drop,

to do anything, but knew I'd never be fast enough to dodge a bullet.

Agony exploded in my shoulder, stealing all breath and thought. Fear shot adrenaline through me, and my power erupted. It raced into every cell, consuming Allen's magic. I dropped to grab my Glock, but the mayor yelped, jerked forward, grabbed the sword, and awkwardly swung it at me, forcing me back.

Brant groaned again, the precursor to another shot. I dropped to the concrete and pain sliced across my cheek. The mayor, sobbing and gasping with tears streaming down his cheeks, swiped at me again.

I rolled out of the way and scrambled to my feet. I needed cover— No. I needed to stop Allen. If Allen was down, Brant would stop shooting, but I wouldn't be able to take Allen down without first dealing with Brant.

I dove for Brant. The muscles in his face twisted in agony, and he heaved his Glock aside just enough for the round to roar past my cheek.

The slide stayed back.

Out of ammo. Thank God.

I slammed my fist into his face with a quick jab that broke his nose and stunned him. His head snapped back, and I rammed my other fist into his temple with all my might. It wasn't easy to knock someone out with a few punches, and I prayed whatever damage I'd done could be healed, but I needed Brant out of the picture.

Please God, let knocking him out break Allen's control.

Brant's eyes rolled back and he collapsed.

I wrenched to face Allen, and he bolted for the back door.

Oh, fuck no. I raced after him, my muscles burning from having fought his possession magic.

Another *thud-thump* made me stumble. *What the fuck now?*

The mayor's sobbing turned to desperate howls. A gunshot roared behind me and blazing agony sliced across my shoulder.

"My spell might not be powerful enough to make the mayor kill himself," Allen snarled at me. "But I can make him kill you."

"I don't think so." I dove for him. He was a little too far away for a tackle, but with my momentum there was a chance I could make it.

I would God damn make it.

My wings burst from my back, catching just enough air for me to slam into Allen. We crashed to the floor. Allen shoved me off him, painfully twisting one of my wings, and the mayor's footsteps pounded toward us.

"Please stop. Please stop," he sobbed.

Another gunshot exploded, the sound monstrous in the mostly empty hangar. The round sliced through my right wing and pinged off a metal filing cabinet.

Allen scrambled to his feet. I grabbed his ankle, yanked him back to his knees, and he wrenched around to punch me in the face, but I hit first.

I slammed an uppercut, palm open, against his chin, and a blade of divine light burst from my palm. My power blazed through every cell in my body and shot out the top of Allen's head.

CHAPTER 24

MY POWER VANISHED, LEAVING ME COLD AND TREMBLING, with agony screaming through my shoulder and throbbing across my cheek. Allen crumpled to the ground, his eyes wide and lifeless, and I gasped out a relieved breath.

The sobbing mayor sagged onto his knees and tossed my Glock away. It skittered across the concrete and everything within me screamed that I needed to go after it, secure my weapon, but I didn't have the strength.

"Essie. Sit rep," Gideon said, his voice ragged. "Essie."

"Son of a—" Marcus growled.

"Just stay there," Kol said. "You too, Jacob."

I strained to hear past the coms and my rushing pulse for any kind of fighting outside, but I couldn't concentrate. All I wanted to do was pass out. At least this time only my shoulder was on fire, not my entire body. That was an improvement over the last couple of times, but I was having trouble focusing my thoughts to enjoy that and a hollow chill had seeped into my bones.

"I'm fine. Essie, answer," Marcus said.

"You're not fine," Jacob groaned.

Marcus snarled. "Well, neither are you."

They were all alive. All of them. They'd all spoken. And no one seemed to be in the middle of a desperate fight.

I staggered to my feet and stumbled to my Glock. Off in the distance, sirens screamed. Backup was arriving, thankfully not in time to join the fight.

"Essie." Gideon again.

Right. He'd asked a question. "Here," I gasped. "The mayor is secure."

"Good," Gideon said, his voice filled with relief. "Priam, where are you?"

"In the SUV, waiting behind one of the hangars." Which was where I'd told him to meet us.

The sirens grew louder, but the mayor didn't rush out of the hangar to his human help. He stared at me wide-eyed, his face white, tears streaming down his cheeks. "I couldn't stop myself. I just couldn't. How could you?"

"I have magic."

His gaze slid to my wings. "Because you're an angel?"

Yeah, duh. But if he was in as much shock as I was, I should give him a break for stating the obvious.

"Officer Keels couldn't do anything, either," the mayor said.

"You're human. Unless you made a demon-deal to become a witch, the odds of you winning a fight with someone like Allen are next to impossible."

Cruisers sped onto the tarmac and red and blue lights strobed into the hangar. Gideon limped to the hangar's mouth and my heart swelled. The rain had soaked his clothes and blood still wept from the gash over his eye, as well as from dozens of other gashes and punctures all over his body. His left arm was badly burned, his right was hugged tight to his side, and his face was pinched with pain. He looked like shit. He'd gotten worse than I had, but he was alive.

Half a dozen cops rushed in behind him, and someone radioed for EMTs. A few seconds later two paramedics rushed in. One went to the mayor, the other to Brant. Allen was clearly dead, his head in a growing pool of blood, his eyes vacant.

The JP SUV pulled up in front of the hanger and Priam hopped out. "Are the witches dead?" he asked.

"Yeah," Gideon said, his tone strange, but I was too exhausted and numb to figure out what it meant. "Take the team to Operations so Jacob can heal Cassius."

"Do we think the poison is still killing him? We killed the witch who cast it," Jacob asked over the coms.

"I don't want to risk it," Gideon said. "I'll stay here and coordinate with UCPD until Chris can get here."

"No, if Priam has enough magic to stabilize me, I'll stay," Marcus shot back, his voice strained. "You should be with your brother."

"Jeez, Marcus," Kol said. "You're bleeding out and your leg is broken. You're not staying."

"You took a full blast of lightning," Marcus gasped.

This was getting us nowhere and I was too exhausted to let it go on. I made eye contact with the closest officer, who thankfully wasn't from my precinct and didn't know I was supposed to be human. "We all need medical attention. A JP agent will be on scene shortly. Pass that on to whoever's in charge."

He gave a tight nod. "Yes, agent."

"We're all leaving," I barked at my guys. "Get in the car."

I staggered to the SUV, blood racing down my arm, leaving a trail on the pale concrete. A paramedic hurried after me.

"Agent," he said, "I know angels heal quicker than humans, but you'll still bleed out before you get to the hospital." He pulled thick wads of gauze from his bag, painfully packed both the entrance and exit wounds in my shoulder, and taped more gauze over that. "Apply pressure."

The rest of my guys staggered into sight, all bloody and all soaked from the storm still pelting rain. Jacob was covered in gashes, and Kol's whole body had been badly burned. Even with the burns, he was still helping Marcus —who had a calf bone protruding through his pant leg— hop to the SUV. God, I couldn't imagine how much pain all of them were in.

"Jesus," the paramedic gasped.

Priam scrambled out of the SUV and pressed his hands to Marcus's chest. "I don't have much," he said, his voice soft and quick over the coms as light flared from his hands. "But this should stabilize you."

Marcus drew in a sharp breath, and his wolf's intensity flared.

"Don't shift," Priam said. "Not yet. You're still too injured."

"I know," Marcus growled.

With Gideon's help, I pulled my wings back into my body and climbed into the SUV. Sebastian was out cold, but his breath was steady and a hint of light, still weaker than it should have been, was radiating again under his skin.

Rain rattled the windshield and the wipers swiped the glass clear, revealing the destruction from the fight. Black marks scorched the pale concrete where it hadn't been ripped up by vines that were no longer around because the spell that had created them was gone. All of the windows of the main building had been shattered, and the mayor's car had taken more damage and looked like it had been crushed with a compactor.

The glyph witches lay among the dirt and broken concrete. Red's battered and burned face was turned toward me, her eyes vacant, and the vine witch's neck was cocked at an unnatural angle, clearly broken. They were both dead.

The rest of the guys piled in and Priam raced us to Operations, driving not nearly as fast as Marcus, but faster than the speed limit. Medically none of us were out of the woods, and we could only pray that he and Amiah had enough to stabilize us so we could wait until their healing magic had been restored.

We were halfway to Operations when our coms were close enough to connect with Amiah's. Cassius was stable and most of the poison was gone, but there was still a thread woven into his essence. Priam gave her a heads-up about our condition, and she and Cassey, along with two other human-looking guys in scrubs, were waiting for us at the garage door with two gurneys.

Jacob and Kol helped Marcus onto a gurney and he was whisked away, while Priam and Gideon put a still-unconscious Sebastian on the other gurney. The rest of us staggered down the white hall with the pale gray vinyl floor to triage, leaving trails of water and blood.

We entered as Amiah put a hand on Sebastian's head. "He's just drained," she said to her team, and they hurried him deeper into the mini hospital, likely to put him in a room to recover.

One of the guys returned with another gurney and Gideon insisted I take it—there was only room for three in triage—and he sagged against it, using it to help him stand while Jacob went straight to Cassius and pressed his hands over Cassius's heart.

Green light with orange sparks burst around Jacob's hands and his head jerked back. A shudder of something fluttered through me and I wondered if I was always going to be feeling spells and magic as a pressure in my chest, not to mention if I'd ever get used to it. But I was too exhausted to really feel anything about that right now.

The powerful stillness in Jacob's brand swept over me and my thoughts drifted—and I hadn't realized they had until I blinked and noticed that Jacob no longer stood beside Cassius. He now sat on the tan leather couch in the waiting area. Cassius groaned and his eyes fluttered open for a second before he sighed and passed out again.

"Is he—?" The light in Gideon's eyes dimmed with worry.

Amiah turned away from examining Marcus's fracture and laid a hand on Cassius's chest. "All trace of the poison is gone."

"Thank God." Gideon pressed his forehead to mine and squeezed his eyes shut. Relief flooded me and I pressed my palm to his cheek. We were alive. All my guys were alive and that was all that mattered.

Amiah stabilized me enough for fresh tightly packed gauze in my gunshot wound to stop me from bleeding to death, and I was wheeled to a hospital room where she told Jacob in a stern voice that I was too weak to heal him. He said he could wait, sagged into the bedside chair, and held my hand as the sedative Amiah gave me helped me fall asleep.

I drifted into darkness, floating in the warm not-water. Panic seized me, so unlike my not-water dreams before that it shocked me. But I had to see my father and know who he was. And yet I already knew I didn't recognize him. I'd dreamed of him before and had no idea who he was.

Far off in the distance something boomed. That something... I knew what it was... why couldn't I remember? It sounded so familiar. I knew I'd recognized it in a previous dream, but now I couldn't remember.

All I really knew was that something wasn't right. *I* wasn't right. The not-water was no longer comforting and I had to get out of this dream and—

And what?

I had no idea. I didn't know what was wrong. I didn't know how to fix it.

Just talk to me. Kol's voice slid like silk over my senses, drawing a shiver of desire.

I don't know what to say. You won't look at me. You don't want to talk to me.

Because I'm afraid.

I know.

Of what I want. His lips whispered over mine. Just a breath of a kiss, but it slipped liquid bliss down my throat and into my heart.

You don't really want me. It was me who wanted him, needed him, just like I needed Marcus and Gideon and Jacob.

How do you know? His lips slid across my jaw to my ear, his breath caressing my neck. The swell of his magic sank low, heating my core, and he brushed his hands up my naked body, the motion slow, sensual, and making me squirm. His thumbs skimmed my nipples on the way up, but didn't stop like I wanted. Instead, he captured my face and kissed me with a wild, almost desperate passion, and his magic flooded me, making my nerves instantly thrum on the edge of climax.

My dream filled in, revealing the hellfire blazing in his eyes with a need for me and only me. His naked body pressed against mine, his heat radiating from his flesh. My breath picked up, my thrumming nerves hypersensitive to every miniscule shift. Each breath brushed my flesh against his.

I ached for him, like I ached for all my guys, needing him body and soul.

He hooked a leg over my hip and pulled me tight, my back to his chest. The length of his hard erection pressed against my butt, and I squirmed against him, drawing a moan of desire from both of us. He trailed a hand down my belly, another whisper of flesh against flesh, that alone almost had me coming, and his fingers—

I was God damn not going to wake up before his fingers reached me, before his magic flooded me. Not like the last dream.

How do you know? he asked against the back of my neck.

The tip of his index finger brushed my clit and shot the first tremor of a climax through me.

How do you know unless you talk to me?

A miniature climax rushed through me, sweeping away Kol, my yearning, everything, leaving me to drift in a darkness that was no longer warm or comforting.

I wasn't sure how long I slept, but when I woke, Gideon had replaced Jacob in the chair beside my bed, and my heart swelled with joy and relief at the sight of him. He looked perfect. His complexion was back to normal and there wasn't a scratch or bruise on him.

"How is everyone?" I asked, my voice setting off a low-level throbbing headache.

"Good." Gideon offered me a gentle smile and took my hand. There were two puncture marks on his wrist. He'd let Jacob feed from him, which meant Jacob wouldn't be up to full, but better than when I'd passed out. "Amiah has finally finished with Marcus and he's giving his wolf a run. Jacob—" His gaze dipped to his wrist. "Marcus and I took turns with a little healing help from Priam, and he's finally back up to full."

"And Kol?"

"He's come and gone and back to full."

And I wasn't going to acknowledge the sting of disappointment at that, because it was selfish and irrational. Kol survived on sex. Even if we were in a relationship, he'd still need to sleep with other people so he wouldn't end up killing me.

Jacob knocked on the open door. His complexion was finally back to normal, and I hadn't realized I'd been beginning to fear that his health would never be fully restored. But there he was, with his vampire intensity mostly hidden and yet radiating powerful stillness.

He sat on the foot of the bed, revealing Marcus standing in the hall behind him, dressed in his jeans and boots but holding his T-shirt in his hand, making my pulse trip at the sight of his beautifully sculpted, undamaged body.

"I told you she was awake," Jacob said.

Marcus hopped onto the bed, squirmed in behind me, propped himself up with the pillow, then helped me settle, my back to his chest, his legs on either side of me. He wrapped his arms around me and pressed his lips to my head. Gideon shifted his chair closer and pressed his palm over his brand on my forearm, while Jacob rested his hand on my calf.

Their love and warmth surrounded me and filled me. This was where I was supposed to be and who I was supposed to be with. There was just one person missing.

Kol peeked in through the door, and a part of my soul sang.

I shoved that as deep down as I could.

Not mine.

"I thought I felt something," he said.

He looked as he always did, breathtakingly beautiful,

his black hair ever so slightly mussed and making me think of wild sex—*yes please!* —with a flicker of red hellfire in his eyes.

I yearned to reach out to him, invite him to join us.

He crossed his arms, didn't draw closer into the room, and slid his gaze away from me.

Really. Not mine.

The only thing that had been right about my dream was that we needed to talk. But he and everyone could have time to recover, regain their equilibrium that had been upset when my wings had first appeared— God, had it only been this morning...?

None of the guys looked like it was still the day I'd fallen off City Hall's roof.

"How long was I out?"

"A full day," Gideon said.

"Amiah wanted to keep you out long enough for your magical channels to heal a bit," Marcus said. "How's your head?"

"Still a little sore." But given how much it had hurt after channeling massive amounts of magic to destroy the key that would have freed Ibizual, I was probably the best I'd ever been.

No buzz. Barely any headache. And there wasn't a single part of my body that hurt.

I had no idea how I'd managed to get through the last few days alive, let alone unscathed, and I really had no idea how I'd gotten so lucky as to have four— er, three soul mates who'd proven they'd accept me even if I was a monster.

"So it's a party in Esther's room," Sebastian said, and

Kol shifted from the doorway to lean against the wall so Sebastian could enter. Sebastian was still dressed in the shirt and slacks he'd worn yesterday, his complexion was still gray, and his internal light wasn't as radiant as I remembered, so I could only assume Amiah hadn't released him from her mini hospital.

"Dude, Amiah will kill you if she catches you out of bed," Kol said.

Sebastian rolled his eyes at him. "Let her try."

"Well," Gideon said, "I'm sure you'll still send us one enormous bill, but thank you. We wouldn't have gotten out of that alive without you."

Sebastian shrugged and gave me a wicked smile that made Marcus tighten his embrace. "Esther did make a large down payment."

"Still," Gideon said. "You didn't have to help. But you did and we prevented an assassination."

"About that." All wickedness vanished from Sebastian's expression. "You know it isn't over, right? We might have killed four witches, but the source of their worship magic is still out there."

"I know." Gideon's grip on my hand tightened and Marcus shuddered behind me. Jacob's hold on his vampiric intensity slipped a little, revealing his deadly nature, and the hellfire in Kol's eyes flared.

It wasn't close to over. There were more witches out there and worse, a goddess. And it was our job to stop them.

Don't miss the next book in the series!

DESTINED RADIANCE
Nephilim's Destiny: Book Five

The darkness could devour her light... but it's a sacrifice she'll make to save her men.

My whole life has been turned upside down and set on fire, but now I'm *Agent* Essie Shaw, full-fledged JP team member. I walk hand-in-hand with Gideon, crave all of Marcus's ferocious passion, yearn for Jacob's intense stillness — and ache for Kol, whose soul is torn so deep he's thinking of doing the unthinkable. Leaving the team.

The timing couldn't be worse for me, my guys, and the dangerous task that still lies ahead of us. The fight we almost lost with those three near-unstoppable glyph witches only scratched the surface. Their source is an evil so powerful, it will restart Michael's war against humanity.

I'll do anything, even risk letting darkness devour my soul, to pinpoint that source and prevent another war. Because I'm done running, done hiding. The future of all mankind is at stake, and the JP team — *all* of us, together — isn't going down without a fight.

Destined Radiance is the fifth and final book in the Nephilim's Destiny series, an action-packed full-length paranormal romance with four irresistible guys and a kick-ass heroine who doesn't have to choose.

OTHER BOOKS BY TESSA COLE

THE NEPHILIM'S DESTINY SERIES

Destined Shadows, prequel story

Destined Darkness, book 1

Destined Blood, book 2

Destined Fire, book 3

Destined Storm, book 4

Destined Radiance, book 5